COLD PURSUIT

A COLD HARBOR NOVEL - BOOK SIX

SUSAN SLEEMAN

EDGE OF YOUR SEAT BOOKS, INC.

Published by Edge of Your Seat Books, Inc.

Contact the publisher at contact@edgeofyourseatbooks.com

Copyright © 2018 by Susan Sleeman

Cover design by Kelly A. Martin of KAM Design

All rights reserved. Kindle Edition Printed in the United States of America or the country of purchase. Without limiting the rights under copyright reserved above, no part of this book may be reproduced in any form or by any electronic or mechanical means, including information storage and retrieval systems, without permission in writing from the publisher, except by a reviewer, who may quote brief passages in a review.

This book is a work of fiction. Characters, names, places, and incidents in this novel are either products of the imagination or are used fictitiously. Any resemblance to real people, either living or dead, to events, usinesses, or locales is entirely coincidental.

1

One Month Earlier

Whitney's mind spun frantically. *Take the children. Run. Now. Fast. Far.*

But how, when a monster with a gun held her captive?

Looking for an escape, she shot a look around the deserted alley. Angry clouds darkened the noon sky, and heavy rain pelted down on her, icing her to the core.

Percy backed her up against the alley wall, a gun barrel jabbed into her stomach. His mouth thinned into a hard, unforgiving line. "Where are my kids, Whitney? They're mine, not yours, and I *will* have them back."

She tried to escape, but he pumped iron on a regular basis, making him strong. Crazy strong. An indestructible wall of cruelty. He glowered at her with hard brown eyes, wet strands of coal black hair falling in his face.

Her breath stilled. She tried to take another. Gasped. Couldn't manage it. The hospital Emergency Department, her place of employment, was merely a few feet away. No one would see her die right outside of their doors.

"Please," she choked out.

He sneered at her. "Just tell me where the kids are, and I'll let you live."

He was lying. *Get a grip. Do something. Save yourself.*

He shoved a corded arm against her throat, his arm crushing her throat.

She opened her mouth. Tried for a breath. Even the tiniest sip of the chilly, wet Portland air. Nothing got through. Nothing but rasping in the back of her throat.

Panic settled in, clawing its way into her core, warning of death.

She felt her eyes bulging. Growing in their sockets.

She raised her hands in defense. Gun in her abdomen, she shouldn't try to fight him, but she had to. Her arm shot up and clawed his face—nails digging, slicing, drawing blood.

He swore, a long curse filled with venom, and backhanded her face, the strike splitting her lip. He stepped back and swiped at the blood on his hand, rain smearing it.

Her lungs unlocked, and she gulped in a sharp breath. Too much too fast, and pain sliced through her chest. Her jacket and scrubs were soaked, and she shivered, gasping for air.

A sudden glassiness in his deep eyes was even more alarming, a slick grin following. He jammed the cold barrel against her temple. "Tell me where they are. You have until the count of ten."

She would never reveal the children's location. No matter the pain he inflicted. No matter if he killed her. She was their protector now.

She didn't move except to breathe.

"Ten," he snapped, a conqueror gloating over his prey. "Nine...eight..."

She tuned him out. So much could happen in ten seconds. Like Percy—her brother-in-law—escaping from jail as he awaited trial for murdering her sister. Her sweet, loving sister, Vanessa.

Escaped. He'd really escaped.

Overpowered a deputy on the way to the courthouse. Now here he was to claim his kids.

And to kill Whitney, as she was the reason he'd been arrested.

"Seven...six...five." He shifted on his feet, drawing her attention.

I'm going to die. Right here. Here, where I can practically reach out and touch my coworkers.

"Four." His face tightened, reminding her of the night three weeks ago when she'd found him standing over her sister's broken body at the base of the stairs in their comfortable suburban home. A glare in his eyes. His chest heaving with anger. His face red, his hands fisted.

She'd run to her sister, checked her pulse, and when she found none, she called 911. He tried to calm her down and claim it was an accident, but Whitney knew differently and told the police as much. He'd been arrested, and as the police hauled him off, he threatened to make her pay.

And now he would.

"Three." He grinned. He was enjoying this. The sick, sick man. No way would she ever let him find his children. Not while she was breathing—which might be only three more seconds.

"C'mon, Whitney. There's no need for you to die." He abruptly stroked the side of her cheek.

She flinched.

"Two." Gone was the smile, a raging inferno burning in his eyes.

He really was going to kill her. Her heart slammed against the wall of her chest.

Please. Please. The kids need me. They can't handle another loss.

Panic crawled up her spine. Her chest froze. Maybe her heart stopped.

He opened his mouth. She waited for the number. For *one*. For death.

A car careened around the corner and screeched to a halt by the ED door. Percy whipped around, mouth still open, that word—*one*—never uttered.

A lumberjack of a man jumped out of the vehicle. He was huge. Could overpower Percy. Not a bullet, but...

Scream!

She screeched with all her might. "Help!"

The driver spun, his eyes catching the scene. "You there. Leave her alone."

Percy jerked back. His gaze darted around.

The monster-sized man came at them with big lumbering steps, bellowing and waving his hands. "Get away from her. Now. I mean it. Move."

Emotions waged war on Percy's face. He glanced at the gun. Lifted it.

"No!" She slammed her shoulder into him. Knocked him off kilter. He stumbled. Caught his footing.

Lumberjack man reached out to grab Percy. He slithered out from under the big beefy arms and sprinted away. Down the alley. Into the fog.

Lumberjack went after him. The sound of Percy's sharp footsteps snapped into the air. Lumberjack's solid thuds followed.

Whitney hyperventilated and fell back against the wall, rain cascading over her hair and running down her face, her mind a jumble of thoughts. She'd only known this level of terror one other time—the day she'd discovered her sister.

She wanted to drop to the rain-soaked ground, but she had to rescue the kids. She'd get to them before he could.

No. No. You can't. The kids needed her to get it together. Act. Move.

Where could she go?

Think, Whitney. Think.

Not home. No way. Percy would find her there. Take her niece and nephew.

He obviously didn't know which daycare she'd selected for nine-year-old Isaiah and three-year-old Zoey. She had to get to them. A plan forming in her mind, she scrambled around until she found her purse on the wet asphalt where she'd dropped it when he'd grabbed her. She snatched up the strap and ran for the parking garage. This could be the last time she ever saw this place since she started her nursing career eight years ago. She couldn't even let them know she wouldn't return.

She would have to cut all ties. Even with her parents.

She found her little Honda in the garage. Fumbled for the keys. Dropped them on the concrete. Scrambled to locate them and get the car open. Inside, she raced the engine and pointed it toward the nearest ATM. She couldn't go home for anything and would need to take out as much cash as possible to survive until she could figure out how to get more. Change her identity. The kids' identities too. And get a job. She couldn't continue to work as a nurse. It would be too easy for him to find her that way.

How in the world would she support the three of them?

A wave of hysteria bubbled up inside.

How had her life come to this? Nearly dying. Planning to assume a new identity. Running with two young kids to… where? She started hyperventilating again. She wasn't strong enough for this.

"Help me, God!" she cried out.

Calm down. Freaking out won't help anyone.

Yes, she had to stay calm. For Isaiah and Zoey.

"Call 911," she said to the car's infotainment system.

The dispatcher answered, and she quickly recounted the attack, swiping at her tears, her voice catching, stopping and swallowing hard too many times to count, but she got out her story. All of it. Every necessary word.

"I've dispatched an officer to the scene," the serene dispatcher said, her voice soothing, almost entrancing. "He'll be with you soon."

"I'm not at the hospital. I left. I have to go now. Find him. Please. Arrest him. He wants to take the kids. I can't let him." She ended the call and had the system dial her mother.

"Percy escaped from jail," she blurted out. "Tried to kill me."

A gasp filtered through the phone. "No. Oh no. It can't be true. Are you okay? Where are you?"

"It's true, and I'm fine," Whitney replied, barely able to believe it herself as she recalled the attack. "I'm on my way to the daycare to pick up the kids. Then I'm taking off. Not sure where I'll go, but I can't tell you or he might try to get it out of you."

"You think he'll come here?"

Whitney hated hearing the frantic fear in her mother's voice, but there was good reason to be afraid and hopefully it would help keep her parents safe. "Yes, and I think you and Dad should get out of town for a while, too. Try not to leave a trail that he can follow."

"Oh, dear...no...oh my."

"Go *now*, Mom. After me, you're his next target."

"Yes. We'll go. I love you, sweetie."

Tears came full force now. Whitney could barely see to drive. "I love you, too, Mom. I'll keep watching the news and call you the minute he's back in custody."

She ended the conversation on that positive note. She had to believe law enforcement would find him and arrest him again.

She instructed her car to dial the daycare center. The phone rang. Once. Twice. Three times.

"C'mon. C'mon." She slammed a fist into the wheel.

One more ring and the director's cheery greeting rang out.

"It's Whitney Rochester." She tried to sound calm, but panic edged through her tone. "Isaiah and Zoey. Are they okay?"

"Fine, why?"

"My brother-in-law has escaped from jail." When she'd registered the kids, she told them all about Percy as the staff had to understand the potential danger. "He knows nothing about your place, but I wanted to alert you and tell you I'm on my way to pick up the kids."

"We should call the police."

"My next call," she said. "I'm ten minutes out. Hide them if you have to, but make sure they're safe. Please. Please. Don't let anything happen to them."

"You know we'll do our best." Her sincerity was comforting, but what could a petite little woman of bird-sized proportions do against the anger-driven Percy should he show up?

Whitney floored the gas, the tires spinning and spitting over the rain-slicked road and prayed that their best was good enough to keep the precious children out of a rampaging killer's hands.

2

Present day

Undercover assignments were notoriously unpredictable. Alex Hamilton ought to know. As a team member of Blackwell Tactical, he'd spent his share of time on them. But never had his success depended on a woman in this way.

But then, never had the mere sight of a woman gotten under his skin and troubled him, either. And he didn't mean his fellow teammate, Samantha Willis, who was sitting at the restaurant table across from him. Sam was pretty enough—blond, shoulder-length hair, greenish-blue eyes, wide friendly smile—but she was a coworker, and that put her in "kid sister" territory for him.

But the woman across the room? The server who drew his attention the moment she stepped through swinging doors with a large tray balanced in her hands? There was nothing sisterly about her.

Whitney, he'd heard another server call her as they served the ski resort's lunchtime crowd. A name that fit her regal posture and smooth way she carried herself. Graceful. Like a dancer. She was tall, thin, with curves in all the right places. Her hair a tumbling wave of chocolate ripples. He wished he was close enough to see her eyes, but she had her focus fixed on the water she was pouring into the annoying jerk's glass.

The jerk, one Frisco McCray, was a known gun runner and the guy Alex and Sam had come to observe. In his early forties, McCray had dark penetrating eyes, bushy black brows, and long unkempt hair. His beard was equally as black and his mouth pursed.

The law hadn't been able to touch him, and a survivor of his vicious assault had hired Blackwell to bring him down. He was drunk and coming on to Whitney, and Alex had barely been able to stay seated, but he couldn't blow his cover. That would jeopardize the whole op.

McCray's hand slid like a slithering snake around Whitney's slim waist, and he jerked her close.

She cringed and glared at him. Alex got his first look at her eyes then, and they were spitting fire.

"Enough is enough." Alex started to rise. "I can't watch anymore. It's a train wreck waiting to happen. I'm going over there."

Sam grabbed his arm. "Wait. You can't blow our cover."

Alex freed his arm and planted his hands on the table. "I can't let a woman suffer, either."

"Gage is going to be mad if we blow this assignment."

Yeah, their team leader, Gage Blackwell, wouldn't like making a client mad. But... "He'll be even madder if he finds out McCray was harassing this defenseless woman, and we did nothing about it."

"True. Though she doesn't look so defenseless."

Alex glanced up to see Whitney had managed to step free from McCray's clutches and was staring down on him, the water pitcher in her hands.

Didn't matter. McCray reached out for her wrist, grabbed hold, and the pitcher tumbled to the floor.

Alex came to his full height. "I'm going."

"Can you at least be discreet?" Sam gnawed on her lip. "Maybe get McCray to go to the bar with you for a drink or something rather than calling him out?"

"I'll try my best, but a woman's honor comes first." Alex took off, and with each step toward the gorgeous brunette he had to wonder about his motives. He'd like to think he would protect any woman in this situation, not only this woman who he desperately wanted to meet.

"Whitney," he said when he reached them, acting like he knew her. "I wondered where you were."

McCray dropped her wrist, and she spun. She ran her gaze over him, and he felt as if in the flash of a moment she somehow had sized him up and found him wanting.

"Do I know you?" A delicate eyebrow raised over eyes he could now see were a color he couldn't put a single word to. Gray, yet blue, with a hint of brown, too. Never had he seen that particular mixture, and he had to admit he liked having them focused on him.

Liked it too much and logical thought melted away.

"Well?" she asked.

Right. Focus, dude. "We haven't met. My name's Alex Hamilton. It looked like you could use some help."

Her eyebrow lifted higher. "I'm fine on my own."

"Yeah, she's fine," McCray said sounding like a parrot with a slurred voice. "We're just getting to know each other is all."

Alex shifted his focus to McCray, and his snide smile took the last of Alex's self-control. He met McCray's gaze and locked on. "It doesn't much look like she's enjoying you pawing her. What say you keep your hands to yourself?"

"I'll put my hands wherever I please." As if proving a point, he slapped Whitney's bottom.

She spun so fast and cracked him across the face, landing a slap equal to the punch Alex wished he'd been able to deliver.

McCray's head jerked back, and his chair toppled over. He crashed to the floor, the other diners gasped, and a wave of whispered conversation rushed through the dining room in a tidal wave of voices.

McCray lay stunned for a moment before his heated gaze locked on Alex. Moving to Whitney, he snarled and issued a growl of warning. He scrambled to his feet. Clumsy. Swaying. His focus never leaving her.

He curled his hand into a fist. "There was no call for that."

"There most certainly was," Alex said, ready to act if that fist should raise to this woman.

Breathing hard, Whiney turned her attention to Alex. "Look, I don't know who you are, but you're making this worse, so step off. I've got this."

He wanted to listen to her and walk away, but there was no way he would budge even an inch. He'd let his temper get to him, and he'd made a mess of the situation. He needed to try to salvage it.

He forced a conciliatory expression on his face and focused on McCray. "Say, buddy, what say we bury the hatchet and grab a drink at the bar?"

"Drink? Me and you? No way." He let his gaze smolder for tension-filled moments then shouldered past Alex. He'd gone only a few steps before he looked back, his gaze going between Whitney and Alex. "You haven't heard the end of this. Either one of you."

Great. Alex has messed things up big time. Both with McCray and Whitney.

McCray stumbled out the front door, and Alex turned to Whitney.

She flashed him an angry look. "Do you have any idea what you just did? That man is a frequent guest, and he spends a lot of money at the resort. I'll likely lose my job for slapping him."

"But he deserved it."

"Sure he did."

Alex frowned. "Then why did you put up with it?"

"Because I need this job. You have no idea how much I need it, and now I might lose it. Thanks to you." Tears formed in those gray-blue eyes, one escaping down her cheek.

Aw, man. This was the worst. He had to fix it. He reached up to gently wipe it away.

Her eyes widened, and she lurched back. *Right.* She didn't want him to touch her any more than she'd wanted McCray to.

"Excuse me." She pivoted and all but ran to the kitchen door.

He'd botched this big time. He was usually pretty smooth when meeting a woman. He knew he was good-looking and women were often attracted to him. Plus, he had a great sense of humor and could charm women easily.

But with Whitney? His brain turned to mush, and he muddled things. Made a big public spectacle of all of them.

He took a look around. Found people watching him. He picked up the chair and pitcher, feeling like he could at least right something. Head down, he crossed over to his table and dropped into the chair across from Sam.

She didn't say anything for the longest time. That made things even worse.

"Go ahead," he said. "Say it."

"That didn't go so well."

"You think?" he snapped and instantly regretted hurting two women in less than five minutes. "Look. I'm sorry. That was uncalled for. I'm just mad at myself, and I'm taking it out on you."

Head tilted, Sam studied him like she did the forensic evidence she collected for the team. "She really got to you."

"Yeah." Why, he had no idea.

He took a long sip of his now lukewarm cocoa. "One of us should see where McCray went."

Sam gestured over her shoulder at the window. "Not like he's going to go far with this storm ramping up."

Alex didn't have to look outside to know the wind howled around them, and a blizzard was on the way. Not unusual in the Oregon mountains as they neared Thanksgiving. Many guests had already left the lodge, but others waited too long and would now have to ride out the storm. McCray was one of them, and—as the people assigned to tail him—so were Sam and Alex.

But McCray didn't need to go outside to access his room. The priciest of rooms at the popular ski resort faced the slopes with ski-in and ski-out lodging where guests could depart for the slope on their skis. But with the blizzard on the way, the manager had moved everyone to rooms with interior access. Why McCray was going outside, Alex didn't know.

The guy was the worst kind of criminal, selling guns to people who had no business owning weapons because they had dangerous criminal records, but Alex didn't want him to stumble around outside and die.

"As drunk as he is, I should probably go after him to be sure he makes it back to his room." Alex started to rise.

The kitchen door swung open, and Whitney stepped out. He dropped back to his chair to watch her. She'd put on an oversized bright blue fake-fur-trimmed parka over her uniform of white shirt and black slacks and wore furry boots. She stormed toward the front door, the boots clomping on the wood floor. She passed by him, casting a glare his way, and stepped into the howling wind.

"You think she really did get fired?" Sam asked.

"I hope not." Feeling lower than low, he watched out the window.

Just after noon, the sky should be clear and bright with the sun reflecting off the brilliant white snow and skiers whizzing down the slopes, but the skies were gray and overcast. The angry swirls of heavy snowfall were in a brief lull right now but hadn't let up before dropping two feet of snow and had brought the ski resort to a halt.

The staff continued to plow the walkways to outbuildings and the main arrival area out front, but the parking lot down the hill and other areas hadn't been touched. Forecasts called for the storm to continue for several days.

He'd much rather it had been sunny where he'd likely be on the slopes trailing McCray down a steep hill. Going top speed, fighting the elements, wind rushing his face and adrenaline pumping. Not sitting in a restaurant watching the guy. Watching Whitney. Blowing his encounter with her.

He changed his focus to Sam. "You're a woman. Should I go after her and try to apologize again?"

Sam frowned. "I would recommend letting it be."

He took another long sip of the cocoa, wishing he could turn back time and have a do-over. Had he really gotten her fired? If so, he couldn't live with that and had to find a way to fix it. First, he had to do his job.

"I need to go after McCray." He got up.

A gunshot cracked through the air, echoing and reverberating through the mountains.

"Whitney." Alex grabbed his jacket and bolted for the

door. He shoved it open, and for a minute was stunned into silence.

A man lay faceup on the snowy ground a few feet from the main porch, a pool of bright red blood already forming on his chest and oozing down into the snow. His eyes were open and vacant.

Whitney was a few feet away, bolting away from the man—her blue jacket a blur, her boots clomping on the cleared walkway to the staff apartments. She kept glancing back before disappearing from view near the workers' living quarters.

"You think she shot him?" Sam asked from behind him.

Did he? There was no one else in the area, including McCray. Was Whitney, this woman he just met, capable of murder?

All Alex knew about her was that he found her attractive and was drawn to her. "I have no idea, but if she ran to get away from danger, coming back inside the lodge would be much closer. Making a mad dash for the apartments left her wide open for a bullet in the back."

"She could've panicked and bolted for whatever building came into view."

"True." He considered following her but nixed that idea. She couldn't go far, and he had to check on the man, though Alex had seen death often enough in combat to know from this man's open eyes that he was gone.

Alex knelt beside the body and felt for a pulse. Found none. Snow swirled to the ground, sticking on the deceased's clothing but melting on his warm face. He wore jeans and a gray parka. No boots, but street shoes, which was odd for the conditions.

"Dead?" Sam asked.

He nodded. "What do you think he was doing out here? He's not dressed for the elements."

Sam shook her head. "It's odd for sure. Maybe he was trying to get a cell signal."

"Maybe. Thankfully, I have the SAT phone to call the sheriff." Alex grabbed his phone from his ski jacket and scrolled down his contact list to find Sheriff Nate Ryder.

"Sheriff Ryder's top-notch." Alex tapped the call button and waited for the signal to connect which always took longer via satellite. "I worked with him on an investigation a year or so back when Jackson caught that case involving Maggie."

Sam nodded her understanding as she'd been fully briefed on the investigation when their teammate Jackson's fiancé, Maggie, had been in extreme danger in a remote Oregon town.

The call connected. "Sheriff Ryder."

"It's Alex Hamilton with Blackwell Tactical. We worked the university investigation together."

"Right. Yeah. What can I do for you, Alex?" His deep voice was garbled by a crackle of static.

"I'm at Powder Point Ski Resort. We have a situation here." Despite adrenaline still lingering in his body, Alex gave concise details of the shooting, including Whitney's abrupt departure, which was at best suspicious.

A huff of air filtered through the phone. "Protect the scene as best you can. With this storm, I'll have to snowmobile in there, but I'll be there soon."

"No way!" Sam cried out. "No. Not now. No."

Alex spun to look at her. "What?"

"Look." She pointed down the hill by the parking lot.

Alex shifted his gaze, searching in the area she pointed. Massive white clouds of snow raced down the mountain and glided across the ground like a curling ocean wave. They swallowed the cars and everything in the path, eliminating them like an eraser on a whiteboard. Gusty wind exploded from the snow vortex, whipping a frenzy around it, creating a blackout situation, the residual winds climbing the hill and buffeting Alex's body.

He turned, planted his feet, and arched against the force, holding his breath until it washed over them and the air calmed. Snow clung to his face, his neck. Slid down into his coat. Icy cold.

"Sam?" he called out and spun to check on her. She stood, back to the wind, her body crusted with snow.

"You okay?" he shouted against the wind.

"Fine." She was staring at the body that was now nearly buried in snow. "I'm going to the manager to see if he has a tent that we can use to protect this scene before all the evidence is obliterated."

"Be careful," Alex said and watched her head inside.

"You still there, Hamilton?" Nate asked.

"Barely." Alex let out a long breath and inhaled a snowy one as he assessed the scene in front of him. Everything was white. Stark. Buried.

"What happened?" Nate asked sounding impatient.

"Avalanche. The quick accumulation of snow and wind must have triggered it. The resort entrance is impassable. Parking lot buried. Can't even see the top of a vehicle."

"Not now! I'll head out to assess the situation. I need to count on you to handle things up there until we can get the road open again."

Alex didn't like the sound of that. Not with already being on assignment, and the murder could very well be related to the ruthless McCray. Nate had a right to know about the job.

"You should know. We're undercover tailing a gun runner. A Frisco McCray. Our guy was out here a few minutes ago and could even be the shooter. Either way, this is going to blow our cover."

"Tough." The word exploded from his mouth. "Your

cover will just have to be blown. The safety of the people at that resort are in your hands until I can get through. As is protecting that scene so we can catch this killer."

Alex knew Nate was right. He got the message loud and clear. "You can count on me to do everything within my power to contain things. And you should know, Blackwell has a new team member, Samantha Willis, who's with me here. She's a former PPB criminalist. She's already talking to the manager about getting a tent to cover the body."

"Good. Good." The call went quiet for a moment, and Alex thought Nate might be thinking about how he could use Sam's former experience in working with the Portland Police Bureau. At least that's what Alex would be thinking about.

"PPB's criminalists are all sworn officers," Nate finally said. "Means if I can't get up there soon, she has the experience that would allow me to deputize her and feel good about the decision."

Alex sure hoped it didn't come to that. "How long do you think it will take for you to get through?"

"No telling yet. Depends on the severity of the damage and the debris field. We've experienced avalanches in that spot before. The slope by the road is forty degrees, which is more likely to trigger one. The last one took four days to dig out, and then the road crumbled, and we had to repair that. I could chopper in there, but not until this blizzard lets up. Which isn't forecasted to happen for days."

At the news, Alex swallowed hard, and ran his gaze over the sea of snow as far as the eye could see.

A bad feeling sent a chill running through him. "So what you're saying is we're stuck on a mountain for days with a killer running free and no law enforcement support on the way."

3

Whitney couldn't breathe. Percy was here. He'd come for her. For them. Killed the man standing next to her. It had to be Percy. A missed shot. Whitney lived—the man didn't. And with the snow piled up over her car she had no escape. The kids had no escape.

Cold shivers racked her body and not from the bitter wind whipping into the protected breezeway between apartments. She fell back against the wall and gaped at the snow, her little Honda Accord vanished. Every inch of it. Her way out gone. Buried under a wall of snow.

Now what? Did she run up to the small staff apartment and lock the door? Cower with the kids, waiting for Percy to come get them? Get her? Lifting his gun. Aiming. Succeeding this time.

She wasn't surprised his aim was off. He was an investment banker. A *sit in the office and sip cocktails with his pinkie finger out* kind of guy. Not a hunter or a shooter.

But he was smart, incredibly smart, which was how he got away with embezzling from his company for so many years. If Vanessa hadn't accidentally found out, he'd still be doing it.

And he was a planner. He likely had cash stashed in multiple places. Maybe fake IDs in case he ever had to run. He would've planned for every eventuality. Except maybe pushing Vanessa down the stairs. And Whitney could have just led him to her apartment building.

She looked over her shoulder. Searched the whipping snow. Visibility was about twenty feet right now, the storm kicking back in. If he was hot on her trail, she should be able to see him, but he wasn't in the snowy courtyard.

Then where did he go? She doubted he was a registered guest. Or at least he wouldn't register under his real name. But if he wasn't staying at the resort, where could he be?

Whitney had to act now, but she felt paralyzed. Frozen in place like the icy banister leading up the stairs to her small staff apartment. If he really did fire the shot, he would come after her. She could ask the kids' babysitter for help, but Whitney couldn't put Yuki in danger, too. Whitney had to get up to the apartment and send Yuki away before Percy came for them.

Mind-blowing terror gripped her, but she carefully made her way up the slippery steps, keeping her eyes focused on the snow swirling around her feet. The last thing she or the kids needed would be for her to slip and tumble down the stairs. They needed her for protection. She had a gun in her room and maybe that was enough.

It had to be.

She reached the landing where undulating drifts of snow packed against the walls. She dug out her keys, but as she reached for the lock, the door swung in and Yuki Fujita poked her head out.

A worried look on her face, her dark eyes narrowed, the little five-foot dynamo of a woman scanned the area. "Was that a gunshot?"

Not trusting herself to speak, Whitney nodded.

Yuki frowned, an unusual expression for the cheerful resort manager's wife who babysat while Whitney worked. "Must be someone hunting nearby. Happens all the time."

Whitney knew better, but she was still totally shaken. How was she going to keep from breaking down enough to coherently tell Yuki that a man had been murdered in front of her?

"Are the kids okay?" A tremor ran through Whitney's words.

Yuki's eyes widened as she studied Whitney. "They're fine, why?"

Whitney shrugged. "What are they up to?"

"Isaiah is having quiet time, and Zoey is napping." She frowned. "What are you doing home anyway?"

That Whitney could talk about. The anger might help. But not out here. Not exposed in the cold, her back to Percy if he climbed the stairs with his gun. She gestured at the door. "Let's go in."

Perceptive, Yuki didn't move, but eyed Whitney. "What's wrong?"

"Nothing." Whitney hustled Yuki inside then twisted the deadbolt and wished the door was made of metal instead of wood. She tried the lock a few times. Just to be sure.

"Whitney?" Yuki's voice was raised now. Alarmed. "Did something happen at the restaurant?"

No outside. "I got into a fight with McCray. Some guy tried to help out. He botched things, and McCray stormed out. Before Tomio could blow up, I asked him to let me go home."

Yuki let out a breath and a hint of a smile came at the sound of her husband's name. "Good. I'd hate to think he got mad and blew his top like he often does."

Whitney felt bad at her relief. Not for Tomio not

blowing his top, but for not sharing about the shooting and the avalanche right up front.

"Um, there's two other things you should know." She took a long breath. "There was an avalanche. The parking lot and road out of here are buried."

"Again, oh, no. That stupid slope. Third time since we've been here." She reached for her jacket dangling from a wall hook by the door. "I have to go. Tomio must be worried sick."

Whitney held up her hand stopping her. "That's not all. The gunshot. A man was killed. I don't know if it's safe for you to leave." *Or safe for you to stay.*

"Killed! Where?" She swiped a hand over graying hair pulled back in a severe bun.

"Just outside the restaurant. Almost on the porch. He was standing right next to me."

"Oh, my word!" Yuki grabbed Whitney's arms. "Are you okay? Do you know who it is?"

Whitney forced out a shaky smile. "I'm fine, and I don't know the man who was killed. Not staff for sure, and I've never served him in the restaurant, so maybe not a guest."

"Could be someone visiting a guest."

"Likely," Whitney said as tears pricked her eyes.

The man. The poor, poor man could have died simply because he had the misfortune of standing next to her and Percy had poor aim.

Yuki lifted her chin. "I'm going to call Tomio. To see if it's safe to leave."

Whitney nodded, and as Yuki hurried to an old olive-green phone hanging on the wall in the kitchen, Whitney went to her bedroom. At first, she'd thought it odd that Tomio kept the landlines connected in the apartments. With the storm, she now knew that it was a secondary option for when cell signals were sketchy, but she expected when the brunt of the storm hit, they could lose the landline connection, too.

Then she'd be stranded here. Percy silently waiting for the best time to approach.

Her knees went weak at the thought, and she dropped onto her bed by her nightstand. She unlocked the drawer with a key she wore around her neck to keep the kids from opening it. She took out the small gun safe and unlocked it. She'd bought the Tiffany blue Glock 19 with a stainless-steel slide the day after she fled from Percy. The same day she'd arrived at this Oregon resort high in the mountains. She didn't need a pretty gun. Just one that got the job done. But this one had recently been traded in, and the gun shop owner said it was small enough that women could handle it fine. Then he'd given her basic instructions.

She'd read more on the Internet and took lessons from a local hunter. She was skilled now, but question was—could she actually pull the trigger and shoot a person? Even Percy?

"Whitney," Yuki called out.

She shoved the gun under her pillow and closed the drawer in the nick of time before Yuki entered the room.

"Tomio doesn't know the man, either. Says he's not a guest."

Tomio. She needed to talk to Tomio and show him Percy's photo to see if he'd registered. Though that was highly unlikely with his picture being plastered all over the news.

Yuki shook her head. "Can you imagine? A murder here? In our sleepy resort?"

"No," Whitney replied, but guilt gnawed on her stomach. The murder was all her fault. She'd brought death to the resort.

Yuki planted her hands on her slender hips. "The sheriff's been called. Nate's great at his job and would handle this well, but of course, he can't get through."

We can't get out, and no one's coming to help.

Panic crept up higher, Whitney barely able to hide it from Yuki now. "So what's going to happen?"

"Nate put some man and woman in charge. They work for a company named Blackwell Tactical. Apparently, the woman was once one of those CSI people. Tomio gave them a tent, and they removed the floor so they could put it over the body to protect it."

"They're going to leave him there?" Her voice skated dangerously toward out of control.

"That's what I thought, too. He said it's a crime scene, and they weren't authorized to move the man. Not even cover him with a tarp or blanket as they could contaminate the evidence. That's why they wanted a tent so it doesn't touch his body." She worried her fingers over a silver cross she wore on a long chain. "I've watched all those CSI shows. Just never thought it would happen in my front yard."

Whitney nodded and swallowed away the lump in her throat. "On the bright side, we have these two people who know what to do, and Tomio doesn't have to take care of things."

"Yes, that's a good thing. And apparently, this Blackwell group is a mix of law enforcement and military. They're top-notch from what Tomio said, and the people who are here have guns if we need protecting."

"That's good, too," Whitney said and really meant it. Maybe she should go talk to them. Tell them about Percy and ask for their help. First, she'd find a way to ask Tomio about Percy.

"There's just one thing." Yuki frowned.

"What is it?"

"The Blackwell guy? You might want to steer clear of him. He was the guy you—"

A knock sounded on the door, taking Yuki's attention and startling Whitney. She jumped to her feet, her gaze going wild for a moment, searching for a foe, before she settled down. "Who could be out here in the storm?"

"You stay here. I'll find out." Yuki bolted for the door before Whitney could recover from being startled and form a solid thought. Or stop her.

It could be Percy. Whitney had to be prepared.

She grabbed her gun and shoved it into her waistband. She felt safer with the gun close by, but she didn't want Yuki to know she was carrying. She slipped a blazer over her shirt, and tugged the front closed. *Drat.* The button had fallen off, and she hadn't had a chance to replace it. But she didn't have another jacket in the room. She would simply have to remember to keep this one closed.

"Come in," Yuki said loudly.

Whitney heard the door closing.

Please don't let it be Percy.

"Whitney," Yuki called out. "The guy from Blackwell is here to see you."

Perfect. She needed to talk to him.

Holding her jacket together, she hurried to the living room. Her gaze landed on the man in the entryway, and her feet stuttered to a stop. There stood the infuriating man from the restaurant. Not the drunk McCray, but the big overprotective guy who thought she was completely helpless. And if her radar was on target, maybe was a bit interested in her, too. As a woman.

Alex Hamilton, he said his name was. She never expected to see him again. Especially since she thought Tomio would fire her, and she wouldn't be going back into the dining room. But here he was. Seeming large and in charge in the small foyer just like he'd been in the restaurant.

So this was why Yuki said she should steer clear of him. She took a moment to look him over, vaguely aware of Yuki slipping into her boots and puffy coat behind him. He wore a stark white ski jacket, dark blue jeans, and heavy snow boots. He was around six feet, had dark curly hair, and his square jaw was covered in dark stubble. He had a curved nose and piercing amber eyes. He seemed larger and more dangerous than in the restaurant. Maybe because he wasn't smiling with the gorgeous blonde. They sat close, whispering to each other, looking quite cozy and comfortable together.

He pulled off his gloves, and she checked for a wedding ring. None. Maybe the woman was his girlfriend, and they'd come here for a romantic ski trip.

"Hello again, Whitney," he said, his tone curt now instead of protective. "I have a few questions I need to ask you."

Seriously, *he* was upset with her? He was the one who messed things up with McCray. Over time, she'd learned to handle the often-inebriated man's advances and brush them off. Even today, when he'd gotten more touchy-feely than he'd been in the past. She could have done a much better job extricating herself without help.

But no, in comes this guy on his white horse, thinking she needed saving, and messes everything up. It was kind of him to care enough to help, she supposed, and should cut him some slack for that. She didn't exactly give him a break when he was only trying to keep McCray in his place, but still…

Yuki looked up at Alex. "Since you said it was safe for me to leave, I'm going to go."

"You're leaving?" Whitney hated that she sounded so

desperate to keep Yuki in the apartment, but she didn't want to be alone with this man. She didn't know if she was ready to tell him or anyone about Percy potentially being the shooter.

Yuki zipped her coat. "I need to help Tomio calm the guests."

Whitney winced. She was being extremely selfish, thinking only of herself and the kids, and Tomio had to be going through a terrible time with guests now stuck at the resort and a murdered man nearly on the front porch. "Let me know if I can do anything to help."

"Thank you." Yuki turned to Alex again. "I'm so glad you decided to vacation here. We—Tomio and I—are grateful for your assistance and feel much better knowing you and your teammate are here."

She grabbed his hand and shook hard. "I look forward to meeting Samantha, too."

Samantha. Was that the woman he was so cozy with in the dining room? Maybe she was his teammate and not a girlfriend. But Yuki said they were on vacation. Odd. Not that men and women couldn't be friends and take a vacation together, it just wasn't common. At least not that Whitney knew about.

Yuki released Alex's hand and added a slight bow of deference as she smiled at him. He offered Yuki a genuine smile in return, and Whitney's heart somersaulted at the charm he oozed. And he wasn't even aiming it at her.

"Nice meeting you." He opened the door for Yuki and stood back.

Well then. He truly was a gentleman. Likely why he came to Whitney's aid in the restaurant, and she shouldn't have snapped at him. She'd taken out her frustration from the handsy McCray on Alex. He didn't deserve it, and she would apologize right up front.

She waited for the door to close.

"I'm sorry for my attitude in the restaurant. I was cranky about McCray and took it out on you."

Alex gave a clipped nod but didn't smile. Whitney expected he would after the way he treated Yuki. He leaned a shoulder against the door, looking casual, but his eyes were sharp and focused with an intensity that concerned her.

"I saw you run off." His tone was equally as lethal as that smile had been. "Left the man behind in the snow."

She hadn't thought about how bad it looked that she ran away when a man lay on the ground with blood oozing from the bullet wound. "His eyes. I have medical training and knew he was dead. I couldn't help him. And I was worried about the children and wanted to check on them."

"You have children?" He sounded disappointed, and he shot a quick look at her hands. Maybe searching for a wedding ring.

"My sister's kids. I took custody after she died." Whitney purposely left out the fact that Vanessa had been murdered. Whitney needed to be extra vigilant. She would only give him the barest of information. She'd never heard of Blackwell, and for all she knew, he could have been sent by Percy.

4

Alex remained in place and watched Whitney carefully. He didn't know what to believe. Did he believe those beautiful eyes staring at him, or did he believe his gut that said she was hiding something from him?

When she said she had kids, his heart had dropped in his chest like a meteor falling from the sky. He hadn't seen a wedding ring so it was a shock for sure. Then she mentioned her sister, and he'd almost flinched at the raw misery he saw there. She was suffering deeply from her loss, and he had the urge to wrap her in his arms and comfort her.

Seriously, he'd just met her, and he was already too emotionally drawn to her to be totally impartial. He was in the exact situation where he'd counseled several of his teammates to back off due to personal connections. Most recently with Riley, whose former fiancé Leah had been accused of murder. Love had blinded the poor guy. Alex wasn't blinded by love, but the way he was reacting to Whitney could sway his opinions.

If only Riley was here to set him straight. Or Gage. Jackson. Alex would even take Coop, who was often too blunt for his own good. He'd tempered it since he got married to Kiera, but still.

There was always Sam or Eryn or even Gage's wife, Hannah. No. He couldn't bring this up with any of them. He'd never confided much in a woman. Not after his mom, and he wasn't going to start now. Nor was he going to let himself fall for this particular woman still watching him as if she had something to hide.

Facts. The investigation. That's what he'd stick to.

"Do you own a gun?" he asked, thinking a blunt question might trip her up and bring out the truth.

A flash of surprise lit her eyes, but she controlled it in record time. Another red flag for Alex.

"I do." Two words, said with rock solid strength.

"Mind if I have a look at it?"

She leveled her gaze on him. "Why?"

Obviously, she needed him to be even more blunt. "Because in my experience at a shooting, people take cover in the nearest location. Not run from it as if they have something to hide."

She started to cross her arms then let them fall instead. "I explained that."

"Yeah, but I'm not buying it."

"Does it matter if you buy it or not?"

"Actually, it does." He paused and firmly held her gaze. "The road's blocked, and Sheriff Ryder just confirmed he can't get up here for a few days. He's officially deputized my partner, and I'm assisting her in finding the killer."

Nate wanted to deputize Alex too, but Alex declined. He didn't want the restrictions of following the myriad of rules when so many people were depending on him.

"A few days. Seriously?" She started pacing, her hand on the back of her neck, looking like a caged animal. "That can't be right? I mean they must have a way to clear things faster."

She was jonesing to leave, and he was positive she was hiding something big. "You can be sure he'll do his best to get up here. As soon as the storm lets up enough, my team will fly him up here in our helo."

She spun to look at him. Her blazer fell open. He spotted a handgun jammed in her waistband.

For a moment, shock kept him frozen in place, but then he drew his weapon and aimed it at her. "Your gun. On the table *now*. Slow and easy."

She blinked a few times as if she didn't know what he was talking about. "Oh. Wait. No. No. You have it all wrong. I didn't shoot him. I was scared and took my gun out when I got home."

He believed her, but maybe because he was interested in her, not because she truly was innocent. A mistake like that could turn deadly for him, and he had to follow protocol. "We'll talk about that when I see your weapon on the table."

She sighed and pulled the pastel blue gun from her waistband and placed it solidly on the table.

He didn't lower his weapon. "Now take a few steps back."

She did as told, and he slowly crossed the room. Sam's constant warnings about not contaminating evidence played in his brain. He pulled down his sleeve to keep from smudging any prints and took a quick sniff of the weapon.

He doubted the gun had been recently fired, but he shoved it into his jacket pocket anyway. The fewer guns in people's hands the better.

"You're not going to like this," he said meeting her gaze. "But I have to search you."

Her face blanched. "No. No way. That's wrong. Just plain wrong."

"Put yourself in my shoes. A man has been murdered.

You ran away from the scene. I find you with a gun. I have to protect myself and others."

She sighed, a long drawn-out hiss as she held up her hands. "Fine. Go ahead."

Alex had searched an untold number of people in his military career, but never had he patted down a woman who he found incredibly attractive.

He stowed his gun and focused on the goal as he performed the task, using a light touch and the back of his hands. But this close, he caught a hint of a coconut in her hair, and when he brushed against it, the strands felt as soft as a fluffy kitten.

Convinced she didn't harbor another weapon, he stepped back.

"Well that was humiliating." She dropped onto the seat of a ladderback chair and glared up at him.

If he tried his very hardest, he didn't think he could come up with a worse way to meet this woman. In the course of a few hours he'd totally offended her. Not once, but twice.

Seriously. Way to go, Hamilton.

He stepped closer. She lurched back.

Yeah, he'd totally alienated her. "I'm sorry about the search. I really do feel bad about it. I hope you can try to understand and won't hold it against me."

She clutched her hands together in her lap. "I understand, but that doesn't mean I like a strange man barging into my apartment and searching me."

Maybe if he wasn't towering over her, she might relax a bit. He grabbed a chair and straddled it to face her. "I'll need to see some identification."

A small backpack sat on the table, and she tugged the strap close to pull out a wallet. She withdrew her driver's license and handed it to him.

Whitney Neilson.

He studied it, looking to see if it was a forgery. Satisfied that it was real, he snapped a picture of the card and gave it back. "Do you know the man who was shot?"

She shook her head, that soft hair swishing on her shoulder. "Didn't he have ID?"

"No."

"No wallet? Phone? Nothing?" she asked.

"No."

"That's odd, isn't it?"

"Yes," he said, unwilling to share more. "What about the shooter?"

She twisted her hands together, and he felt bad for having to put her through this, but it couldn't be helped. She was the nearest thing they had as a witness to the crime, and she had to be interviewed. He wished Sam was here instead. She'd know the right questions to ask for a murder investigation, but she was still securing the body, which was top priority next to guest safety.

Alex could easily put himself in Whitney's place as he remembered sitting across the table from the detective investigating his mother's death. Whitney might not know the deceased, but he was still gunned down next to her, and that would be difficult to recover from.

But he had to ignore her emotions and stay focused. Do the job Nate tasked him to do. "Did you see the shooter?"

"It all happened so fast. My head was down against the wind. I saw the victim's feet. He was heading inside. I glanced up when the gun sounded, and he dropped to the ground." She shuddered violently and wrapped her arms around her stomach.

An answer, but not a direct one. "Is that a yes or no? Did you see the shooter?"

"No." She eyed him. "Are you a former cop or something? Because you sure sound like one."

He shook his head. "Recon Marine. Been with Blackwell Tactical almost four years now."

"Recon as in reconnaissance?"

He nodded. "Force Recon. A Marine spec ops group. We collect relevant intelligence of military importance, observe, identify, and report adversaries."

"Ah, that explains the attention to detail."

She was right about that. It was a very detailed and demanding job behind enemy lines. Silence and stealth were vital to prevent compromising the team's position. They deemed their mission a failure if a single round was fired. And that would hold true here, too. He and Sam had to bring in this killer without another shooting. But he wasn't serving as a marine right now. He was here working for Blackwell and now under the direction of Nate.

"Yuki said you have another Blackwell person here," Whitney said.

"My teammate, Samantha Willis. She's a former criminalist with the Portland Police Bureau and served five years as a patrol officer. She'll likely have additional questions for you as we work the investigation."

Whitney relaxed her arms but didn't seem to know what to do with her hands and ended up folding them together on the table. "Then why didn't she come up here?"

"We were able to cordon off and protect the scene best we could, but she's gathering any evidence she can before we lose it in the storm."

Whitney nodded. "Yuki said it was like having CSI right in her front yard. I guess she was right."

He appreciated that Whitney didn't seem angry with him at the moment, but he wondered if her small talk was an attempt to try to throw him off the track from additional questions. He needed to keep questioning her to eliminate her as a suspect.

He settled back and tried to relax to lessen the intensity that he'd been told could be "over the top" when on a mission. "So why do you own a gun?"

"Protection."

"How long have you owned it?"

"Two weeks."

"Where did you get it?"

She rattled off the name of a local gun shop, and he made a mental note to check it out online when he got back to his suite. At least he'd find out if she'd been convicted of a felony. If the gun shop was legitimate, they would have run a check on her, and they wouldn't sell a firearm to a felon.

"Did the store run an instant background check on you?" he asked.

She nodded, her lips pursed tight, and she paled.

Interesting response. Did she have a conviction she somehow managed to hide?

"The owner said it was the law," she continued. "And before you ask, it came back clean, or I wouldn't have the gun."

Right. *If* she gave him her legal ID. "So two weeks ago, you suddenly felt a need to own a gun. What changed?"

She shrugged.

"Did you have prior experience with handguns or was this purchase a whim?"

"No experience." She looked down at her hands, but suddenly looked up, fiery conviction in her eyes. "But trust me, it wasn't a whim. Not with kids in the apartment. I thought long and hard about it first."

Desperation had crept into her tone, at odds with the laidback vibe she was trying to portray. Was it simply that she was worried about the kids?

He saw toys laying around, but no sign of the children. "Are they here?"

She tipped her head at a short hallway. "Zoey's three and napping. Isaiah is older, but he has a quiet time now. If I know him, he has his nose in a book." Her mouth softened in a smile, and her eyes sparkled with love for the children.

He'd thought she was attractive before, but with her defenses down and a soft glow to all of her features, her beauty cut straight to his heart.

Man, she got to him. Totally.

He looked away from her for a moment, pulling his reaction under control. "How long have you lived and worked at the resort?"

"Two weeks."

So she'd bought the gun when she came to work here. Or maybe she came to work here with the gun. Why? Was she intending to kill someone who frequented the resort? Possibly, but she could have also been trying to protect herself. And the kids. This would be a good place to hide out from someone. But who and why?

He shook his head. He was already more interested in solving the puzzle of why Whitney was here than locating a killer, and that wasn't good. But if the two things were wrapped up together then... "Where did you live before here?"

"Portland."

He was getting tired of her short answers. "And were you a waitress there, too?"

She shook her head.

"You're going to make me work for every detail, aren't you?" he snapped.

She frowned and looked hurt. She was sending out such mixed signals. On the one hand, open and sincere. On the other hand, evasive and secretive. Which was the real Whitney?

Either way, he regretted losing his cool. "What job did you have in Portland?"

"Nurse," the word was barely whispered out.

"And now you're a waitress living in a remote resort." He didn't bother keeping his skepticism from his voice. "Did something happen on the job to make you move and buy a gun?"

She shook her head again.

Okay, so not job-related. "You're not going to tell me why you bought the gun."

"No."

"Then you have to know that I have no choice but to believe it has something to do with killing the guy."

"It doesn't."

Frustrated, he stood, but managed to keep his tone professional. "Did you think that maybe that bullet wasn't meant for him? That with the low visibility in the snow, the shooter missed."

"Yes."

"See now," he said locking gazes. "That's not the kind of answer the average person would give. It's the answer of a person who believes someone wants to kill them."

Her gaze fixed somewhere over his shoulder and, her back went rigid, but she didn't respond.

"Okay, fine, Whitney Neilson—if that's even your real name." He bent down and palmed the table. Got in her face until she looked at him. "You give me no choice. I will be keeping my eye on you, and I will find out why you bought that gun. On that you have my word."

He wasn't making much progress here, and it was time to throw in the towel. Maybe Sam would have better luck. But before he left, he needed to search her apartment.

"I need to have a look around before I go. We're searching all guest rooms, staff quarters, and outbuildings, looking for the shooter."

"You think I'm harboring the killer." Her voice rose an octave.

"Not really, but I have to do my due diligence."

She stood. "Fine, but try not to wake Zoey."

She led him down the hall, and he went through the master bedroom with zero personal items or décor, a bathroom, and then into the kids' room. A lanky boy with dishwater-blond hair sat on a twin bed, his nose in a book as Whitney predicted. He looked up, his fair face dotted with freckles, a worried expression furrowing his forehead. On the other bed, a little girl with blond hair in curly pigtails was snuggled down under the covers.

Isaiah started to speak, but Whitney held a finger up to her lips. "Everything is fine. My friend Alex just wanted to look at the room."

"Hi," Alex whispered but got a blank look in response. He made quick work of looking in the closet and an adjoining bathroom then backed out.

Satisfied she didn't have a killer lurking around, he started for the front door but turned back. "We'll be enforcing a curfew for the duration of the storm. Guests won't be allowed outside at any time and must be in their rooms by ten at night. Tomio will approve staff members to come to work, but that is the only time you are to be out and about."

"Don't worry, I won't be hanging outside in this weather."

"Anyone caught violating the curfew without a good reason will be dealt with." He had no idea what he and Sam might do in way of a punishment, but he didn't think anyone would break curfew unless they were up to no good, and he hoped it was a way to find their killer. Because the one thing Alex knew about lawbreakers was once they broke the law, they began to think they were above it, and it was often a slippery slope from there into complete lawlessness. Which, in this case, could mean another murder.

Frustrated, Alex left Whitney's apartment and stepped to the next door. He was tasked with the staff apartments and questioning the occupants while Sam went room by room through the main building. Then, together, they would tackle the outbuildings.

He found the workers cooperative, and he quickly finished the small apartments. He marched through the wind that was kicking up higher and higher, the visibility seriously reduced to maybe two feet—with squinting.

He spotted a light glowing in the tent erected over the body. Sam must have finished her search and was waiting for him there. The fabric flapped in the wind, and he managed to secure the opening behind him.

"Man, am I glad to be out of that snow," he said and shook layers of it from his cap.

Sam looked up from where she was squatting next to the body. "Any luck at the apartments?"

"No, but I did pass the curfew information on to the people I talked to. How about you?"

"Same. I didn't see McCray. But I figured you wanted to be with me if I did approach him."

"I do. But honestly, he was so in the bag he could be passed out in his bed."

"Maybe we can get a key from Tomio then."

"Yeah, I can try that when we get back from the outbuildings. We should get going. I can only imagine how much snow there will be if we wait until morning."

Sam looked up, a worried expression on her face. "We're going to have a hard time keeping access to this tent open."

"On the bright side, if we can't get in here, no one else can either."

She frowned.

"What's wrong?"

"I keep thinking about the bullet that killed this guy, and how badly I want to find it. With every passing minute it gets buried even deeper."

"So it was a through-and-through then?" he asked.

She nodded. "Exited the middle of his chest, and I believe I'll find it lodged in the porch. I know the direction the shot came from, but if I can find the slug, I'd have the two points I'd need to calculate the trajectory and might be able to figure where the shooter took his stand."

"And then maybe find where he went from there."

"Exactly."

Alex was all for that. "Any way we can make that happen?"

"I've already got Tomio working on it. He's trying to get a few of the guests to help him tarp the porch in the general area where I think the slug came to rest." She set down her tool and settled her cap on her head. "But now we do it old school. Finish the search and keep our eyes open as we clear the nearest outbuildings."

Alex nodded. "Visibility's going to be a problem."

She tugged up her hood and stared at him. "There's nothing about this investigation that's going to be easy. You know that, right?"

He got that, but hard or not, they had a killer to find and people to protect. And if that wasn't challenge enough, he had a mystery to unravel around one stubborn, and yet, infinitely intriguing woman.

5

Whitney got what she wanted, right? Alex would be keeping an eye on her and the children, but not in the way she'd hoped. Maybe she should just tell him about Percy. No. Not yet. She had the children to think of and she didn't know enough about him. She couldn't trust anyone with her secret. Not until she knew it was safe to speak up.

She opened the Internet on her laptop and was thankful to see it connect. She made a mental note to thank Tomio for using top-of-the-line computer and network equipment. She typed in Blackwell Tactical. The first link was for their website. She clicked on it and a military-looking site opened. She selected the About page and learned the team worked out of Cold Harbor, Oregon on the southern coast.

The owner and founder, Gage Blackwell, was a former Navy SEAL who was injured on the job, thus ending his navy career. He formed Blackwell Tactical to employ former military or law enforcement personnel who had also been injured on the job and were forced to retire from their chosen careers. The company provided law enforcement training for employees and professionals as well as protection and investigative services for the general public.

All very interesting. It also meant that Alex had suffered a career-ending injury of some sort. But what? She didn't notice a limp or other disability. He looked fine. Better than fine—fit—and, she suspected, a capable warrior. That was the vibe he gave off.

She clicked on other pages looking for any information on him. She soon confirmed he was a former Recon Marine and discovered that he taught classes in tactical tracking. Made sense, she supposed. She searched for Samantha and verified she was a former police officer and criminalist just as Alex had said.

So he'd told the truth. But what he hadn't mentioned was what he and Sam were doing at the resort. Were they on vacation or working? If working, what were they doing? Could it have something to do with McCray, and was that why he'd been watching her?

She clicked on a few more links and found a section detailing the protection services they provided for people in danger or in need of a bodyguard. She could easily imagine Alex as a bodyguard by the confident way he carried himself. Imagine him watching out for her and the children. It would be such a relief if she could hire a company like Blackwell to help her.

But would there be a conflict of interest for them since Samantha and Alex were investigating the murder, and he made it clear that he thought Whitney could be involved. Her fault, she supposed, since she was being so evasive with him.

The kids' bedroom door opened.

Isaiah poked his head out and looked around. "Is your friend gone?"

"He is." She closed her laptop before Isaiah got a look at the information she'd been reviewing.

"Zoey is waking up." His forehead furrowed as he came

into the room, his body stiff, apprehension eating away at the childish features of his face. "Why are you home now?"

Oh, her poor, sweet little nephew. So leery any time their routine changed a fraction. Before his mother was killed, he was such a carefree boy. Now he was always anxious.

"The lunch crowd was light from the blizzard. Everyone's ordering room service instead." She got up and went to him. "Nothing to worry about."

His expression remained apprehensive. "I thought..."

"I know, bud. But you've got to stop being fearful."

He nodded, but she could see he didn't really buy it. "I heard your friend talking."

She should have thought of that and talked to Alex out in the breezeway. She was still learning how to be a mother, and she screwed up all the time. She tried to put the kids first, but sometimes when her own life got stressful, she didn't immediately think of their well-being. She had to do better.

"Something kind of shocking happened," she said.

"What?" He froze.

"An avalanche."

"Really?" His eyes widened.

"Really. I don't think anyone was hurt, but it covered the parking lot and the road is closed."

"Yay, no school." His body relaxed a little.

"There's no school anyway. Thanksgiving break, remember?"

"Yeah. That." His lips turned down in a mega frown.

Since this would be his first holiday without his parents, he wasn't looking forward to the day. They had a lot to be thankful for, but honestly, she wasn't looking forward to the day either and was downplaying the holiday. She would scale back Christmas for him, too. No tree, per his request. No presents. He just didn't want to celebrate at all.

Her heart ached for him, and she drew him into her arms. He was stiff and unyielding, but she kept holding. He accepted that she was now his parent, but he had yet to really acknowledge that his mother had died. And his father? How in the world did he come to grips with the fact that his father killed his mother?

What nine-year-old could accept that? What adult could even wrap their head around something so mind-blowing? She couldn't and couldn't expect him to do so either. She simply had to love him through this.

She tightened her hold.

She had to protect him. Now. Forever. From Percy.

And they were all sitting ducks right now. Percy was likely at the resort. All of them were stuck until who knew when.

She had no option. She had to trust Alex. Starting right now. This very minute. And tomorrow, when she could hopefully make her way through the storm that was raging outside, she would find him and hire his team.

Even if she had to beg for the help of this infuriating man, she would, because she would do whatever it took to protect Vanessa's children. Anything. No matter the price.

Alex rushed into the lobby and stomped his feet. He was cold to the bone from their trip to the outbuildings, and his clothing was etched with snow. They'd failed to locate any sign of the shooter, and Alex was starting to get frustrated. Sam went back to the tent. He had no idea how she wasn't as cold as he was, but she said she was fine to continue working on the forensics.

That left Alex to talk to McCray. He stepped up to Tomio at the front desk. The manager wasn't much taller than the raised level of the counter, his hair an inky black laced with strands of gray, his eyes narrowed, and his gaze sharp.

"I see that you have cameras around the resort," Alex said, getting right to the point. "I need to get a copy of the video to review."

Tomio frowned. "I can't give you that."

"Sheriff Ryder told you we are working on his behalf, didn't he?"

"Yes, but even if Ryder stood here himself, I wouldn't hand over video files. Privacy laws and all."

"This is an unusual situation."

Tomio's lips pressed tight as he tapped a few keys on his keyboard.

"I also need a key for McCray's room."

"Same issue," Tomio said, but continued typing and then took a keycard, swiped it through a reader, and set it on the front of the keyboard.

He opened a drawer and plugged a flash drive into this computer then looked up. He leaned forward and lowered his voice. "You know, I feel a need to use to the restroom. With the blizzard I don't have anyone else to man the desk. I sure hope no one tries to take the key for Room 232 or sees that I left the surveillance footage open."

He stepped away, and Alex almost gaped after him. Almost. Looking around, he saw no one in the area, so he ran around the other side of the desk and started copying the video files to the flash drive just as Tomio had planned. When it finished, he closed the files, pocketed the drive, then grabbed the key. Checking the area again and ensuring no one was around, he headed to the stairs and took them two at a time. At McCray's door, he pounded with his fist to make sure the guy heard him.

No answer.

He knocked again. "Open up, McCray."

No response.

Alex figured the man was passed out or gone, so he swiped the key and the door popped open. He looked around the guest room and saw McCray sprawled across his bed, facedown. Alex walked into the room and shook McCray's leg. He didn't stir. Not even a fraction of an inch. Alex went around and thumped him on the head. No movement.

An empty pint of vodka lay next to the bed. McCray had come back here and drunk himself into a stupor. The team's prior research on the man said he recently split with this wife and developed a serious drinking problem. They believed that could be the key to taking him down. It just might be.

Alex snapped on a pair of latex gloves and took the opportunity to look through the room. He didn't expect to find any information regarding McCray's gun running operation. McCray would never leave anything like that laying around, but there was no telling what else Alex might find that would be helpful to the murder investigation and the gun running, too.

Alex riffled through the bedside drawer and found a 9mm gun at the bottom. Alex wasn't a weapons expert, but he smelled the gun just as he had with Whitney's little blue number. In his opinion, this gun hadn't been fired recently, either. Unless McCray cleaned it. Alex moved through the room, keeping his eyes open for any gun cleaning supplies.

Thankfully, Alex hadn't been deputized so he didn't have to abide by investigative protocol. He pocketed the gun for Sam's review. Though she wasn't a firearms specialist, she'd seen her share of guns over the years and could provide a more accurate analysis. If it turned out the gun *had* been fired, Alex may have screwed up the investigation by taking it, but he was willing to risk it to disarm McCray.

He finished searching drawers and under the bed, then slid his hands along the mattress edges. He checked out the guy's suitcase and ski equipment. Coming up empty-handed, Alex slipped out of the room and went straight outside. The wind had picked up, biting into his face, the snow feeling like shards of ice sandpapering his face.

He wanted to bend his head down and protect his skin, but with a killer on the loose he had to keep his head on a swivel. He grabbed the tent zipper and slid it up, his cold hands refusing to work efficiently. He felt like sighing in relief protected by the tent. The sides rattled in the wind. Still, he felt cocooned. But with a dead body.

He found Sam squatting next to the victim, lifting a frozen blood sample from the snowy ground. She looked up. "Any developments?"

"I got video files for the last month and a key for McCray's room. What about you? Locate anything here to help?"

"Unfortunately, no. I took the victim's prints with my electronic scanner earlier and sent them to Nate. Just heard back from him. No match in AFIS. So we have a bona fide John Doe on our hands."

All law enforcement used the Automated Fingerprint Identification System to look for matches to lifted prints. AFIS held fingerprints for all convicted felons and also for law enforcement officers.

"If he's never been arrested it could shoot down my theory that he's here to meet with McCray."

"Or not. Maybe he's just careful. Or lucky and hasn't been collared."

"Could be." But Alex doubted it.

She put the blood sample in an evidence bag. "You brought the drone, right?"

He nodded. "But flying it in this storm would be nuts."

"Agreed, but if it clears a bit and Nate still can't get a chopper in here, I can fly the sample out. DNA could give us an ID if he's in CODIS, and at a minimum, we can get a more exact age than our estimated age of forty."

"Seriously, you can get age from a blood sample?"

"Yes."

He had no idea that was possible. "That could help us I suppose, but right now I don't see how."

"Every piece of the puzzle adds up in an investigation. You know that, but maybe your brain froze out there." She laughed.

He chuckled, too. "You do know joking is my thing with the team, right? And you're not going to try to step on that."

"I get it, but come on, lightening the mood when faced with murder is a cop's go-to response, so you have to cut me some slack here."

"I get it. Trust me." Marines did the same thing. Civilians not so much. They thought the officer or marine was being disrespectful. But climb in their shoes or boots for a few days, and they'd soon understand it was a defense mechanism that allowed them to continue to do their jobs.

Sam's expression turned serious. "What's with the joking anyway?"

Right. Like he was going to discuss that with her. "Can't a guy just like to kid around with his buddies?"

"Sure, but something tells me you're using it as a cover-up for something else."

"What is this? Sam's Psychology 101?"

"Nah, just my old cop sense tingling."

The last thing Alex wanted right now was to be analyzed by Sam—or anyone else for that matter. He took out the gun from his pocket and gave it to her, planning to hand over Whitney's next. "McCray's passed out like we thought, and I found this in his room. Doesn't seem like it's been fired recently. No sign of gun cleaning supplies in the room, either. I doubt he cleaned it here. And his sorry state makes me wonder if he could possibly be our shooter."

"He was in good enough shape to fire a gun when he left the restaurant. Maybe not hit his target, but fire it." She lifted the gun to her nose and inhaled. "You're right. Not fired recently, but let me check for gunpowder residue in the barrel, too."

"If you find any, that'll just tell you it hasn't been cleaned since it was last fired."

"Right, but with no cleaning supplies in the room, if it comes up clean we can assume it's not the murder weapon." She went to a folding table they'd set up and took a swab from her kit then inserted it in the barrel and withdrew it. "Clean. This isn't our murder weapon. Doesn't mean McCray didn't have another gun that he ditched after killing this guy."

Alex had to admit he was disappointed. "I knew it was too easy, but still..."

"You wanted us to nail McCray and find this killer all in one."

He nodded.

"And you hoped it proved Whitney was innocent, too."

He didn't know how to answer that, so he didn't.

Sam raised an eyebrow. "Avoiding your interest in her won't make it go away. Might even make it seem more interesting."

"I'm *so* not having this conversation with you."

"Okay." She grinned. "I'll back off...for now."

Alex rolled his eyes. "She was carrying when I went to her apartment."

"She—what?"

He dug out Whitney's gun from his other pocket and relayed their conversation before he handed it over.

She studied it. "The gun's pretty cute, isn't it?"

Alex groaned. "'Cute' and 'gun' are words that should never be said in the same sentence."

She laughed and tested it as well. "There's residue here."

She sniffed the barrel. "Doesn't seem to be fired recently, though."

"I thought as much," he said, and was surprised at how relieved he sounded.

"This isn't proof she didn't shoot it, you know?"

"I know. We'll need the slug to compare."

"Exactly."

"Anything I can do to help you here before I go watch the videos I got from Tomio?"

She nodded at the south side of the tent. "That side looks like it's going to come free so if you could secure it, that would help."

"I'm on it." He wasn't eager to go back into the cold, but he *was* eager to get away from Sam's psychoanalysis. The last thing he needed was for her to try to dig into his past relationship with his mother when that's where he wanted to leave it. In the past.

6

The next day the storm hadn't abated even a fraction, and Alex spent the day researching and watching most of the CCTV footage without any leads. Now he sat across the table from the infamous McCray. Sam perched on the edge of a chair just to his right. Alex could hardly believe McCray showed up on time for his interview. Actually, that he showed up at all. And sober. But he had. Even a few minutes early. Now the conference room seemed darker somehow... as if he brought evil with him. He had that look. Darkness. Danger. Just this side of sane and balanced, and any action could push him to the dark side.

"So we meet again." McCray's snide grin sliding through his bristly whiskers grated on Alex, and he wanted to deck the guy. "You dis me and now you want me to cooperate with you."

"*Want* isn't the right word, Mr. McCray." Sam eyed him and clasped her hands together on the table. "I'm fully deputized, and I *expect* your cooperation."

His grin widened, confident, cocky, and he turned his full attention on Sam. "Well, now, little lady. You're a different story. I'm glad to answer any and all of your questions."

He tried to rest his hand over hers. She jerked back, but her rebuff didn't faze McCray in the least. In fact, his interest grew, and he leaned toward her while running his gaze over her head to toe. Pausing along the way. Holding. Lingering.

Alex wanted to say something. Put the man in his place and warn him not to treat Sam like that. But Alex knew Sam wouldn't appreciate him coming to her defense any more than Whitney had wanted him to yesterday. Sam was a tough, confident woman. One who'd held a lot of authority as a police officer, and she'd dealt with guys like McCray on the job. Of that Alex was certain.

She took a deep breath. "What did you do when you left the restaurant after lunch yesterday?"

"Headed straight back to my room."

Sam picked up a pen and twirled it for a moment, then snapped it down on the table. "Can anyone vouch for that?"

He took a long moment before answering. Maybe making up an alibi. Alex could read people well but, in this case, he couldn't tell what was behind the man's dark gaze.

McCray picked a piece of lint from his sleeve and flicked it away. "Not sure why anyone would need to do that, but no. I'm here alone on a breather from work."

"What's your line of work?" Alex asked and couldn't wait to hear his lie.

"You hear something, missy?" He cupped his hand behind his ear. "Sounded like a bug to be swatted."

"Just answer the question, Mr. McCray," Sam said, his name coming out like a hurled insult.

He frowned, and his black eyes darkened to shiny obsidian. "I'm in the import/export business."

"What kind of products do you handle?"

He shrugged and seemed to relax, but his expression

remained tight. "A little of this and that. Depends on the market."

Alex doubted they were going to pin him down with questions. It was time to try to bluff his way to getting an answer. "You mentioned being alone here, but you were seen with another man."

A flash of surprise lit his face before he scrubbed his hand over his chin and mouth. Could Alex have been on target? Had McCray actually met with his contact and they'd missed catching them in the act?

"Was a maintenance man. Had a bulb out in my room."

Alex was impressed with the quick response but he wasn't going to let it go. "So this maintenance man came into your room to change a lightbulb?"

McCray gave a single nod of his head.

"When was that?"

"Don't rightly remember. And before you go asking Tomio about it, I didn't have to bother the front desk. I saw the guy in the hallway and called him in."

His story was growing, providing unnecessary details. Embellishing a story was a perfect example of someone who was lying, but there was no way for Alex to dispute McCray's statements. He took out his phone and swiped it open to reveal the deceased's photo.

"Did the maintenance man look like this?" He shoved the phone at him and kept his focus on McCray's face to gauge his reaction.

Recognition sparked in his eyes, but he quickly erased it. "Nah. Never seen this guy. I assume he's the guy who was shot. At least he looks dead in that picture. I hear you're having a hard time ID'ing him. Too bad you don't have the skills to get the job done." That snide smile returned as he taunted them.

Alex refused to take the bait. "So you've been alone here the entire time? No friends? No business associates?"

"Yep. Not that I really want to be. Or deserve to be, if you know what I mean." He looked at his fingernails and buffed them against his shirt. "Was looking for some action with that hot waitress, but you botched that for me."

"You botched it all by yourself." Alex had managed not to respond to the taunts thus far, but McCray's comment about Whitney had Alex's fingers curling into fists under the table. He held them tightly balled. If he didn't, he'd surely slam a fist into McCray's face. "She's a classy lady and doesn't deserve your Neanderthal pawing."

McCray arched an eyebrow so high that Alex thought it might merge with his already receding hairline. "Sounds to me like you've got a thing for her. No way you could score with her over me. So tell you what." He leaned back in his chair as if he owned the world, or at least this room, then brushed off his sleeve as if covered in lint. "I'll back off and let you have her."

Alex clenched his hands harder, his nails biting into his palms, raw anger building to explosive proportions.

"Let's stick to the interview questions," Sam said, drawing McCray's attention.

Alex knew she was doing it on purpose to let him cool down, but with the slimy way McCray ogled her, she had to be cringing inside. And he had to give her props. If she was indeed troubled by his behavior, she was doing a bang-up job of not showing it.

She continued to toss out questions for the next twenty minutes, and McCray whipped out non-answers. Vague. Deceptive, like the man they'd come to know. A snide smile here. Another there. Leering looks at other times. Just plain nauseating behavior if you asked Alex, but Sam persevered until she ran out of questions.

She set down her notepad. "Please be aware that we might have additional questions, so I need you to make yourself available when we ask."

"Oh, honey, I'm available for you day or night." He leered at her as he pushed to his feet. "I was just heading in for some dinner. Maybe you want to join me."

Sam glared at him.

He winked. "What can I say? You're a real hottie."

Sam slapped her pen down on the table. "Good day, Mr. McCray."

He chuckled and sauntered toward the exit.

The moment the door closed, Alex slammed his fists on the table, then jumped up, fury boiling inside him. He wanted to punch holes in the wall.

Sam exploded from her chair and started pacing, her hands planted rigidly on her waist. "Oh, man. *Man*. Not giving him a piece of my mind was the hardest thing I've ever done."

Alex took a breath to calm himself, allowing him to focus on helping Sam. "I'm impressed by how you handled yourself. I couldn't have done it in your shoes. I wanted to deck him."

"Why do guys like that always get away with breaking the law?"

Yes, why, God?

Alex thought about John Doe. About the violent ending of his life. The shooter could act again, and Alex suddenly felt a need to go check on Whitney.

He stood and grabbed his jacket. "I've got this hinky feeling about Whitney and the kids. Not sure why or what. Maybe because of the way McCray talked about her, and he might go looking for her."

Sam paused to look at him. "He doesn't strike me as the

kind of guy who would battle the storm for that. He'll just hit on the nearest female who captures his interest."

"Yeah, maybe, but I gotta follow my gut." Alex slipped into his jacket and zipped it up. "This won't take me long, and then we can meet up for dinner and recap the day."

"You could just call her."

"I could, but then if she was under duress I might not pick up on that."

"Good point." She dropped into the chair and grabbed her phone. "I'll go ahead and update Nate while you're gone."

Alex was out the door before she even connected her call, and as he strode across the nearly empty lobby, he put on his hat and gloves. On the porch, the storm hit him like the concussive wave from the bomb that stole his hearing, and he had to pause then arch his body to get moving.

Down on the ground it was more protected and easier going. He moved, but just ahead a figure darting through the snow caught his attention. The person followed along the rope strung by Tomio, likely a staff person, but Alex couldn't be too careful. He hurried forward, and in a protected corner of the apartment breezeway, he found Yuki brushing snow off her jacket.

"You must be nuts to come out in this weather," he shouted over the wind.

She shot him a look. "I could say the same for you."

"Point taken, though I'm working the murder investigation, and it doesn't stop for a storm. Why are you out?"

"I got a desperate call from Whitney. She needs me to watch the kids so she can go somewhere."

So maybe this is what his feeling was about. "Where?"

"She didn't say."

Alex gestured at the swirling snow. "And you didn't ask where she could be going in all of this?"

"None of my business." Without another word, she turned and climbed the stairs.

Alex turned, too, in the opposite direction and took a stand between two tall junipers to wait for Whitney. He could go up to the apartment and ask about her plans, but her earlier cagey behavior said she'd clam up. Better to catch her in the act of leaving. He really didn't like her for the murder, but his opinion was based on gut instinct. It never served him wrong in the past, but then... in the past he had a basis for what his gut told him. Here he only had a pair of gorgeous eyes that he couldn't forget. Nothing to base a decision on in a murder investigation.

The wind howled around him, and he could barely see three feet in front of his face, but he fixed his gaze on the breezeway and waited.

Whitney didn't disappoint. She appeared as a spirit through the snow, her bright blue jacket a beacon in the whirling white flakes. Her hood was up. Her head down. She came his way. Battling the wind with solid steps planted in the mounting snow.

She reached him.

He took a step forward. "Going somewhere, Whitney?"

7
———

Whitney whipped around. A man spoke. Here in the middle of the storm. Calling her name, his voice garbled and lifting on the biting wind.

Percy?

Her heart raced, and she searched the wall of snow for him. How she wished she had her gun, but Alex had taken it.

She spotted the frame of the man. Tall and dark-haired like Percy.

Please don't let this be the end. Take me if you have to, but don't let him get to the children.

"Show yourself," she demanded and crouched in a defensive posture.

He stepped forward.

"Alex," she sighed out his name and gulped in a breath of the frigid air. "You almost scared me to death."

He moved closer, his expression an iron mask of indifference. He didn't apologize or even acknowledge her fear, simply continued with the intimidating stare that raised her hackles.

"Where are you going?" he asked. "We instituted a

curfew—remember?—and you're not on Tomio's list of employees to report in today."

He was right. She shouldn't have come out, but she had to. She'd spent the day waiting for Yuki to be freed up to watch the kids, allowing her to come talk to this man. But with his cold reception, she didn't know if she'd made the right decision.

Was this unyielding guy standing before her really the man she should confide in? This crazy handsome man whose intensity might indicate a harsher side—a side like Percy's? If so, would Alex direct his anger at her the way Percy had?

Remember the information you read on Blackwell's website. They're the good guys. The knights in shining armor.

He would point any anger at Percy. At the person who could take innocent children. She had to count on that.

She steeled her mind to continue with her plan. "I was coming to find you."

"Why?" Suspicion deepened his baritone voice.

"I need to tell you why I bought the gun and ask for your help."

For a moment there was no response. Then he took her arm. "C'mon. We can go to my room to warm up and have some privacy."

His room? Seriously? She didn't want to go to his room with him. Alone. She did want to speak in private, though.

"Don't worry," he said, obviously sensing her distress. "Sam and I have a suite and there's a living area where we can talk. And even if there wasn't, I'm not *that* kind of guy. I'm not McCray. You have nothing to fear from me on that count."

Right. On that count. *What about other counts*, her heart screamed, and she hated that her heart was screaming anything. Her emotions whipped her through a gauntlet of fear, doubt, attraction, warning. She wanted to run toward him and run from him at the same time.

"And I'll make sure Sam's there as chaperone if you like," he offered.

She did like, but it was hard enough talking about this with one person, let alone two. She'd seen the suites in her first week of employment at the resort when she'd been hired to deliver room service trays. She could handle being alone with him in the living area. After all, she was going to trust him with her most prized thing, her secret, so she could surely trust him to be a gentleman. He'd shown himself to be a man of honor in the restaurant. And he had been truthful in everything he said.

But she still would like Sam nearby. Just in case her intuition was off—a good possibility as she never even suspected Percy of any wrongdoing and look how that turned out. "Maybe she could hang out in her room."

"Sure," he said. "If that's what you want."

She gave a quick nod and didn't wait for him to lead the way but grabbed onto the rope Tomio had strung from the breezeway to the lodge for the employees when the storm had started in earnest. She kept a tight hold of it, her ice-crusted mittens clinging to the rough line. She sensed Alex behind her, but she couldn't feel his movements on the rope. With his tracking and scouting experience, she doubted he needed any type of guide.

Inside the foyer, she pushed her hood down and shook off the snow like a wet dog. She untwisted her crusty green scarf from around her neck and shards of snow fell to the floor.

Alex stomped the snow from his boots, and shook his head, too, the hair she'd thought was totally brown looking almost red in the cool entry lights. He ran his fingers through it, putting every strand back into place.

"Let me call Sam." His beard held sparkling crystals like little diamonds, and for some reason she couldn't even begin to fathom, she reached up to brush them away.

He gaped at her for a moment, then his gaze heated up. She stepped back. So she hadn't imagined it at the restaurant yesterday, he really was interested in her. She knew the look. She'd endured her share of awkward advances over the years. But despite her ban of all men after Percy's deception, she liked seeing that Alex found her attractive.

Seriously, what was wrong with her? She was here to discuss protection for the children, and she was flirting with the man who could provide it.

Unbelievable, Whitney. Get a grip.

"You're calling Sam." Her words extinguished that spark of interest like the foam spray from a strong fire extinguisher, and his closed expression and commanding presence were back.

He phoned Sam, and Whitney heard her agree to join them before he ended the call.

"Follow me," he said and led the way to an ancient elevator that took its sweet old time getting started.

The motor churned and groaned, the car creaking as it took them to the third floor. He stepped down the brightly lit hallway over carpet of abstract multi-colored skis. He swiped his keycard on a door and held it open for her. A moment of hesitation stalled her, until he gave her a pointed look, and she stepped into the sitting area. She looked around at a sofa, two arm chairs, and a coffee table. A kitchenette with coffeemaker, microwave, and refrigerator filled one wall. A small oblong table and four chairs sat in front of it.

Sam poked her head out of the bedroom on the right. "I'm here if you need me, Whitney, but you can trust Alex."

"Thank you," Whitney said.

Sam nodded before backing away and leaving the door open a crack.

Alex shrugged out of his jacket and hung it on a chair.

Whitney unzipped her coat.

"Let me help you with that." He reached for her shoulders.

She almost protested, but why? Here was a rare gentleman who practiced the long-lost art of civility. He grasped her jacket, and she slipped out of the wet garment.

He draped it over the nearest dining chair. "Can I get you some coffee or tea to warm up?"

A good host, too.

She wasn't here for a social visit, but she *was* cold and a mug would give her something to do with her hands. "Tea would be wonderful."

He pointed at the sofa. "Take a seat. I'll have it ready in a minute."

He went to the special hot water dispenser at the sink, and she headed for the sofa. Unlit logs filled the large stone fireplace sitting between two oversized windows with heavy velvet drapes closed against the cold. Real pine garland and pinecones stretched across the solid wood mantle, perfuming the air, and plaid Christmas stockings hanging from brass holders spelled out the word NOEL. The scene made her heart ache with pain at losing Vanessa.

Memories of warm, wonder-filled holidays came flooding through her mind. Their magical childhood Christmases filled with toys and joy. Their teen years baking cookies and belting out carols while decorating the tree and wrapping gifts. Their young adult years coming home from stress-filled lives to relax with their parents. Then Isaiah and Zoey's joy-filled expressions of wonder on Christmas Day. Vanessa simply alive with love for her children. Smiling. Laughing. Loving.

Whitney's heart overflowed and tears blurred her eyes.

Would she ever enjoy holidays without her sister? It would get easier over the years, right? But that didn't help now. Now she couldn't even fathom a Thanksgiving meal or Christmas morning without her older sister.

The sound of Alex's boots thumping across the floor grabbed her attention, and she quickly looked up toward the ceiling to stop the tears. When she regained control and looked down, she discovered he'd set a Christmas mug and a basket holding an assortment of tea on the coffee table.

She reached for the mug, remembering when she'd helped Yuki switch out the usual mugs for holiday ones. That day, as they'd worked side by side, Yuki shared her faith. Whitney was thrilled to hear that Yuki and Tomio were practicing Christians. Whitney's faith might be suffering right now, but it comforted her to know she had fellow Christians to turn to if she needed support.

"Help yourself." He lifted another mug. "I'm going to take this to Sam and get some cocoa for myself."

Wow. More thoughtful behavior. He really was a good man—as Sam kept hinting at. When he stepped back into the room, Whitney had selected an apple spice blend tea bag. She dunked it in the mug and discretely watched him from a distance as he swiftly stirred a packet of cocoa into a cup of hot water. He attacked the cocoa with intensity, the way he seemed to tackle problems he encountered. Perhaps he really would be able to help her.

He returned, holding up a matching mug and grinning. "Not like the real stuff you serve at the restaurant, but I'm not a tea drinker."

He balanced on the arm of a plush chair, his intense eyes laser-focused on hers. She looked down and drew in a breath. She could do this. Tell him about Vanessa and Percy. But could she do it without falling to pieces? He was going to challenge her story. No question in her mind, as he seemed to doubt others. Or maybe it was just her. Probably because she'd shut him down at every turn. With that kind of behavior, what was he to think? Or maybe because he caught her breaking curfew. That would surely make him suspicious.

"You wanted to tell me about the gun," he said, his tone softer than she'd heard so far.

She took a sip of tea before starting and stared at the mug, her fingers gripped tightly around it. She just couldn't look at him when she talked about Vanessa or she would start blubbering.

"My sister was murdered about a month ago." Her throat felt like it was swelling closed with the grief.

He shifted, leaning closer, maybe hoping she would look up at him, but the anguish kept her head down.

"I'm so sorry for your loss." His sincere tone was almost the end of her emotional control.

If she looked at him and saw compassion in his eyes, the tears would flow for sure. So she kept her focus on the mug. "Her husband, Percy, killed her. He'd been embezzling from his company for years. Vanessa found out and was going to report him. He got angry and shoved her down the steps of their house."

"That's the reason you have custody of the children." He got up and came toward her, moving slowly, then sat on the sofa next to her. Too close for her comfort. She noticed his long fingers splayed around the mug resting on expensive jeans that stretched taut against solid muscles.

She looked up. His eyes were the color of dark honey, filled with kindness now. She couldn't think with him this close, so she scooted back a bit, earning a raised eyebrow, but better that than encouraging her wayward thoughts.

"What happened next?" he gently prodded.

She looked away and fidgeted with her mug. "Percy should be in jail awaiting trial, but he escaped about two weeks ago and found me. Tried to kill me."

She took a long breath and tried to tell the story—each gory detail—as if it happened to someone else. But the fear and horror came back full force. The terror. The seconds counting down to death. Percy's hot breath on her. The cold gun on her body. Everything jumbled in her brain, and her voice shook with fear.

Alex reached out. Patted her hand. His touch was like a shock, and she jerked back.

Disappointment flashed across his face. She'd hurt his feelings when all she'd meant to do was protect her own emotions.

"So you bought a gun," he said, his voice intense again, the tenderness gone.

Maybe it was for the better. She put her mug on the table. "I didn't buy it until after I took off with the kids. Percy threatened to get them back—and kill me. We ran. I got a fake ID and this job. My last name's not Neilson, it's Rochester." Her anger at Percy now under control, she felt free to exchange gazes with Alex without crying. "I couldn't let him take the kids. *Can't* let him take them. I need your help. I think Percy might be here. He might be the shooter, and that bullet could've been for me. He could be here to kill me and take the children."

Alex set his mug on the table, too. She caught the spicy scent of his aftershave. He was such an enigma. Tough. Hard. A fierce warrior who she thought would be more at home in athletic attire or rugged outdoor wear. And yet, he was perfectly groomed, his clothing expensive. She ought to know. Her dad was a doctor, and his clothes cost big bucks, so she could recognize the quality of Alex's jeans and navy button-down shirt.

He took several long breaths, his chest rising and falling as if the thought of Percy going after the kids and her made him angry. She found that powerfully attractive and waited for him to offer his services.

He met her gaze and held it. "So you want *what* from me exactly?"

Not the answer she expected, and with those golden-honey eyes fixed on her, it was such a loaded question. "I looked at Blackwell Tactical's website and saw that you offered protection services."

He blinked. "We do."

"Then I want to hire you to be with me twenty-four seven," she stated bluntly. "With me and the kids, that is."

He sat back, running his fingers over his hair. Thinking. Not looking at her.

She held her breath. She didn't know him well enough to read him.

"I don't know," he finally said, his tone hesitant.

Was he going to turn her down?

No. Please don't say no.

She was so sure once he heard her story and asked all questions to prove she was telling him the truth that he would agree. He would stand up and fight for her—for the kids. Goes to show she shouldn't be trying to judge him by his looks or his behavior in the short time she'd known him. Didn't Percy's deception teach her anything at all?

He scrubbed a hand over his carefully groomed whiskers. "I hate the thought of you and the kids being in danger, but I've already made a commitment to the sheriff to find this killer and keep everyone here safe. If I hunker down in your apartment with you, I can't fulfill that commitment."

She was relieved to hear his reasoning and almost sighed. He made perfect sense. He was thinking of the greater good. She wanted the others to be safe—of course she did—but she had to admit to selfishly wanting Isaiah and Zoey to take priority.

They couldn't advocate for themselves. She had to do it for them, and she wouldn't give up easily. "Can we find a compromise?"

"Like what?"

That was the question of the hour. The day. Her life. The kids' lives. "I don't know. Maybe we can move Isaiah and Zoey to a room where no one knows where they are except us and Yuki and Tomio. That would remove them from the danger of being with me."

"And what about you?" He raised his eyebrow.

Yeah, what about her? The only thing that really mattered was that the kids were safe. Well, she did matter to the kids. They couldn't survive another loss, and she had to think of staying safe for them, too.

"I don't know what to do." She thought for a moment and saw a vision of Alex investigating the murder. "What if I accompanied you when you do whatever you have to do? You know, sort of be under your protection that way."

His full lips turned down in a mega frown, and he gave a solid shake of his head. "That could put you right in the line of fire, an even more dangerous position than hunkering down by yourself."

"Okay, plan C, then." She tried to come up with it as desperation settled in. "What if Sam handled the investigation and you take care of our safety?"

Another shake of his head. "I can't bail on her either. We're a team, and I can't let her do all the work."

His continued *no* was echoing in her head so loudly that it was all she could hear, and she couldn't think logically. Couldn't sit. Especially not next to a guy who was turning her down flat when she needed him.

She jumped up. Paced back and forth, her thoughts still clouded and no solution coming to her.

"Come back and sit down, Whitney," he said softly. "We can work this out."

She ignored him and kept walking, her mind moving as fast as her feet, thoughts coming up, her common sense flinging them aside as quickly as they came.

She was vaguely aware of Alex standing. Heard his boots on the floor. Felt his presence. He stepped into her path. She flashed an angry look up at him. Her non-protector. The man she hardly knew but already had so many expectations of. She should move around him and keep going, but she felt the magnitude of his presence. Imposing. Holding her in place.

He tipped her chin up and forced her to look at him.

She wanted to rebel but gave in and looked at him.

"You could be wrong, you know," he said, letting his hand drop. "You might simply have been in the wrong place at the wrong time, and Percy isn't even here."

"It's him," she said adamantly.

"I'm going to share some information with you that I shouldn't. I'm not going to give you a name, but Sam and I aren't here on vacation. We're tracking a gun runner who we think planned to do a deal here. He's a very dangerous man. A killer. Maybe his deal went bad. Maybe he's been double-crossed."

She stilled. Okay, not at all what she expected to hear. No wonder Alex felt like he needed to protect everyone.

Had she seen this very dangerous man? This gun runner? Maybe served him in the restaurant in their idyllic little resort? Well, no longer idyllic with a felon here, a poor man laying lifeless in the courtyard, and no way out.

A chill raced over her body. "You really think that's a good possibility?"

"I do," he said. "But I also don't want to downplay the possibility of it being Percy. I'll call our boss, Gage Blackwell. We'll get the team searching for him. If he's out there, they'll find him. What's Percy's last name?"

He sounded so confident. She wished she could be, too. "Masters. Percy Masters. I'll take your help for sure. But if the police haven't been able to hunt him down, how can—"

"We find him?" he finished for her. "We have sources and skills that they don't have. And more importantly, we have a team dedicated to finishing the job no matter the cost. We never stop, and we never go back on our word once given. Never."

His vehemence caused a sudden dawning in her brain. His reluctance to be her bodyguard wasn't just about helping others. Sure, he planned to do that, but she'd been looking at this from only one point of view. Hers. She realized the magnitude of what he had to do.

He was a man of honor. He'd given his word, and he would keep it. He continued to prove he was honorable as well as capable. And her interest in him grew tenfold. Sure he was ruggedly handsome with a buff body, but it was what was inside the man that was important. He was starting to look like he was the whole package, and she had to cut him some slack. Show him some understanding.

"That's why you have to handle the investigation," she said, putting a smile in her voice. "You're a man of your word."

"Exactly. I want to help you. I do. The thought of you and the kids alone with this Percy guy nearby?" He clamped a hand on the back of his neck. "That cuts me to the quick. Honestly, it does. But so does the thought of the guests and staff getting hurt because I'm focusing my efforts in one direction."

She couldn't fault him for caring about everyone. In fact,

she respected him for following his commitments *and* his compassion for all the people here.

He looked into her eyes, and she saw concern. Kindness. And something else she couldn't place.

He huffed out a breath, and his gaze searched the room. Gone was his inner calm but his eyes suddenly cleared. "Tell you what. Why don't I arrange a conference call with my team to discuss this? Putting together the brains of some of the most capable people I've ever known might give us a better solution."

Perfect. He wasn't giving up on her. On them.

Thank you! Oh, thank you!

"I'd appreciate that and thank you," she said, doing her best to hide her elation and relief.

Thankfully, he was going to get his team involved in finding a solution. That was perfect, but until then, she was on her own with no one to protect her or the kids.

She turned away before her disappointment slipped out.

He hesitated again. "I can't guarantee anything, but we'll see what we can do."

Percy's enraged face when he had her by the neck razored into her mind. She shivered and wrapped her arms around herself. She wanted to cut Alex some slack but she couldn't let this go. Not yet. Not for the kids. She lifted her head and prayed that when these men and women met, they would find a solution to keep her and the kids alive and safe, and they would do so quickly.

8

Alex escorted Whitney back to her apartment, each step through the brutal cold heaping guilt and disappointment on his head for not being able to come up with a way to protect her niece and nephew. Protect Whitney, too, because though he downplayed the danger while talking to her, he couldn't in all honesty say that Percy wasn't the shooter, and she wasn't the target. She could very well be right, and that scared him more than he wanted to admit.

But he couldn't abandon everyone else for her. After seeing her safely back, he would return to his suite to finish reviewing the video files until he could get everyone gathered for a call.

"I'll let you know what the team has to say," he said at the door. "In the meantime, stay inside and keep your door locked. I know cell service is sketchy right now, but the landlines are still working, so you should be able to get through. Also, I have a satellite phone, so don't worry."

"Thanks. We'll be fine." She opened the door.

Before she could step inside, Zoey came running across the foyer. She charged past Whitney, slammed into Alex's leg, and nearly bounced off. Yuki trailed after her, her hair frazzled.

The child cast a sweet smile up at him. "I'm Zoey."

Her crooked little smile and trusting expression melted his heart into a big puddle, and he didn't know what to say.

Whitney detached the child and scooped her up. "Sorry if you didn't want a hug. Zoey has always gravitated toward men and isn't afraid to let them know how she feels."

"I'm three." Zoey held up three chubby fingers.

One look into that face, and Alex could barely stop from pushing into the apartment and proclaiming that he would stay by this little family's side until the killer was apprehended.

He stayed put and returned her smile. "I'd never turn down a hug."

She lifted her arms and nearly hurled herself at him, dangling between him and Whitney. He took hold before she fell, and she settled an arm around his neck as if she'd known him for all three of her years.

Whitney gave a wry smile. "As I said. She prefers men. My mom said I was like that as a child, too."

"Why don't you come in and warm up?" Yuki suggested. She circled behind him and all but shoved him into the small foyer before securing the door behind him. "Give me your jacket."

He did as told and caught the scent of fresh-baked bread and a savory smell, too. He spotted a loaf of bread cooling on a wire rack on the counter and a Crock-Pot plugged in nearby, the lid chirping against the crock. His stomach grumbled in appreciation.

Yuki watched him, her eyes narrowed. Why, he didn't know, but she was proving to be very observant. Maybe she'd seen something regarding the shooting. He would be remiss in his job if he didn't question her, but not in front of Zoey.

He turned his attention to the living room where Isaiah sat on the sofa, a book on his lap. The boy looked up and ran a cautious gaze over Alex, worry sparking fear in eyes that reminded him of Whitney's. Isaiah shot a look at her, his gaze seeking comfort.

The kid was afraid. Of him or something else. That was a kick in the gut, and a feeling Alex could totally remember. Isaiah likely hadn't even processed his mother's death, let alone learned to live with it. He was waiting for the other shoe to drop. Another tragic blow to hit.

Alex knew what that felt like. Totally. He was eleven when his mother took her own life. He wasn't as young as Isaiah, but still a kid, and the boy's angst drew Alex like an invisible cord tugging him across the room.

He set Zoey down and nodded at the book as he approached. "Whatcha reading?"

The boy's eyes flitted from his happy sister to Alex, and he visibly relaxed. "Captain Underpants. The Attack of the Talking Toilets." A tight grin found his mouth as he flipped it closed to display the fun cover.

Alex had to smile, too. Potty humor. Perfect for a young boy. Alex remembered those days, but maybe not as fondly as most adolescent boys. Living with a mother who suffered from depression, Alex always had to be on his best behavior. How many times had he heard his father say, *Don't upset your mother*? Daily at least. And so he'd taken on the job of trying to cheer her up. Everything at home was about improving her mood. Until she took a bottle of pills and never woke up again. Then he had to encourage his dad. His younger sister. His aunt. Everyone in the family. Twenty-three years later, he was still doing it with everyone around him. The joker, the clown—keep things light.

Relating to the kid was going to make it even harder not to give in and provide individual protection for him, Zoey, and Whitney. Alex should turn and walk out that door. Leave the adorable little girl behind. Leave this angst-torn boy before he started to care even more.

He started to turn, to force his feet to move, but he couldn't go. He just couldn't. He pasted on the best smile he could muster. "Mind if I look at it with you while I warm up?"

The boy shrugged.

Alex took that as an *okay*. "My name's Alex."

"Isaiah."

Alex sat on the sofa. "How old are you, Isaiah?"

"Nine. Almost ten." He lifted his chest at the end.

That saddened Alex even more. Here was a kid who should enjoy being a kid. But his mother's death and his father's actions had forced him to grow up way too fast.

Zoey came running across the room, a joy to behold as she moved at light speed. She slammed into the cushion next to Alex, a stubborn look on her face.

"Up," she demanded and lifted her arms to Alex.

Alex couldn't stop the smile that spread across his face. Here was a suffering boy sitting next to him, but this little tyke's enthusiasm tempered it.

He picked her up. He was comfortable with a young child. His sister was seven years younger than him, and he virtually raised her after their mother died.

"Read," Zoey said, and before he knew it, he was reading the book to both kids and they were quietly slipping into his heart and settling comfortably in.

When Isaiah turned the page, Alex looked up to find Yuki and Whitney watching them, soft smiles on their faces.

His thoughts jetted back to Whitney's surprise announcement. Did Yuki know about Percy? Did she figure out Alex had turned Whitney down flat? That getting to know the children and changing his mind was Yuki's plan when she invited him in?

Zoey shook the book. "Read."

He turned his attention back to her and finished the story. He needed to get going before he was totally invested in these kids. He set Little Miss Zoey on a cushion and patted Isaiah's knee before getting up.

"Do you have plans for dinner?" Yuki asked. "There's hearty stew in the Crock-Pot and it's ready."

The smell made his mouth water, but he shouldn't stay. "I have video files to review, and I should check in with Sam. Then I need to get my team together for a conference call as soon as possible."

Whitney looked relieved by his response. Of course she did. From the moment they'd met, she'd proved that she didn't want to be near him, and it hurt that she wanted him to leave. That was precisely the reason he should leave. But maybe her response wasn't personal. Maybe it was simply because he turned her down earlier.

"You have to eat dinner and those files aren't going anywhere," Yuki said. "And Sam has a phone, right?"

He nodded.

"Then call her and invite her, too."

He ran his fingers through his hair. "The signal could be iffy this far from Tomio's external antennas."

"I thought SAT phones worked everywhere," Yuki said.

"They pretty much do, but you can't get signals inside a building, car, or even a boat. They require an external antenna with at least an eighty percent view of the sky for a good signal. So we've been counting on Tomio's strategically placed antennas."

Yuki looked offended as she crossed her arms. "Tomio

has top-of-the-line equipment installed for emergencies, and I'm sure it will work. Check it."

He looked at Whitney, whose expression now gave away nothing. Yuki tapped her foot, so he took out his phone and waited for it to connect. It did, and he lost his excuse to take off. Besides, Sam could use a hot home-cooked dinner after her time out in the tent, and he didn't want to deny her that. He made the call and offered the invite.

"Sounds amazing, but someone should stand watch at the crime scene whenever possible," she said.

She had a valid point. They still didn't have others who could guard the tent twenty-four seven to preserve the evidence and maintain chain of custody. The two of them had split the duty for the most part. When they couldn't man the tent, they secured the zipper with a zip tie that they could see hadn't been cut. Not ideal, but it was what they had to do.

In this case, though, he could find another way. "You come up and eat, and I'll stand watch at the tent."

"No. No." Yuki forcefully waved her hands. "I will stand guard while you eat."

"You?" Alex almost laughed.

She lifted her shoulders. "I'm a black belt, and no one is going to get past me."

Alex opened his mouth to say being a black belt wouldn't stop a bullet, but the odds of someone busting into the tent with guns blazing was low. Watching the body was more about keeping away any guests who might be adventurous enough to come out in the storm to take a look.

"You hear that, Sam?" he asked.

"Sure, it's fine with me. In fact, I asked Tomio to work on a schedule of volunteers to stand watch and free us up to investigate."

He caught Isaiah watching him and gnawing on his lip.

Alex needed to cut this conversation off, as he assumed that no one had told the boy about the murder. "We can talk about that after dinner."

He hung up and felt awkward standing there. He didn't know if he should sit back down on the couch. At the table. Offer to help. He was never socially awkward, but something about Whitney turned him into an adolescent boy with a serious crush. All gangly and awkward.

"Now." Yuki shooed him toward the table. "Sit. Enjoy. I will go relieve your Sam." Yuki shook her head. "Why a girl would want to be called a man's name I don't understand."

She slipped into a black parka that dwarfed her tiny body, kissed Isaiah and Zoey's heads, then stepped out the door.

Alex felt like a mini-blizzard had just whirled thorough the room, this one warm and comforting. How in the world was he letting this little dynamo of a woman direct his steps like this? He was a grown man. A strong operator. And she was—what?—all of five feet tall and ninety pounds? Sure she was a black belt, but still, he shouldn't be letting her push him around.

Seriously.

He caught Whitney looking at him, her expression confused, and he felt even more out of place.

"It was nice of Yuki to invite me, but I can go if you'd rather," he offered.

"No. No. You should have a hot meal. Stay."

"Are you sure?" he asked, giving her one more chance to back out.

She nodded. "Let me get the table set."

"I'll help," Isaiah volunteered and raced to the kitchen ahead of Whitney. He stared up at her. "Why does someone have to guard a tent?"

Alex instantly felt bad for not thinking of the young ears

that were listening to his conversation with Sam. Especially this boy who was already hurting and vulnerable.

Whitney placed her hand on Isaiah's shoulder and lowered her voice. "I hoped you didn't have to know, but a man was shot and killed outside the restaurant."

Isaiah's freckled face paled. "Is he? Do we know him?"

Whitney shook her head.

Isaiah let out a long slow breath, deflating like a Christmas lawn blowup, then he went back to the sofa, clearly forgetting all about helping Whitney.

This kid was suffering, and Alex desperately wanted to help him. And he would. Somehow. Some way. He wouldn't end the conference call tonight until they'd figured out how he could protect this family *and* the others.

And while he was at it, maybe he could depart to Isaiah a little wisdom he'd learned after his own mother's tragic death to help the boy cope and move forward.

9

Whitney served the savory stew into bowls, steam rising up and curling into the air while thoughts of dining with Alex filled her mind. She had such mixed feelings about him and didn't know if she could sit quietly across the small table from him.

She glanced at him under her lashes. After offering to help and she'd given him a pass, he'd taken a seat at the dining table and was staring at his phone. His feet were planted flat on the floor, his posture perfect. His mere presence seemed to fill up the room, and she couldn't avoid her growing interest in him.

It would've been rude to tell him he wasn't welcome in her home, but oh, she didn't want him here. He was off limits for her. Every man was. After what happened to Vanessa, there was no way Whitney would risk marriage. Ever. On the surface, Percy was a great guy. Had been a great husband for eleven years. Then *bam*. Vanessa discovered his dark secrets, and he killed her, proving you could never know anyone, and Whitney wouldn't put her heart at risk.

She sighed, drawing Alex's questioning gaze. She didn't like being caught watching him and jerked her attention back to the stew. She had to stop thinking about him as anything other than their protector. *If* they could figure out a way for him to help. After dinner and the kids were in bed, she planned to talk to Sam and get her on their side.

But for now, she needed to be a good hostess and get the meal on the table and Alex out of there. "Isaiah, can you grab some clean napkins and set the silverware for me?"

He got up without complaining and came to grab the needed items. She appreciated his help, but wished he was less compliant. Wished he would grumble about chores like a typical kid might do, but he was worried that if he didn't act like the perfect child, she might not keep him. She'd told him over and over that no matter what he would always be with her, but he hadn't gotten to the point of embracing it yet, and she had no idea how to change his feelings.

A knock sounded on the door, and she jumped, dropping the ladle in the crock and splashing hot liquid on her hand. She jerked back and rushed to the sink to run it under cold water.

Alex got to his feet. "You okay?"

"Just clumsy." She offered him a tight smile.

He had to know the reason she'd burned her hand, but thankfully kept it to himself as Isaiah was watching them.

"That will be Sam," he said. "Want me to let her in?"

"Please." She started carrying the bowls to the table and on a return trip, she stopped to greet Sam.

She was slender and an inch or so taller than Whitney's five nine. She tugged off a stocking cap revealing blond hair that fell out and cascaded to just below her shoulders. She had brilliant blue eyes and was in a word—beautiful.

Sam took off her gloves and shoved them into her jacket pocket. Alex took her jacket and hung it on one of the hooks by the door. It felt natural to have him do so, but also wrong, like it established a personal connection that Whitney didn't want to create.

He turned to Whitney. "Whitney, meet Samantha Willis."

"It's Sam." She smiled and held out her hand.

Whitney shook hands, not surprised that Sam's was chilly. She introduced Sam to the children.

"Nice to meet you, Isaiah." Sam shook hands with him, and he seemed surprised to be treated like an adult. She smiled at Zoey. "I like your pigtails, Zoey."

She looked up from the book on her lap. "Me too."

"Dinner's almost ready," Whitney said. "If you want to take a seat at the table."

"Can I help?"

Whitney shook her head. "I just need to cut the bread and get the rest of the stew on the table."

"I'll do the stew," Alex offered, and before she could object, he stepped into the small kitchen, an even bigger invasion of her personal space.

She waited for him to exit with a set of bowls before going to the cooling rack and placing the bread on a cutting board for slicing. He came back for the last bowls. She inched closer to the counter as he slipped behind her, and still he brushed against her setting off all kinds of senses. Her hand slipped on the knife, and she knocked her finger.

"Ouch." The word came out involuntarily when she hated to draw attention to her dumb mistake.

"You cut yourself." He set down the bowls and took her hand.

"It's nothing." She pulled it back.

He eyed her for a moment, then shrugged and carried the last bowls to the table. He must think she was the biggest klutz ever. She wrapped a paper towel around her finger to stem the bleeding, then took the bread to the table.

It hit her then that they didn't have enough chairs for everyone. She lifted Zoey's booster seat from one of the chairs and set it aside. "Dinnertime, Zoey. You'll have to sit on my lap."

She toddled into the room and stood looking up at Alex. "Want to sit on your lap."

"No!" Isaiah shouted, shocking Whitney. "You can sit with me."

He picked her up and plopped down on a chair, settling the struggling Zoey on his lap.

"Want him." She kept squirming to get free.

"You can sit with me," Isaiah insisted.

"No." Zoey's lower lip popped out.

"It's okay. I don't mind." Alex held out his arms, and she grabbed onto him.

Isaiah fired Alex a testy look then pushed away from the table and stomped to the bedroom, slamming the door behind him.

"Sorry about that," Whitney said, but honestly, she was glad to see Isaiah show some emotion for once.

"I'll be right back." She started for the door.

"Can I weigh in before you talk to him?" Alex asked.

Really? What could he have to offer on this topic? She looked over her shoulder at him. He seemed very sincere, and she didn't want to be rude. "I guess."

"Not that I have any idea how to parent a child, especially one who has recently lost their parents, but..." he rubbed a hand over his jaw, "my mom died when I was eleven...so I totally get what he's feeling. Back then, I wouldn't have wanted you to come talk to me until I cooled down."

Whitney stopped, slowly turning back. "Your mom died when you were eleven?"

Sam looked startled, too.

"Yes." He shoved his fingers through his hair. "I was so angry at times, but I didn't want everyone else to see it. They were already suffering, and I thought it would upset them more if I got mad. I just kept it all bottled up inside me. Until...I couldn't." He looked at Whitney and tipped his head toward the bedroom door. "Let him blow off the steam. Then talk to him. Or I'll even talk to him if you want. Tell him about how I felt."

Wow. This wasn't what she expected at all. This guy had a sincerity and depth to him that she would have never guessed—and deeply appreciated. He was being very generous to offer to talk to a sulky nine-year-old. Plus, she honestly didn't know what Isaiah was going through or how to help him. But Alex knew.

She came back to the table and sat. "I truly would appreciate it if you would talk to him."

"All right. Let's give him a little time first."

"You're a good man, Alex Hamilton," Sam said with conviction.

Whitney agreed and bit her tongue to stop all the burning questions she had from pouring out. It wasn't her place to ask for more details, but she seriously wanted to know more. She picked up the bread plate and passed it to Sam.

"Thank you. This all looks so good." Sam took a piece and handed the plate to Alex.

Zoey grabbed a slice and chomped off a bite.

"Remember we pray first," Whitney said to her niece and glanced between Sam and Alex. "Do you mind if we pray?"

Alex shook his head. "It's routine for both of us."

So he was a Christian, too.

Seriously, God, you've got to stop showing me this guy's strengths. How about a fault or two so he's easier to resist?

She took Sam's hand, and instead of taking Alex's, she grabbed Zoey's free hand. Alex's long fingers wrapped around Zoey's tiny hand—still holding the bread—and joined his other hand with Sam's. Whitney didn't know what he was thinking, but her actions had obviously caused a reaction.

She bowed her head and offered thanks for the food and added a prayer for Sam and Alex to accomplish their mission. She finally asked for healing for Isaiah's wounded heart and had to fight to keep her voice from breaking.

She released hands and took a long cleansing breath before looking up. "Zoey, you can sit in Isaiah's chair until he comes back."

"Don't want to." She bit off another bite of her bread.

"Sorry," Whitney said to Alex.

"No worries." He reached around her to butter his slice. "My sister, Faith, is seven years younger than me. After my mom died, I had a big part in raising her, so I know how to eat with a kid on my lap."

Sam took a bite of the stew and moaned. "This is perfect on such a cold day."

Whitney smiled at Sam who seemed like such an open and friendly woman. "Thank you."

Whitney dug into her stew and the meal passed with pleasant, yet generic conversation. Alex did a great job of helping Zoey eat her stew, but she still had gravy-covered hands that found their way to Alex's sleeves.

Whitney got up to take Zoey and offered him an apologetic look.

"You should see what we often get into. This isn't a big deal." He smiled up at her. A wide, even smile, and she had to consciously think to breathe.

She hadn't expected that. Hadn't expected the intensity of her response to his smile. She gained her composure. "I'm going to go ahead and bathe her if you don't mind being on your own for a while."

"We're good," Alex said, that smile coming back wider and sending her heart tripping faster.

She nodded and hurried away, her mind a jumbled mess. She wanted his protection for the kids. For herself, too. But having him around her all day? Was that such a good idea?

She could end up head over heels for him before she could blink. Since she'd sworn off all men, that could only mean one thing for her.

A world of hurt.

"Wow." Sam sat back in her chair and eyed Alex as the bedroom door closed. "You two have progressed a long way in little more than a day."

Alex clearly knew she meant there was chemistry between him and Whitney that no one could miss, but he didn't have to acknowledge it. "I don't know what you mean."

Sam rolled her eyes. "I get it. None of my business. I know when to keep my mouth shut."

"See that's what I like best about you, Sam." He laughed.

She punched him good-naturedly. "Before Isaiah comes back I need to tell you a guy came to the tent before I left. A Brandon Everett. He's a PPB officer, and he's up here with two fellow officers on a vacation. He offered their help. I don't know him or the other guys, but it would be good to have some assistance."

"Interesting." Brandon and his crew could be the answer Alex was seeking. "I've scheduled a conference call with the team tonight. Since Riley's a former PPB officer maybe he knows them or we can have Eryn check them out."

He quickly explained Whitney's situation.

Sam blinked a few times. "Wow. I mean...wow! I had no idea."

"She doesn't want us discussing it outside the team."

Sam nodded. "What are you going to do about it?"

"At the moment, I'm thinking if this Brandon guy and the others check out, we can move Whitney and the kids to our suite and have an officer stand duty when I have to leave the room."

Sam sat quietly, her thoughts racing across her face, but she didn't speak.

He needed to know what she was thinking. "Go ahead and say whatever you're thinking. I can take it."

"Okay. You asked for it." She leaned closer. "Do you want to move them to our suite because you think this Percy guy knows about her apartment but wouldn't think to look in our suite or..." she locked gazes, "you just want her close?"

"Yes," he said firmly, not bothering to deny his interest in Whitney right now, but tonight on the video call, he'd have to find a way to hide it from Gage. "They can have my room, and I'll bunk on the sofa. That is, if it's okay with you."

She relaxed back. "Sounds like a plan to me."

The bedroom door opened, and Isaiah slowly stepped out. Alex wasn't sure of the best way to break the ice, but food was always a good topic for a growing boy. "Want me to reheat your stew and you can join us?"

"I can do it." Isaiah took his bowl to the microwave.

Now would be a perfect time to have that talk with Isaiah. Alex signaled for Sam to take off.

She stood. "I need to check in with Yuki."

"I never got around to asking her if she saw anything

today," Alex said, trying to be cryptic to keep Isaiah from worrying. "Mind handling that when you see her?"

"Glad to." She looked at Isaiah. "Nice to meet you, Isaiah. Tell Whitney thanks for the dinner."

"Yeah," he said flatly.

Sam gave Alex a *good luck* look, and after slipping into her coat and hat, took off. Alex got up to turn the deadbolt behind her and sat back down.

When Isaiah took his chair, Alex grabbed another piece of the amazing rosemary bread and chewed while the kid ate. Alex didn't want to broach the subject of his loss before getting some food in the boy's belly.

"You into sports?" Alex asked.

"Soccer," Isaiah replied around a bite of stew.

"Me too. I'm into skiing, too. Hang gliding. Scuba diving. Parasailing. You name it, I like it."

Isaiah flashed a look of approval. "My mom woulda never let me do any of those things."

"Mine, either," Alex said, thinking this was his opening he needed.

"You're a grown-up. You don't have to listen to your mom."

"I meant when I was your age. She didn't even like me playing soccer. She worried a lot."

"My mom was cool with soccer." He frowned and stabbed his fork into a potato dripping with rich brown gravy. "I don't know what Aunt Whitney will say."

"It's hard, right? Suddenly having a new person in charge of you."

He jutted out his chin in challenge. "Like you would have any idea."

It was painful to see such a skeptical expression and tone in a boy so young, but Alex likely had the same look when his mom took her life. Maybe even worse because she chose to leave. "My mom died when I was eleven, so I totally know what you're going through."

Isaiah paused, fork midair. "Really?"

Alex nodded.

He sat quietly for a minute then set down his fork. "Was it sudden? You know...like my mom?"

Alex nodded again, the memory of finding his mother lying on the floor in her bedroom, the empty pill bottle at her side came rushing back, and he had to clear his throat to keep the tears at bay even at this age. "She swallowed a bottle of sleeping pills."

Isaiah's eyes widened. "Like did it on purpose?"

Alex nodded again. "She suffered from depression. Do you know what that is?"

"Being sad."

"Yeah, except it's not like when we get sad. It's far deeper, and the person can't see a way out of it." Alex paused to keep his emotions under control. "She just couldn't go on living like that."

"Did you live with your dad then?"

Alex shook his head. "He was this big-time company executive and didn't have time for me. So I went to live with my aunt like you."

"Was is it really hard at first?" Isaiah asked, his voice trembling and tears sparkling in his eyes.

"Yeah, but here's the thing." Alex moved closer and thought about resting his hand on the kid's. No, that was too much. "It gets better, and the sooner you accept the change, the easier it will be. I was like angry all the time. Especially at God."

He nodded like a sage old man. "Me, too."

"And I was sad. Real sad. Felt like crying a lot."

"Did you?" He peeked up out from under his eyelashes as if embarrassed to ask the question. "Cry, I mean?"

"Yeah, at her funeral, but after that only in my room. And I never let anyone see it because I was embarrassed. But there's nothing to be embarrassed about. Even grown men cry."

Isaiah studied Alex so intently he felt like squirming under the kid's penetrating focus.

"Seems like you got over it."

Alex wished he could make this part easier for Isaiah, but he couldn't. "I'm not going to lie to you. You never totally get over it, but that's okay. If you did, you wouldn't be keeping a part of your mom with you, and it's good to remember her."

Isaiah's nod was less convincing this time.

"Plus, here's the thing. Your mom wouldn't want you to be sad, so it's okay to smile and laugh and have fun. I know it feels like you're betraying her, but you're not. Honestly."

Isaiah crossed his arms and fell back in chair. "I don't want to smile or laugh."

"I know, bud. I get it. But you will. Trust me. You will."

He started shaking his leg, frantically, looking lost and so very alone. "And my dad? What do I do about him?"

That Alex felt far less qualified to weigh in on, but he'd try anything to help this boy. "See here's the thing. My dad wasn't in jail, but he was always gone, so it was kind of the same. I hardly ever saw him. I'm thinking I had similar feelings about him. Was maybe even madder because he chose not to be with me. But I finally got tired of being mad all the time and decided that no matter what, I was going to go on. It wasn't easy and it took time, but I did."

Well mostly, anyway.

The bedroom door opened, signaling for Alex to wrap this up. He rested his hand on Isaiah's shoulder. "If you feel like talking more, I'll make sure Whitney has my cell number and you can call me. Okay?"

"Yeah, sure. Thanks." Isaiah sat forward and started eating again.

Alex turned to the door to watch Whitney step out. Her face was glistening and her hair was at odd angles where she'd pushed it off her rosy face. Her shirt was wet, and she looked a bit defeated.

She met his gaze and shook her head. "Bathing a three-year-old should be an Olympic sport."

"You do look like you've just earned a gold medal, doesn't she, Isaiah?"

The boy looked at her, and a hint of smile turned up the corner of his mouth before he whisked it away.

Alex got up. "Let me clear the table and do the dishes while you relax a bit."

Whitney looked like she was going to say no, but then a firm resolve tightened her face. "We can do it together."

A huge step, he thought, when she'd been keeping her distance as much as possible.

In the kitchen he stepped close to her and lowered his voice. "What time does Isaiah go to bed?"

Her eyes darkened in worry like a cornered animal. Did she think he was coming on to her in front of her nephew? Seriously?

"I want to have that conference call but might as well do it from here where I can keep an eye out for all of you."

"Oh, right." She glanced at her watch. "He gets ready in fifteen minutes then reads for an hour in his bed."

"Sam will be joining in the call, and it would be good if you could, too." He figured it would help the team personalize this investigation and work even harder to locate the evil Percy. "Can we meet while Isaiah's still awake or might he overhear?"

She frowned for a moment. "We could go into the other bedroom, I suppose. My room."

She probably didn't like the thought of him in her bedroom even with Sam joining them, but it was the best option, and he wasn't going to give her a chance to rethink it.

"That would be great." He took out his phone. "I'll text Sam and the team to be ready."

A quick nod and she turned her attention to the bread, which she bagged. He leaned against the counter to text and receive responses as they came in. He expected most everyone would join in. Team members were on call twenty-four seven on a rotating schedule, which meant they always had a minimum of four people at the ready. The others got a pass after regular business hours, but everyone was so committed to making a difference that they often responded anyway.

He set his phone on the counter as Whitney packed away the leftover stew in the refrigerator. He grabbed a dishrag and wiped the counter, feeling incredibly comfortable simply hanging with her in the kitchen. His phone kept chiming, and he soon received a reply from everyone. Jackson was getting married in December, and he begged off to spend time with Maggie. Coop claimed he had big plans with his wife, Kiera.

Plans. A significant other. Wedding.

Such foreign thoughts to Alex that he almost shook his head. He had no idea what any of that was like. Sure, he'd dated in the past. Had a few relationships that could've gone somewhere if he'd let them, but he didn't let it happen. He always felt like he was *on* when he dated. Like he had to keep up the joker role he'd established as his identity. But that was tedious and tiring, and he didn't want it every minute of every day.

He needed to get away from cheerful Alex. Be real. Be himself. Not spend his time worrying about the other person's happiness and trying to cheer them up. He couldn't do that all the time, but it was so ingrained in him that he couldn't let it go, and that left him perpetually single.

Problem was, he'd recently watched everyone on the team find their significant others, and he was starting to want the same thing in his life.

"You're going to rub a hole in my counter," Whitney said.

"What?" He blinked hard as he had no idea what she was talking about.

She pointed at his hand. "You've been rubbing that same spot for some time now."

"Oh, right. I was just thinking."

"About the call."

"No," he answered quickly before he blurted out what he'd been thinking about. "But we're all set if we can get a clear signal with the SAT phone. If not, we'll do a landline call. Two of the guys can't make it, but the others will be there."

"Let me make sure things in my room are...well, you know. Not a mess." Her face colored a bright red.

Her innocent response was totally refreshing, and she was so adorably cute that he couldn't resist and touched her hand. "No one will care."

"I care, though." She slipped her hand free and almost bolted for her bedroom.

Alex watched her go. This woman was easily getting to him. And then it hit him like the blizzard force wind outside.

He didn't feel a need to be *on* for her. He only wanted to be real. Not the joker. An odd feeling. Too odd. Now what was he going to do about that?

10

On the way to her bedroom, Whitney quickly ran through the state of the space as she'd left it that morning. She'd made her bed. She always did as it made her feel organized and her day seemed to go better. But what about other things?

She pushed through the door. Spotted her robe on the back of a chair. Grabbed it. Hung it in the closet. Tossed a pair of shoes inside, too. She threw lip balm into her nightstand drawer and followed it with a book she'd been reading when she couldn't sleep and to take her mind off Vanessa.

She ran her gaze over the room. Fluffed her pillows.

There. Good. It was the best she could do this quickly. She wasn't about to start dusting or pull out the vacuum. That would be overkill. But how her fingers itched to do it.

She went into the adjoining bathroom to run a brush through her hair and stood stock still in front of the mirror.

Oh my gosh. Seriously.

Strands of her hair stuck out at all angles. Likely from when she pushed it out of her face in the muggy bathroom. Her face was beet red from the steamy bath water. She was a hot mess. Literally. And Alex hadn't said a word.

She grabbed the brush and tamed the strands with a hard yank of frustration. Frustrated because she looked so disheveled in front of Alex, but even more frustrated that she felt a need to look her best for him. She didn't want anything from him but his protection, and it didn't matter how she looked for that.

She tossed down the brush. Planted her hands on the edge of the counter and stared.

Okay, fine. She needed some lip gloss, too. It was for meeting the team. Not for Alex.

Right. Tell yourself that.

By the time she got back into the living room, Sam had returned. Alex had the dishwasher loaded and running, and Sam was wiping off the rest of the counters that Alex hadn't scoured. Whitney felt invaded, and yet, oddly touched by their caring.

The two of them seemed to get along so well, but it was perfectly clear there wasn't any romantic interest there. Still, they had a connection just the same. Whitney supposed when your job was life-or-death a lot of the time, you had to have a strong bond with your fellow teammates.

She watched Alex for a moment. She didn't like the thought of him risking his life like that. Didn't like it at all. Sam, too, but it was different.

He looked up and caught her watching. That flirty half smile tipped his lips up. Was this a smile he gave every woman when she wished it was hers alone?

Oh, knock it off already.

She turned her attention to Isaiah who was playing Tetris on Vanessa's old Game Boy. "Time for bed, buddy."

He didn't complain. Didn't ask to save his game. Just nodded.

"You can finish that level if you want."

"It's okay. I wasn't doing very well anyway." He clicked it off.

Whitney had to wonder if he'd also clicked off his heart forever. She made a mental note to talk to Alex to see how their talk had gone and to ask if he felt like Isaiah might survive. Sure it was too soon to tell anything, but she needed some reassurance that she wasn't making things worse for her nephew. She loved the kid more than she thought possible and would do anything to help right his world for him again.

She bent down and kissed the top of his head. "Good night. I love you."

"Me too." He got up and trudged to his room like a ninety-year-old man, and her heart cried out for him.

Sam came over and put an arm around Whitney's shoulders. "Seeing him like that has got to be breaking your heart."

Whitney's throat clogged with tears, and she couldn't speak.

Sam hugged Whitney closer. "I can tell how much you love him and want to help him."

Alex joined them. "It's gonna take time, but don't quit trying. He needs your caring and love. He just doesn't realize how much yet. But he'll figure it out and be glad you're there for him."

Whitney appreciated the opening to ask about his earlier conversation. "Did your talk go well with him?"

Alex cocked his head. "It was about like I expected. I could relate to his emotions, and I know it helped him to talk. I told him I'd give you my phone number so he could call me if he wanted. Not just while we're here, but any time after that, too. If it's okay with you, that is."

"Thank you, Alex." She squeezed his arm. "I'm very thankful for your kindness."

A rush of red started at the base of his neck and flushed over his face. This intense, physically powerful man who seemed fearless *blushed* when she thanked him, and his humility knocked a large chunk of ice off her heart frozen by Percy's lethal actions.

"We should get set up," he said quickly. "I thought we could take the dining chairs in if there's room instead of sitting on the bed."

She hadn't even thought about seating. "There's room."

They picked up chairs and were soon set up. Sam put her iPad on Whitney's low dresser, then attached her SAT phone to it for their Internet connection.

"Now cross your fingers that we can get through." She made the connection. The screen was fuzzy, but the camera captured a group of men and women clustered around a table in a small conference room.

Alex greeted his teammates, his tone flat and businesslike. Whitney had no idea why he was relaxed with Sam but tense now. It was such a change that Whitney didn't know what to think. He almost seemed cold and untouchable. Not the guy she thought she was getting to know. But then, Percy proved that there were far more sides to a person than you could ever know, and Alex's change in behavior shouldn't surprise her.

He introduced her to each person. Gage, the boss, was dark-haired and serious looking. No smile when he said hello. The woman, Eryn, had even darker hair and a big smile. Sharing the screen with her was a redheaded man named Trey, her fiancé who had recently joined Blackwell. The last guy, Riley was blond and had a kind smile.

All of them comfortably wore a fierce warrior look, even Eryn. Whitney wished they could hop a helicopter right now and come stand guard over her precious niece and nephew.

Alex gave a concise overview of the situation, telling them that Whitney was their main witness, which drew raised eyebrows and their stares intensified—if that was possible. But the attention didn't seem to bother Alex, he continued reciting point after point about his and Sam's findings.

He paused for a moment to take a long breath. "We lucked up. There are three Portland police officers vacationing here. They approached Sam just before dinnertime and offered to help in the investigation. An officer Umbel, Everett, and Yablonsky."

That was welcome news to Whitney's ears, and she wondered why Alex hadn't mentioned it.

"I wish I could tell you more about them, but they're all relatively new recruits," Sam said. "I didn't meet them before moving to forensics."

"You know any of these guys, Riley?" Alex glanced at Whitney. "Riley's a former PPB sniper."

"Sniper. Wow."

"No biggie," Riley said looking a bit embarrassed at her reaction. "I don't recognize the names."

"I was hoping you'd be able to vouch for them." Alex frowned, the downturn of his lips so severe it was looking more like a scowl.

"What's wrong, Alex?" Gage asked, his dark eyes piercing on the screen, and she could easily see him leading the team of tough men and women.

Alex tipped his head. "What do you mean?"

"The jokes. We've been talking for five minutes and you haven't cracked a single one."

"Exactly." Sam eyed him.

He poked her knee with his and gave her a pointed look. Whitney had no idea what was going on, so she kept her mouth shut.

Eryn snorted. "Our connection might be hideous, but there's no way we missed that look to silence Sam."

Gage pursed his lips. "Something I need to know?"

"No." One word from Alex, but it was firm and resolute. "And we should move on before we lose this signal. Whitney's here because she wants to hire us, and I'm not sure how we can accomplish that." He glanced at her. "Do you want to tell them your story or should I?"

"Go ahead." It was a bit intimidating to have all the faces staring at her, and she was already emotional. If she had to talk about Vanessa, she'd likely end up blubbering like a baby by the end.

Alex explained her dilemma concisely, but when he mentioned Isaiah and Zoey, his voice cracked, and she knew that he cared about the kids. That Percy killing Vanessa was now personal to him, too. That he would do whatever it would take to protect them.

What a guy. A sigh wanted to slip out, but she swallowed hard to stop it.

He finished the story and glanced at her. "Did I get that all right?"

She nodded and smiled her thanks.

He gave a quick nod of acknowledgement and held her gaze longer than she expected with everyone watching them.

"Sam and Alex," Gage said. "You're both there. Have evaluated the scene. Is this a case of the shooter missing his mark?"

"I'd be leaning that way except the deceased has no ID," Sam said. "Nothing, and we know he's not a registered guest because Tomio has confirmed they're all safe and accounted for. That's raising red flags for me."

"Could he have been visiting a guest and left his ID in a room to go out skiing?" Trey asked.

"He wasn't dressed in ski attire," Whitney said and all gazes moved to her. She ignored the pressure she felt and continued, "He was wearing jeans and a parka. No boots. Street shoes. And there's a blizzard going on."

"And Tomio also said none of the guests admit to having a visitor," Alex added. "Fortunately, most people left when the blizzard forecast came out, and we only have thirty-five guests on site with a hundred rooms. We searched every one of them, plus the staff quarters. Twenty staff remained here on duty. We also searched the outbuildings for the shooter but didn't find anyone or evidence that a person was staying there. So wherever Percy—or the shooter if they're different people—is hiding out, we haven't located it."

Whitney had no idea they'd done all of that. It must have been while she was holed up here trying to decide if she should tell Alex about Percy.

"Could he have gotten away from the resort?" Trey asked.

"Not via the parking lot," Alex replied. "He could've hoofed it cross-country I suppose. But if he did, with the way this storm ramped up, he's likely dead by now."

"It's that bad up there?" Riley asked.

Alex nodded. "Unless the shooter's prepared to withstand this blizzard out in the open, he's a goner. Even with prep and proper equipment, it would be a challenge even for us."

"I think he's hunkered down somewhere on the resort," Sam said. "And we just haven't found him. He's likely waiting for the storm to abate. And if John Doe wasn't his mark, he'll try again."

"I agree," Alex said. "His prints didn't return a match in AFIS, but I still think the odds are good that John Doe was here to do business with our target."

Target. Had to be the gun runner whose name Alex wouldn't mention.

"Why's that?" Gage asked.

"He's the most likely guest to deny having a visitor where the other guests most likely wouldn't have a reason to. And so far, we haven't found a reason for the staff to lie about knowing this guy."

"Unless they're into something illegal," Gage said.

"True, and when we sit down tomorrow for formal interviews of the staff and guests, I hope we can ferret that out," Sam said. "And even *if* the deceased was working with our target, it might not be related to the gun running. John Doe could've happened to be in the wrong place at the wrong time. Would also be true if he was visiting a staff member up to no good. In both cases, the bullet could still have been meant for Whitney."

"Which is why I want to hire you all to protect me until Percy can be found." Whitney held her breath as she waited for Gage to say it wasn't possible and shut her right down.

Instead, he shifted his gaze to Alex. "Is that feasible while looking for the killer and keeping the other guests and staff safe?"

"If the PPB officers check out, I think it is," Alex said. "We can move Whitney and the kids to our suite under cover of darkness. If Percy is at the resort, he won't know where to find them. I'll post one of these officers at the door at all times when I have to be out of the room." He shot a look at Whitney. "Assuming you're okay with that. You and the kids can have my room, and I'll bunk on the couch."

Essentially, he was asking her to spend as many of the next waking hours as possible together. In that amount of time, she would surely learn more about him, and it scared her that it would bring her closer to him, when she was already drawn to him like a magnetic force field pulling at her. But she had the children to think about, and his plan seemed solid.

"It sounds good," she said. "Thank you."

He faced the screen. "Eryn, how long will it take for you to confirm that these officers are legit?"

"An hour tops."

Alex looked at Whitney again. "Eryn's our cyber guru, and she can find out most anything about anybody."

"Good thing I don't have any secrets then," Whitney chuckled and the others laughed with her. She did have a secret though. A big one. She was falling for Alex Hamilton. Falling big time, and at this moment when he was smiling at her, she didn't care a bit that it was happening.

"What else can we do?" Gage asked.

"I have an idea," Sam said. "If this storm lets up enough to get the drone up, but not the helo, I can send blood and hair samples out if someone can meet it. I've mapped out a drop point and will need someone on standby."

Trey leaned forward. "I'm not teaching any classes right now and am on maintenance detail so I'm free." He sounded like he was dying of boredom.

Eryn wrinkled her nose at her fiancé. "You just want to get your excitement quota in for the week."

"You know it." Trey laughed.

Eryn joined in, and Whitney admired their ease with each other. She made a mental note to ask Alex how long they'd been together.

"We'll also get started on finding Percy," Gage said. "We'll formulate a plan tonight and should have an update for you in the morning."

"That fast?" Whitney gaped at the screen. "But the police haven't found even a hint of his whereabouts."

"We aren't the police." Pride filled Alex's voice. "We're a cut above."

"As a former deputy, I can attest to that," Trey said. "This team has resources and contacts we never had as a deputy."

"I concur," Riley weighed in.

"Then thank you for taking this assignment on such short notice," Whitney said.

Gage waved a hand. "It's what we do. Step in when people are in crisis and help them sort it out. And if they're in danger, we make sure they're safe."

She nodded as if this was normal, but it wasn't normal at all. These men and women were exceptional and modest at what they did. And they were here for her. All of them. Even the two who weren't on the call, she suspected.

Her heart swelled with gratitude, and those tears that never seemed far away since Vanessa died threatened to fall again. She looked up and took a long breath.

Thank you for looking out for me and the kids. For letting me meet this team.

"I've gotten video files for the resort," Alex's voice startled her. "I've reviewed most of them with no leads, but I'll finish them tonight. I don't expect to see much of the actual shooting due to the blizzard, but maybe I can catch Percy or our victim earlier on."

"If you confirm he's there, let me know so we don't waste resources trying to find him," Gage said.

"I'll text you when I finish going through the files. Then, if Sam and I are freed up with the PPB officers standing guard tomorrow, we'll begin the day by interviewing guests and staff. We can show them a picture of the deceased to see if they recognize him or have seen him around. And we'll also ask their permission to do a detailed room search. Might be pointless, as if the killer is in the group, he'll most likely have disposed of his weapon by now."

"The PPB officers can help us with these searches," Sam added.

Gage nodded. "Sounds like you have a solid plan. Let me know if you need any additional resources."

"Not sure how you can help other than with information since there's no way in or out of this place."

"We can provide moral support," Eryn said.

Trey circled his arm around Eryn's shoulders. "And my sweet almost-wife is very good at that."

The others made gagging noises and started laughing.

Whitney appreciated the change in mood as things had gotten so heavy in her life lately and on the whole, she was a happy, fun-loving person who enjoyed laughing.

"Okay, as much as I want to join you all in mocking Trey," A grin slid across Alex's face. "We need to get Whitney and the kids moved. I'll wait to hear from you on the officers, Eryn, and then tomorrow we'll do an update on our progress."

His teammates started to say goodbye and wish them well.

Alex leaned forward to disconnect the call.

"Just a minute, Alex," Gage said, his tone sharp.

Alex sat back, and Whitney leaned forward as she didn't want to miss whatever Gage was going to say.

"Something's off with you tonight. Don't know what it is and don't care unless…" He locked gazes with Alex. "Unless you let yourself get distracted and underestimate this killer. Then we need to have a talk."

Alex curled his fingers into fists and remained locked in on Gage. "Don't worry. There'll be no need to have a talk. I'll protect this family and everyone here with my life. You can count on that and so can they."

11

Alex packed up his clothes and supplies from the bathroom. The sheets and towels were fresh from the morning, and now, the room with double beds was free for the family who he was starting to care for deeply to move in.

Gage's warning words came back. Alex wouldn't let his boss or Whitney and the kids down. He would keep his head. No matter the way she turned it just by walking into a room, much less sitting next to him in her bedroom. He'd had to work doubly hard just to concentrate on the call and that's what Gage was picking up on. His boss didn't miss a thing.

Get a grip, dude, or you will fail.

He shouldered his tote with more force than necessary and went into the living area. Isaiah and Whitney sat on the sofa, a sleeping Zoey resting on Whitney's chest, and Isaiah's head propped on her shoulder. Zoey wore adorable reindeer fuzzy footie pajamas and had a small blanket tucked up next to her chin. Her soft blond curls contrasted with Whitney's dark hair, but otherwise he could have mistaken them for mother and daughter.

An instant mother. Just like that. One day single and on

her own, the next day responsible for two children. That had to be a huge shock. In all of this, he didn't ask or even wonder how she was handling it. And on top of it, a killer, someone she once trusted and likely had even come to love over the years, was hunting her down.

A need to care for them coursed through Alex. He'd never felt such a protective desire in his life, and it left him feeling like the very floor was shifting under his feet. Fearful, too, of the heavy responsibility. Sure he'd been on missions to rescue and protect others plenty of times in the past, but it had never felt so deeply personal before.

And he'd never shouldered the majority of the weight on his shoulders.

If only the pass was open and reinforcements could get through. But there was no *if only* in this situation, only what was—a roadblock. A big, dangerous roadblock. Mounds. Piles. Mountains of snow blocking what Alex needed most. Help.

The theme in his life of late. Something he'd been dialoging with God about. With all his teammates pairing up and getting married, Alex was starting to see how empty his life was. So he'd been consciously trying to change that. To think about dating. Not that he'd succeeded in moving forward. He kept hitting walls, mountainous walls in his heart, and he had been finding every which way around them. Now he had to face them square on. Did God orchestrate for him to meet Whitney and the kids so that he'd be forced to face his past?

Well, it was clear God *did* want him here to protect them. There was a killer here, and no way out for any of them. And right now only God knew why.

If He changed His mind, He could move mountains to affect the change. Could do anything He had a mind to. Problem was Alex had come to believe that God wanted him to learn something while blocked by the mountains in his life. Maybe that's why he was finding himself literally hemmed in.

Maybe he had to change so those mountains could move.

Still, God was here with them. That Alex knew, and he couldn't rely on his skills alone. He needed God's help. He stood for a moment and lifted his head. Tried to think positive and focus on what he *did* have at his disposal.

Thank you for putting PPB officers here. For Sam being here. For her skills and the ease in working with her. Give me the wisdom to coordinate all of our efforts. To stay vigilant and do the right thing to keep this family and everyone at the resort safe.

Feeling more optimistic, he continued around the sofa and set his bag on the floor. "The room's all set."

Isaiah got up and stared up at Alex. His eyes were narrowed, and he gnawed on his lower lip. *Man, oh, man.* The poor kid. He was wearing fear like a boa constrictor, clinging and strangling him.

What had happened to make his suffering worse?

Alex could hardly look at the boy without hugging him and promising that everything would be okay now. He swallowed and forced a smile. "S'up, bud?"

"Aunt Whitney told me Dad might be here. Might be wanting to hurt her and take us." He rubbed his head in nervous little strokes.

Alex rested his hand on Isaiah's shoulder. "I'm sorry, bud. But you don't need to worry. I'm here with you and so is Sam. We'll keep you safe." Alex felt like he was lying to the kid, because he couldn't make a promise like that. No one could. Still, he couldn't leave the boy feeling this distraught —he would never sleep.

"See?" Whitney said. "That's what I said. We have the

very best person looking out for us, and we'll be fine as long as we listen to everything he tells us to do."

Isaiah started to rock back and forth on his feet, and his focus landed at Alex's waist where he'd strapped his holster to his belt. The boy's eyes went wide, and he stared up at Alex. "Are you going to kill him?"

What? Oh, man. Alex shoved a hand into his hair. How did he answer that loaded question? If Percy attempted to hurt them, Alex could indeed end up killing him, but Alex sure wasn't going to tell Isaiah that.

He took a breath, eased it out, and prayed for an answer that would comfort Isaiah not hurt him more. "I never want to use my gun. Never. But you need to know that I'll do whatever I have to do to keep the three of you safe."

Isaiah stood silent for a long moment then suddenly gave a firm nod of his head. "Thank you."

Seriously? This kid kept surprising Alex. He was acting so grown-up. So worldly-wise and he was only nine. With one swift, thoughtless act by his father, Isaiah had been forced to grow up. Alex knew the feeling. Knew from the day his mom checked out of his life.

"I got your back, bud." He held out his hand for a fist bump.

Isaiah reciprocated. He looked like he wanted to say something, but then picked up his suitcase and headed for the bedroom.

"You're good with him," Whitney said as she tried to scoot to the edge of the sofa.

"Let me take Zoey for you." Alex's emotions were stripped bare from Isaiah's terrible situation—loving his dad and probably hating him at the same time. Add Whitney's compliment to that, and Alex wanted to run the other way. Forget facing and feeling all the pain and heartache. Just slip back into the joking façade he was comfortable with.

He pushed the thoughts away and scooped up Zoey's warm little body. She didn't wake but shifted to snuggle against his chest and plugged her thumb into her mouth. She reminded him so much of Faith when she'd fallen asleep in his arms on the day he'd discovered their mother.

He just stood there staring at Zoey's precious face surrounded by blond curls. The innocence of a baby with none of the world's hurts written on her heart. None of the devastation or danger. None of man's sin against other men.

"Don't worry about waking her," Whitney said. "She sleeps through everything."

"I'm not."

Whitney picked up their suitcases and paused to stare at him. "Is something wrong?"

He didn't know what to say. Didn't know if he could trust his voice. He swallowed hard. "It's not fair. These kids losing their parents like this. But then, life isn't fair, is it?"

A shaky breath escaped between her lips as she shook her head. "We can never know what God's purpose is in anything, but yeah...yeah...I'm struggling with this. I've always believed the verse that says He brings good from a bad situation, but..." She shook her head harder. "I'm wrestling with figuring out how that can possibly happen here."

"I thought the same thing when my mom swallowed that bottle of pills," he said bluntly. He was testing her by the way he blurted out the way his mother died. He had to find out what she was made of.

He watched and waited for her gasp or offer a horrified look that his mother killed herself. After all, that's what most people did, and he felt like a freak growing up.

She set down the suitcase, rested her hand on his arm, and stared up into his eyes. There was no horror there. No shock. Just compassion. And impossible understanding of his pain.

"That must have been doubly hard," she whispered. "Losing her and knowing she left you on purpose."

Of course, Whitney would be kind. Compassionate. He was learning that about her, and it was a quality he always sought in people. That's why he loved his team so much. They were all big tough guys who would deny having any emotions until the cows came home, but each and every one of them cared deeply and wanted to right the world's wrongs.

Gage was the catalyst for that attitude, and he drew like-minded people to work with him and join their team. It was an honor to know, work with, and call each of them *friend*.

"I'm sorry you had to go through such a life-altering trauma," Whitney continued, her hand still resting on his arm. "But it's allowing you to connect with Isaiah. I can see how much you're helping him, and I can't ever repay you for the invaluable gift you're giving him."

Heat flooded his face. He never could accept a compliment. He didn't know why, but it almost bothered him.

"God finding the good from bad, I guess," he redirected.

She squeezed his arm and let go. "I like that you're so humble, but please accept that you're helping him and that I appreciate it. You deserve someone to appreciate you."

How had he gotten into this deep of a discussion with her?

He held Zoey up. "We should get her to bed."

Whitney looked hurt at his sudden change of topic, but he'd been flooded with so many emotions in the past two days that he couldn't deal any more. He hadn't connected with anyone like this since his mother died, and everything was all jumbled up with that. Point-blank, he didn't know how to handle it.

He headed for the bedroom. Isaiah had turned back the sheets and was in his pajamas sitting in the bed. "She can sleep with me."

Alex glanced at Whitney to be sure that was okay. She nodded. He laid Zoey in the bed. Her hair covered her face, and he gently moved it away.

He wanted the best for these kids. Besides keeping them safe, he wanted to help them adjust. Especially Isaiah.

He held out his fist again. Isaiah met it with his. "'Night, bud."

"'Night."

Alex nearly fled out of the room and found Sam in the kitchenette making a cup of tea.

She looked up. Watched. Assessed. Evaluated. "Want something?"

Yeah. Understanding of what in the world was going on with him. He needed to get it together because if he didn't, he would be distracted. And distraction led to errors that he couldn't afford to make.

12

Alex hoped to wake up to sun streaming through the window, but when he looked outside he couldn't see more than a few feet through the swirling snow. And the forecast said temperatures had dropped ten degrees overnight. If their shooter had escaped, he was facing even more extreme conditions.

Alex closed his computer from reviewing the last of the resort's video files and cupped his hand around a warm coffee mug. He'd stared at the computer screen until three a.m. and then tossed and turned on the sofa until six and started reviewing files again.

"Good morning," Whitney said from behind.

Her warm voice washed over him, and he was unreasonably happy that she'd finally gotten up to join him. He swiveled slowly to savor that first look at her this morning. She was wearing a pine-green sweater that brought out her beautiful eyes and her soft, creamy complexion. She looked fresh and well-rested, a sweet smile on her face.

He returned her smile and hooked an arm over the back of the chair. "You look like you slept well."

"I did. Surprised me. I must have been exhausted from the stress. What about you?"

He shrugged. "But that's not unusual when I'm on a protection detail."

Her smile evaporated. "I'm sorry about that. I wish it could be different. I can't begin to tell you how grateful I am for your help."

"Glad to do it." He gestured at the kitchenette. "I made coffee if you want some."

"Thank you." She crossed the room, and he watched the subtle sway of her hips and very long legs in dark jeans. She glanced over her shoulder. "Once the kids get up, I'll order room service, but if you're hungry, you don't have to wait for us."

"Sam grabbed breakfast for us at the restaurant about an hour ago." He glanced at his watch. "Our first interview is in fifteen minutes."

"What time is it?"

"Quarter to eight."

"Oh, wow. That's late for me." She poured the coffee. "I guess I really *did* need to sleep."

"I used the time to review the final video files."

She poured creamer into her mug. "And?"

"No sign of Percy in any of them. The cameras caught John Doe entering the lodge two days ago, but it didn't record him anywhere after that. Not a surprise. They don't have many cameras inside other than at the front desk, and he doesn't show up on those videos. Means he never registered or checked out."

"What about your gun runner? See anything interesting with him?"

Disappointed, he shook his head. "None of the guests seem to be up to anything unusual. And I didn't see our target meet with anyone in a public space."

"That's disappointing." Stirring her coffee, she came near him, and the cheerful mood she brought into the room earlier had disappeared.

He tried not to frown. She seemed discouraged about the lack of progress, and he wanted to alleviate her concern. "Investigations are a step-at-a-time kind of thing. There's never an easy answer. It's really trial and error, so don't get down with every lack of a lead. This is normal." He gave her a half-grin. "It's not like on TV or in the movies where obvious clues lead straight to the suspect."

She smiled at that. "I'll do my best to stay optimistic."

The SAT phone rang from the table, and when he saw Gage's name, he grabbed it. "Morning, Gage."

"Yeah. Hey, listen, I wanted to see if you saw Percy in the videos."

"No sign of him."

"Okay, then let me update you on what we know so far."

"Whitney's with me. Let me turn on speakerphone so she can hear, too." He pressed the button. "Go ahead, Gage. What's new on Percy?"

Whitney's expression perked up, and she came closer.

"Eryn and Piper have been working with a contact at the Marshal's Service."

Alex looked at Whitney. "Piper is Eryn's friend. She's also an FBI agent who specializes in cybercrimes, and she helps us out when we need it. She's on leave due to an injury and has been working with Eryn a lot lately."

"That's great," Whitney said, turning her focus to the phone. "Did she find something with the Marshals?"

"They've obtained a list of all the locations where Percy's potentially been spotted," Gage replied.

"But those didn't pan out, right?" Whitney asked. "At least the news stories say they didn't."

"Right," Gage replied. "So you may think it's a waste of

time for our team to review the sightings, but Eryn has mad computer skills that they don't have and has often found leads that have been passed over by law enforcement."

Whitney gave a firm nod as if Gage could see her. "I continue to be impressed with your organization."

"It's the team. I'm blessed to have the best people." Sincerity rang through his tone, and Alex knew his boss really meant it. "So anyway, she's written an algorithm to see if there's a pattern in the sightings."

"And?" Alex urged him faster.

"And she may be on to something. She's not sure yet. But she's retrieved as much CCTV footage as she can easily locate to support her theory and is reviewing it. If these files don't pan out, she said she can look for additional footage from private sources."

"How long will all of this take?" Whitney asked.

"Eryn figures she'll have preliminary information by lunchtime."

"And you'll update us again then?" Alex asked.

"Absolutely. Talk to you—"

"Wait," Whitney interrupted. "Does Eryn really think one of the people actually saw Percy? That one of those sightings will actually pan out?"

"She says there's a potential pattern of movement. So yeah, she does think it's possible."

"Then he may not be at the resort, and John Doe was the target." She looked at Alex. "I could have just been in the wrong place at the wrong time."

"Don't be too quick to jump to any conclusions," Alex warned. "Sure, Eryn has a theory, but we can't let our guard down here. Nothing is going to change in my protection plan for you."

She nodded vigorously, her coffee sloshing in her cup. "Right...right...yeah. I hear you."

"Okay, then," Gage said. "Anything I can do for you before I disconnect?"

"Just tell Eryn thank you for me," Whitney said. "Oh, and Piper, too. I owe them both big time."

"Will do, and keep me updated on the interviews, Alex."

"You got it." Alex disconnected and stood. He locked gazes with Whitney. "Promise me you won't leave the suite or stop being vigilant with your safety."

She held his gaze. "I promise."

He reached out to touch her arm to make sure she knew how serious he was. "I mean it. Stay focused."

"Now you're scaring me."

"Sorry. I...it's...when I think about you and the kids..." Worry crept up in voice and almost choked it off. "I hate having to leave you, and I want to be positive you're safe while you're out of my care."

"Don't worry about us. We'll be fine here." She patted his hand then stepped back.

He clamped a hand on the back of his neck. "Officer Everett or one of the other officers will be right outside the door until I come back. Is there anything you need before I go?"

"No. You've thought of everything already." She smiled at him, that same tender smile of thankfulness and gratitude that went straight to his heart.

He had to force himself not to pull her closer for a hug.

Seriously. Who was this guy who'd taken over his brain? This was so not him.

"If you have an emergency, talk to the officer on duty first, and then call me if you have cell service or use the landline as it's still functioning," he managed to say. "If you need something that's not urgent, text me if you can."

"We'll be fine. Just be sure you're careful, too." She came

close. Nearly toe-to-toe. Smiled up at him again. Rested a hand on his bicep, nearly melting his resolve.

"I wouldn't want anything to happen to you." The smile widened, a beautiful sight to behold.

He could hardly resist, but he had to. He gave a quick nod and stepped back. She looked hurt, which honestly surprised him. Was she feeling the same thing? With his recon training, he was usually overly observant, but he couldn't think straight when she was around.

He made a mental note to pay more attention to her. Hah! Just what he needed. He started to roll his eyes then caught himself. "I'll come up on our morning break to check on you."

She nodded, clipped and precise.

Right. He'd offended her. He couldn't stay around to explain because he wasn't about to tell her that he was interested in her, and if the coffee swimming in his gut told him anything, he *was* developing strong feelings for her. Even when that was the last thing he wanted with any woman.

Panicking, he wanted to bolt out the door. Instead, he forced himself to take slow even steps until he was in the hallway.

Officer Everett stood right outside. He spun, his hand going to his holster at his belt.

"Relax," Alex said, but had to admit he was glad this guy was on extreme alert.

Everett let his hand fall. "Can't be too careful."

Music to Alex's ears.

Everett was Alex's height, had buzzed blond hair and a thick neck. Alex put him in his late twenties and he'd only been an officer for four years. But when Alex had interviewed him that morning, he got a good feel for the guy's grasp of proper procedures for a protection detail, and Alex was confident he was up to the task at hand.

"I'm off to our interviews," Alex said. "You've got my cell number. Reception's been spotty for most cell phones, but use it if you have even a hint of any problems."

"Roger that."

"I'll be back in a few hours to give you a break." Alex stepped off then looked back. "You have Percy Masters' picture memorized, right?"

He nodded.

Alex eyed him for a minute. "Wouldn't hurt to look at it a time or two just to keep it fresh."

Everett held up his phone. "Will do."

Alex liked the guy's attitude, and as he headed down to the meeting room he felt a sense of relief that the trio of officers happened to be vacationing at the resort. Some would say that it was coincidence, but Alex wasn't sure how he felt about that. Like did he just coincidentally happen to be here when Whitney needed protection, or did God place them both here at the same time for a purpose? Alex always had a hard time grasping what to believe because an infinite number of things could change in a flash. He knew God was all-powerful, and Alex wished he could believe God orchestrated everything, but the magnitude of such a task boggled Alex's mind.

He entered the first-floor meeting room where the interviews would take place. He would have preferred a smaller, less-intimidating space, but this was the best Tomio could do.

Sam was already sitting at the table, her jacket hanging on the chair behind her, the hood crusted in snow. Her cheeks were rosy, her boots dripping with melting snow. She was looking at a paper, likely the interview schedule that Tomio had set up for them. He'd really stepped up, doing whatever Alex asked. When this was all over, Alex needed to do something nice for the manager.

Sam looked up from her phone. "What's wrong? You're flushed."

Flushed? He touched his face. Was it from his crazy reaction to Whitney? If it was, she had to have noticed it, too. *Great.* He turned around to take his coat off, then flipped a chair around and straddled it. "Must've been the trip down here. I was in a hurry. Wouldn't do to be late."

"Right." A skeptical look said she didn't buy his story, but she waved the printed schedule, and he was thankful she was letting it go. "You ready for a full day of interviews?"

"I'd rather be in here than standing watch at the tent. It's even colder today."

"Tell me about it. Tomio and I just finished getting the tarp up over the porch. I can now start looking for the slug."

"How long do you think it will take you to find it?"

"If I'm looking in the right place, it'll probably take me all day at a minimum. It's going to be a long, tedious process. Snow has drifted nearly up to the roof, and I'll have to remove it a small shovelful at a time and sift through the snow for evidence before discarding it."

He drummed his fingers on the table. "Maybe I should handle the interviews and you should do that."

"That's what I was thinking. But I need to warm up so I'll sit in on the first one. And then I can pop in when I need a break throughout the day."

"Sounds good." He pulled out his phone and set it on the table. "I'm going to record the interviews and take a picture of the guests to show Whitney in case she might recognize one of them. You could listen to the interviews later, if you want."

"Yeah. Good. I'll do that tonight. Maybe I'll come up with questions you miss."

Alex continued to be impressed with Sam's willingness to go with the flow. "I hate to keep you up late, when it's probably a long shot, but I'm not going to ignore any possibility."

She waved him off. "We have to step up here and make sure nothing goes south."

"True that. Have you talked to Nate today?"

She shook her head. "I did send a picture of John Doe to Eryn last night to have Piper run it through facial recognition. I have to say it's pretty sweet that Eryn has a fed for a friend. One who's willing to help us out anyway."

Alex nodded as having an insider who had access to top-of-the-line forensic and electronic tools was indeed invaluable. "Bummer that her foot hasn't healed, and she's still on medical leave."

"You know…" Sam tilted her head and studied him. "I've heard about everyone's injury that took them out of their past jobs, but not yours. Is it some super-secret thing that others are under penalty of death from repeating?"

"Nah, nothing like that. I just don't talk about it." *And don't want to mention it now.* "It's so minor I honestly feel kind of like an imposter. I mean Gage almost lost the use of his arm. Jackson his knee. Shoot, Riley even lost a kidney."

"And Coop's back is a nightmare at times."

"Yeah, plus Trey's bum leg and your shoulder."

"Okay, we ran down everyone's issues, and yet…" She raised an eyebrow. "Yours is still a mystery."

He slowly reached up to his right ear and pulled out a hearing aid. "I've lost a substantial portion of my hearing in this ear. Bomb."

Her eyes narrowed. "That's not minor."

"Yeah, it really is." He settled the small hearing aid back in place. "I hardly notice it. But take Riley. If he takes a bad hit, he could be in a life-or-death situation."

"True, but then any one of us could find ourselves in a

life-threatening situation. Prior injury or not. It's all just part of the job, and we deal."

She was right, and yet... "I'm thinking Piper doesn't quite feel that way yet."

"You think she's going to be sidelined by the FBI?"

"Odds are good."

"They'll probably give her a desk or analyst's job."

He snorted. "You've met her, right? Like that's something she'll agree to do."

"Yeah, I kinda got that feeling from her. She loves the cyber part of her job, but she wants some action thrown in, too. I totally get that and loved that I got to do both at times as a criminalist. And on the team, it's a perfect balance. Maybe Gage will have a place for her if her foot doesn't heal."

"Maybe." Alex considered the idea. "Eryn and Trey *are* talking about having more kids after they get married. Maybe she'll quit working or switch to part-time and something will open up for Piper."

"Well, all we can do now is pray for Piper."

Alex nodded and thought about asking Sam to pray for him, too, as he clearly needed help in figuring out his life, but then he'd have to tell her why, and he *so* wasn't going to do that.

Better to get back to the investigation. "Let me know when you hear from her on the facial recognition, okay?"

"Of course." Sam sat back and crossed her legs. "So what's your gut feel? About Percy being here?"

"It varies depending on the moment, but we have to assume he is. And in that vein, I want to move Whitney and the kids to a different location tonight."

"You think Percy knows where she's staying?" Sam frowned.

"I can't honestly say, but if we keep changing things up, he'll have a harder time figuring it out, right?"

She blinked a few times. "Or there'll be a greater chance he'll see you move her."

"We can mitigate that."

Sam cocked her head. "What did you have in mind?"

"I don't know. I'll have to check in with Tomio and see what he might suggest."

She gave a firm nod. "If that's what you want to do, I can see the value in it."

"I honestly do."

She got to her feet. "Then let's open the door and start the interviews. The sooner we get started today the sooner we can move them and keep Percy off track."

13

This was the worst job for Alex, sitting in a windowless room asking questions. He was a take-action guy, not a sit-around guy, and only two hours into the interviews he was already antsy.

An older couple, Herb and Martha Norman, crossed the room and sat down across from him. She had curly gray hair, he was bald, both faces were lined with wrinkles and plenty of laugh lines, but neither of them were laughing now.

Martha clasped her hands primly on the table. "I don't see how we can be of any help to you. We don't know anyone here."

Alex had heard this from each interviewee he'd talked to, and he offered a practiced smile. "You never know what you might have seen that could be of help."

Herb frowned. "We're law-abiding citizens, not some hoodlums bent on killing each other."

"I fully understand that, Mr. Norman." Alex took out his phone to move things forward. "I have a picture of the poor man who was murdered. Would you mind looking at it to see if you happened to notice him here?"

"A dead person?" Martha clutched her chest.

"I'm sorry, yes, he's deceased."

"I'll look at it, Martha. You don't have to." Herb reached for the phone, grimaced, but then took a good long look. "He doesn't look familiar at all."

Martha shook her head. "You would've only noticed him if he ran you down—with your head in the clouds all the time." She held out her hand. "Give it to me."

Herb *tsked* and passed her the phone. She glanced quickly at the screen then looked away and kept sneaking quick peeks as if it wouldn't be as bad if she didn't actually stare at it.

"No." She shook her head hard, her curls bouncing. "No, I've never seen him."

Herb patted his wife's hand. "And if my Martha says she hasn't, she hasn't. She knows her mind for sure."

Alex took his phone back and looked at the room roster. They were staying in the room right next to McCray. Some pointed questions were in order here.

"Have you seen anything out of the ordinary happening near your room?" he asked.

"No," Herb said. "Should we have? Are we in some kind of danger?"

"No, no. I'm only asking to see if you noticed anything odd since you've been here."

Martha looked at him. "There was that one thing."

Herb rolled his eyes. "Don't bother him with *that*."

"Go ahead," Alex said and smiled at her. "Bother me with anything you want to share."

Martha sat up a little taller. "Well, this man in the room next to us. I came out to get ice. He was heading to the ice machine, too. He was real nice, and we talked for a few minutes. His name is Frisco McCray. He seemed sad to be at the resort alone. Said he'd recently ended a long marriage, and he had to get away, but it wasn't fun being alone."

"And of course, being the busybody you are, you commiserated with him and pried more." Her husband gave her a fond smile.

"Oh, you." She laughed. "We did talk a bit more, but he really didn't have much else to say."

"So what was it that concerned you?"

"We got our ice, and then we went back toward our rooms. He opened his door and a man spoke to him from inside his room." She frowned. "I thought that was odd when Frisco said he was alone."

Yeah, it is. But McCray said he had a maintenance man in his room. "Did you hear what the man had to say?"

"Yeah, he said, 'I'm out of here.' And then, Frisco said rather sternly, 'We aren't finished yet'."

Could this have been John Doe? "Did you see this other man?"

"No. Frisco pushed him into the room and quickly closed the door before I could get a look."

"And let me tell you," Herb said. "If it was earthly possible, my Martha would have accomplished it."

She swatted a hand at him, and they grinned at each other, a wash of love following their teasing.

"When was this?" Alex asked.

"Sunday night. About eight. I know because I was getting ready for my show to come on TV when I saw that Herb let the ice run low."

"Is there anything else that you noticed about this Frisco guy?"

"No. That's it."

Herb's bushy gray eyebrows furrowed, and he leaned forward. "Something about him we need to know, seeing we're next-door neighbors?"

Alex held up a placating hand. "Please don't read anything into my questions. Like I said, it's often the things that don't seem significant that are, and I like to be as detailed as possible so I don't have to call you back down here and waste your time."

"Right. Right. Well, okay, then. Nothing else odd. And believe you me, Martha has been keeping an eye on things for us." He chuckled.

"Do you mind if I take your picture for my records? It helps us keep track of the people we've spoken to."

"Fire away." Herb circled his arm around Martha and leaned close to her. They smiled, but it was forced and tight.

Alex handed his card to Martha. "If you think of anything else, my cell number's on the card. Or if there's no service, Tomio can always find me."

They stood, and Herb offered his hand. "Lucky for all of us that you and your teammate were vacationing up here."

"Glad to be of help." Alex shook hands and walked them into the hallway. He bid them goodbye and locked the meeting room door to take his mid-morning break and check in with Whitney.

He pretended to look at his phone but really his mind was all over the information gleaned on McCray. It sounded like he'd met with the guy he'd planned to do business with up here and odds were good that this man could be their victim. But it was equally possible that this man could still be at the resort and a danger to them all, too.

When the Normans disappeared from view, Alex turned and took a circuitous route toward his suite. He really was liking McCray for this murder and was still holding out hope that Percy wasn't at the resort. But he couldn't let his guard down and allow himself to be followed. If he did, he could be leading a killer to Whitney's door.

He approached Officer Everett whose hand went to his gun. He was either proactive or jumpy.

"Something happen while I was gone?" Alex asked.

"It's probably nothing, but a rowdy group of guys insisted their buddy was staying in this suite. I told them they were wrong and to take a hike, but they could've been on a scouting mission."

"Did you get their names?"

"One of them, yeah. And the name of the guy they were looking for."

Alex didn't like the sound of that. Maybe he should move Whitney now. But he didn't want to alarm Everett. "Text them to me, and I'll follow up with Tomio."

"You think I'm overreacting."

"Could be, but I'd rather that than failing to act when we should." Alex didn't think he could ever overreact when it came to keeping the trio inside safe. "Send me that text now. And FYI, we were planning to move Whitney and the kids to another location tonight, but after this I'm going to head down to finalize it now."

"Okay." Everett got out his phone. "Texting the names now."

Alex heard his phone ding in his pocket but he didn't stop to look at it. He headed straight to the lobby and found Tomio in his office behind the check-in desk.

"Alex," he said, his accent messing with the enunciation of Alex's name.

"I need you to tell me what you know about these guests." He got out his phone and displayed the two names.

"Oh, them." Tomio rolled his eyes. "They've been a problem since the day they arrived. Drinking and carousing around the lodge at all hours. I almost asked them to leave. But honestly, they're big spenders, and a wing we're remodeling fell behind schedule so we need the business. I've been doing my best to rein them in."

"Are their room numbers similar to my suite?"

He clicked his computer keys. "Yeah. The one guy's in 212."

"And I have 312. So if they were drinking, they could've made a mistake and gone to the wrong room."

"Exactly."

"Still, I'm not taking a chance and want to move Whitney and the kids. What do you have to offer?"

He tapped his chin. "Another suite is the only thing I've got other than single rooms."

"What about something away from other guests where guys like this won't happen to wander up. Do you have a place like that?"

"I could..." He snapped forward eagerly, then frowned. "Nah, probably not."

"Could what?"

"The wing I mentioned. The one that's under renovation. It's closed to guests. Chained off actually. You can only access it from outside. Several of the suites are ready."

"That's it. Sounds perfect."

"Yeah, except I don't have an occupancy permit for it while under renovation."

"It's not like you have to worry about an inspector showing up."

"True."

"Is the area safe to occupy?"

He nodded vigorously.

"Then let's do it."

"Okay."

Alex glanced at his watch. "I need to get back to the interviews but we could move them during my lunch break. Can you have the rooms ready by then?"

"Sure."

"Hey, thanks, man." Alex held out his hand to shake. "You and Yuki have been very helpful. I won't ever forget it."

"So maybe if I need a favor someday, you repay me."

"You got it." Alex took out his phone. "I'll call Whitney and tell her to pack up and then come see you when I break for lunch."

"Sounds good."

Alex spun and left the office. He would have to make sure no one saw them move, but with the PPB officers' help they could block off hallways and visible areas to keep others out or see what they were doing. At least Alex hoped they could make this move without anyone taking notice.

Whitney wasn't used to sitting around, but once she unpacked in the new suite and settled down in the living area with the kids who were playing a game of Candy Land, she had nothing to do. She'd always been active in her personal and professional life. Nurses never had downtime. Especially not an ED nurse. And she was a problem solver, too. Observe, assess, and act. That was her motto. It always worked to give her patients the most professional and compassionate care. It allowed her to discover their greatest need right off the bat, and she could begin to address it right away and give them relief from their suffering. Pending the doctor's order, of course.

But with Percy, she'd been in panic mode from the moment she'd discovered Vanessa. Flight mode—avoidance —and she was feeling helpless. Totally helpless. She hoped by now that Eryn would have found Percy, but Eryn said she needed more time to gather additional files. She was still optimistic that Percy wasn't at the resort, but as Alex said,

Whitney couldn't count on that and let her guard down. So her nerves were strung taut and vibrating.

She jumped up and went to the small kitchen to rinse out mugs used for a hot chocolate snack. It was something to do. To keep busy while Isaiah and Zoey played together, much as they did in the old home routine, which was something Whitney was trying to foster. Zoey was just learning the game rules and simply enjoyed moving her little plastic person around the colorful board with Isaiah's guidance. Whitney almost stepped in but then realized it was good for Isaiah to help his little sister. This eliminated his habit of sitting around and brooding about his loss. With nothing to do, Whitney could brood, however. She had plenty of time for that even if she knew it was detrimental to her.

She glanced back at the pair, their heads bent over the board. Isaiah's hair had been pale blond as a baby but continued to darken over the years, and his longer chin and big eyes resembled his father's features. Zoey was a spitting image of her mother. Vanessa was fair and blond like their mother. Vanessa was also eight years older than Whitney, who'd gotten her dark coloring from her father, and people rarely thought they were sisters.

God handpicked the characteristics for each child so interestingly. At the moment, she was very thankful for Zoey's appearance as Whitney could simply look at her and feel close to her sister.

But then that brought pain. Deep agonizing pain. All because of Percy. How on earth was Isaiah going to survive this betrayal by his father? How was she, for that matter? She'd once blindly given her trust to others. At least to her family. Now her whole foundation was rocked to the core.

And yet, it seemed as if she hadn't learned a thing. Here she was trusting Alex and Sam—the entire team—to keep them safe. Maybe she shouldn't. Maybe she should be trying to help herself, too. Help find Percy.

But how? She couldn't leave this room.

She finished rinsing the mugs and turned back to the space. Her laptop sat on the table. If the Internet was still up, she could access the world that way. Maybe figure something out. She hurried across the room and turned it on. She'd read many stories about Percy's escape, but hadn't checked them lately. She opened a browser window and sighed when it connected. Tomio's investment in technology was really paying off.

She entered Percy's name in a search engine. It returned a long list of links, and she started with the first one, even though she'd seen it. She grabbed a resort notepad and pen from by the telephone to jot down any information that would help her track his movements.

By the time she was done with the links on the first page, she'd created a list of sightings in locations all over Oregon and even as far away as California, one person even reporting they'd seen him crossing the border into Mexico. The authorities had ruled them all out.

She heard voices from the hallway, and then the click of the lock. It was likely Alex, but she couldn't be sure, and her heart pounded. If only he'd returned her gun, she could protect herself and the kids. But he said Sam had to keep it until they recovered the slug that killed John Doe and could prove she hadn't shot him.

The door opened, and Alex stepped in. His concerned gaze raced around the room, lighting on her then the kids before his shoulders visibly relaxed.

"Candy Land?" he called out. "You played Candy Land without me?"

He charged across the room and knelt by the coffee

table. "Oh no...looks like you're almost done. Can I get a quick game in before heading back downstairs?"

"Yay." Zoey jumped up and down and clapped.

"She doesn't really know how to play," Isaiah said, his old-man, serious demeanor in place. "I'm helping her. Cut her some slack, okay?"

Alex gave a serious nod. "Gotta help your little sister. Mine is seven years younger than me, and I did the same thing."

Isaiah issued a nod of approval and looked at Zoey. "Want to quit this game, Zo-Zo, and start another with Alex right now?"

"Yes!" Her eyes sparkled with delight, and she threw her arms around Alex's neck to hug him hard.

Whitney had been on the receiving end of Zoey's fierce hugs many times and knew it could feel like a stranglehold. But still, there was nothing more priceless than the warmth of that little sweetie snuggled up close. Vanessa's baby. So precious.

Oh, Sis. I'm so sorry. So, so, sorry.

Vanessa would never know her little girl's warm hugs again. See her children grow up. Be there for big days like sports or band concerts, prom, graduation, and weddings. Isaiah in a sharp tux. Zoey in a flowing white gown. Grandchildren.

Oh...oh.

Vanessa's precious babies. Without their mother or father. The safe and secure life they'd known. Gone. In the blink of an eye. Just gone.

Tears flooded Whitney's eyes, and her vision swam. She hadn't thought beyond the present when she needed to focus on their safety. With Alex and his team on the job, she'd relaxed a bit and been very distracted. But now the full weight of her responsibilities hit her hard. She had two tiny humans counting on her for everything...protection, provision, emotional support, and solid guidance so they would grow into healthy, godly adults.

Could she do it? Really do it well?

Maybe, but as well as Vanessa would have done?

Oh, Sis. I want to. I do.

Tears flowed in earnest.

God, please help me.

"Be right back," she got out over a throat closing with grief and worry and ran to the bedroom. She closed the door, went into the bathroom, and closed that door, too. Even then, she grabbed a towel and held it over her face before unleashing her anguish.

The first sob drew her deeper into the soft white towel, her moans sounding like a wounded animal as the muffled sounds echoed from the tiled walls. She'd decided the very first day the children came to live with her that she would never let them see her cry. Sure, she let them know she was sad and missed their mother. She had to. She couldn't hide it all the time. Plus, she wanted them to see it was okay to be sad, too. But they didn't need to see her extreme pain. See this mess. The ache was so deep it felt like a knife plunged into her flesh.

She rested the towel and her face on the counter. Clutched her arms around her body and sobbed. Her chest burned with the pain, her stomach convulsing. Minutes passed. Maybe ten. More and more, but she couldn't stop. All her pent-up agony, fear, stress, worry, and pain exploded through her in raging waves.

Panic took over. She couldn't breathe.

She'd never cried this hard before. Never given in to it. And she didn't know if she could find her way out.

Help me! Please help me.

A knock sounded on the door. She jerked her head up

and swallowed, her chest rising and falling in deep chest-convulsing hiccups.

"Whitney," Alex asked from the other side of the door. "You've been gone for a while. Is everything okay?"

"Fine," she got out on a choke.

"You sure?"

"Yes." Another croak.

"Okay, I wanted to talk to you, so I'll wait with the kids."

She heard his footsteps fading and looked up at the large mirror. She was a mess. Tear-streaked face with big red blotches. Red-rimmed eyes. She grabbed a tissue and blew her nose, then repaired her appearance as best she could by applying dabs of concealer and putting eye drops in. Alex would know she'd been crying, but hopefully Isaiah would miss the signs.

She pulled in enough oxygen to empty the little room and blew it out. In and out. In and out. After a few more times, she stepped out and ran a hand over her hair as she walked.

Put on a smile. Relax your tense body. Fake it until you feel it.

She found Alex sitting on the sofa, Zoey on his lap. Isaiah next to him. A Mario Kart video game was playing on the large television. The guys each had a steering wheel in hand and were racing a vehicle on the screen. Zoey's pudgy little hand rested on Alex's long fingers, surely slowing him down as he drove Princess Peach through the track in a pink car—obviously chosen by Zoey—and Isaiah raced Yoshi on a motorcycle.

Isaiah was winning hands down, and he was smiling. A wide beaming smile that Whitney hadn't seen since Vanessa died. Whitney had tried to get him to play video games with her, but he'd refused. She wondered how Alex had managed it.

But, oh, what a sight! A wonderful sight. Isaiah could

still smile. The sun would come out again for him. For her, too.

Thank you for showing me the possibilities still ahead.

She took a seat at the table and simply watched the trio. Maybe watched Alex a bit more. His profile was rugged and chiseled, his jaw covered in whiskers trimmed at a precise length. His nose was a bit hooked and seemed to add to the strength he conveyed.

And yet, here he was playing with children and grinning like a kid himself. What a contrast.

"Yes!" Isaiah pumped his fist and fired a superior grin at Alex. "Take that."

Alex laughed, and Isaiah joined in, his sweet boy laughter ringing to the ceiling and bouncing around the room while it mixed with Alex's deep rumble.

She joined them. "Well done, bud. You skunked him."

"I know, right?" He started to laugh again, and then an iron curtain dropped over his face.

"I..." He glanced around the room as if he'd come out of a trance and didn't know where he was. "I shouldn't...I'm sorry...oh, I..." He dropped the steering wheel and raced for the bedroom. The door slammed.

She feared he headed there for the same reasons she had, and she felt tears rising up.

Alex gave Zoey the steering wheel and restarted the game. She couldn't actually play this either, but she was having fun turning the wheel.

Alex shifted to look up at Whitney and grasped her hand but didn't get up. "It'll get better for all of you. I promise."

She clung to him and reveled in the feel of his rough skin...in the comfort of his gentleness and empathy.

How in the world had this guy remained single all these years? What was wrong with him? It had to be big, and maybe her trust in him was misplaced. And even if it wasn't, she had no business letting herself be drawn closer to him. Not when she had more than enough to deal with without adding the terrifying risk of getting into a relationship.

She slipped her hand free. "Would you mind sitting with Zoey while I go talk to Isaiah?"

Alex's eyes narrowed. "Can I suggest that you let him be again this time? Let him figure this out on his own?"

"But he..." She shook her head and bit her lip. "I just want to hug him."

"He might be open to that, but having been in his position, I know this could be another one of those times he needs to figure things out alone. In addition to hurting, he's embarrassed, maybe mad that he let himself be happy. Remember how sometimes you wake up in the morning eager and joyful for the day, and then suddenly you remember Vanessa and everything crashes down on you."

Boy, did she. She nodded.

"That's what hit Isaiah. He had a happy moment, then *bam*. He remembered his loss, and he feels bad about laughing. Let him process."

She looked at the closed door and sighed. "I'm not sure I'm up to that."

He set Zoey on the sofa and came to stand toe-to-toe with her. He locked gazes, and she was entranced by how being this close she spotted a tiny scar hidden in his facial hair just above his mouth. She wanted to know about that scar. Know about his emotional scars, too, and learn from them so she could help Isaiah.

He lightly rested his hands on her shoulders and looked deep into her eyes, probing, searching...for what, she had no idea.

"I haven't known you for long, but I can already see how strong you are," he said softly, yet with conviction. "And I know you can do whatever Isaiah needs. Even if it means leaving him alone with his heartache."

Could she? She wasn't as certain. But here was this big, powerful man with a tender heart who could help her navigate these treacherous waters.

Wouldn't it be wonderful to have a man like him by her side to help Isaiah all the time? She'd love that support, but she couldn't give in. Couldn't let her fears go. That was too great of a risk to take.

14

Alex watched as Whitney took a giant step back. It reminded him of when he played Simon Says as a kid. She didn't look at him, but peered over his shoulder. "You mentioned wanting to talk about something."

She'd seemed so open to him. Open to his touch. Then she closed down and stepped back. He didn't like it. Not one bit.

He got out his phone to show her pictures of the people he'd interviewed when what he wanted to do was press her to find out the reason for her sudden change in mood. But what would the point be when he should never have touched her in the first place? It only led to wanting more. Like the whole hands-on-her-shoulders thing. He didn't know her well enough to be doing that, and yet, it felt like he *did* know her. Very well. Like they'd been friends for years.

How could that even be possible?

Is that you, God?

"You want to talk or are you going to make a call?" She pointed at his phone.

Focus, man.

He tapped the screen to bring up his photos. "I took pictures of each person I've interviewed, and I want to run them by you in case seeing them might jog something in your mind that could help us."

"Okay, sure." She glanced at Zoey, and Alex did, too.

Zoey had set down the steering wheel and was playing with the Candy Land people, bouncing them on the game board as they talked to each other about the Chocolate Swamp.

"I'm glad to have something to do," Whitney said. "But I really should spend a little time with Zoey before her nap time. Could I do it afterward?"

"Sure. I'll AirDrop the pictures to you, and you can look at them then." He pointed at her iPhone laying on the table so they could change her settings, allowing him to send her the pictures via Apple's Bluetooth file transfer system.

She picked it up and tapped the screen, and as they worked through the process, it felt like he'd gone from being a close friend to an awkward stranger. Had a simple touch done all that? Put a wall between them and erased the obviously growing connection?

"I wish I could sit in on the interviews," she said, watching her screen as the files transferred. "But leaving this room would be foolish, and the kids need me here."

"I recorded the interviews for Sam. She's clearing the porch in hopes of finding the slug and wants to listen to them later. You could listen in, too."

"Yes. Yes, please. I'm going stir crazy up here. I even went to the Internet to look for information on Percy thinking I might discover something." She held up her hands. "And before you say that's a waste of time, it was something to keep me busy."

"I wasn't going to say that." He smiled. "I think you should keep going. Read every story you can find because something might stick out for you that doesn't mean anything to anyone else."

"Oh, okay, good. I'll keep going then." She pulled her shoulders back, a resolute look claiming her face.

"Just remember not to get discouraged if nothing pans out. It's—"

"The way investigations go," she interrupted. "I remember that from when you said it earlier, and I'm trying to stay positive."

Zoey toddled across the room carrying *Goodnight Moon* in one hand, her blanket in the other, and her eyes were drooping. "Read book."

Her focus was on him, and he honestly wanted to sit down and read to her, but he had a killer to find. And almost as important, he was already letting this little family distract him. He couldn't give in every time they needed him, could he?

Whitney closed the video of Alex's interview with Herb and Martha Norman and leaned back on the dining chair to stretch her arms. A soft glow from the fireplace where Alex was adding another log warmed the room, but the howling wind and pelting snow against the window left the place still feeling cold.

She shivered and got up to join him near the warmth curling up over the distressed wood mantle.

He glanced up at her for a moment, then continued to stir the flames dancing in the box. They reflected a reddish hue on his glossy dark hair. He was squatting close to the fire, his pants taut over muscular thighs, and he hefted large logs with little effort, balancing gracefully on the balls of his feet as he moved. He brushed his hands off over the wood pile and closed the screen.

He came to his feet with grace and welcomed her with such a sweet smile, she could swear her toes curled in her shoes, and she had to look away before she touched that little scar by his mouth.

"Need a break?" he asked.

She forced herself to look back at him. "I have a question."

"Go ahead."

"Your target. The gun runner. It's Frisco McCray, isn't it?"

Acknowledgement flashed in his eyes for the briefest of seconds. If she hadn't been so focused on him, she would have missed it.

"Even if it is, and I'm not saying it is, you know I can't tell you that."

"You don't have to. Your eyes just did."

He frowned and looked angry. "I'm still not going to confirm anything. And honestly, I'm not sure how much it helps you to know."

She didn't know why he was mad, but she didn't like being in the dark. "I get that, but it would explain a lot of things I've seen this past month."

"Like what?" he asked, his monotone voice belying a flicker of interest in his eyes, confirming in her mind that she was right on track.

She sat down on the sofa and held her hands out to the fire in hopes that he wouldn't see how interested she was in getting to the bottom of this. "He's always alone for meals and on the slopes, but then I've seen him talking to different men. Usually in out-of-the-way places. Hidden spots where no one but staff might happen upon them. And there's this one man in particular I've seen him with a few times. I almost asked him about it one time."

Alex widened his stance, his nose flaring, as he took a deep breath. "I'm glad that you didn't. There's no telling what he might have done. We've both seen his disrespect for you. I can't help but think he'd get mad at you for butting into his business and take it out on you."

She could see that. Totally see that. She shuddered. Another man who couldn't be trusted. She shook her head. "How has my life blown up like this? My brother-in-law's a killer. Someone shot a man next to me and the bullet could've been meant for me. And this gun runner has to choose *me* of all the waitstaff to get familiar with. Why?"

He leaned against the mantel. "I can't honestly explain the first ones, but the last is obvious. You're a beautiful woman, Whitney. What man wouldn't hit on you?"

"You haven't."

"Not because I don't want to."

Wow. Oh. Wow.

"So what's stopping you?" she asked boldly, as she had to know.

"First, I don't even know if you're in a relationship, and I wouldn't want to step on another man's toes."

"Not dating anyone at all."

"Then, second." He ran a hand through his hair, those long fingers searching out and righting strands. "I'm not relationship material. Totally not. Maybe if it was just you I would've pursued my interest, but you have the kids now. You have to think about any man you might date as a potential father for them. I am so far from that possibility that I wouldn't want to lead you on and make you think it could ever happen."

Crazy. She had no idea he'd thought this all through. Meant he was feeling things between them as deeply as she was, but he'd closed the door. Tightly. Firmly. A good thing.

So why did she unexpectedly want to delve deeper and try to open it?

She couldn't. Not a good idea at all. Better to make light of things and get them back to business.

"So you've got us married already, huh?" She chuckled.

"No, it's not...I mean...I don't know." He dropped onto the far end of the plush sofa. "I just want to be truthful. I like you. I am attracted to you, and yet, I will do my very best to avoid those feelings."

"It's for the best anyway."

"Why's that?"

"For starters, I'm in this big mess, but then beyond that, when Percy is behind bars and I can resume life again, I have so much to figure out. Being a mom is a new and all-consuming thing for me. Adding a man to the picture wouldn't be a good idea until I get things resolved."

"That makes perfect sense. Give it some time before dating." He sounded sure and disappointed at the same time.

"Even then, I doubt I will want to," she rushed on so he didn't get the wrong impression that she might be interested in something down the road. "Not after seeing what Percy did to Vanessa."

His eyes widened. "You don't want to live the rest of your life like that, do you? Judging all men by what Percy did?"

"Want to? No. *Will.*"

"But..." He shrugged.

"I get that odds would say I won't meet another murderer in my life, but the murder really isn't the issue. Don't get me wrong, his actions stole my precious sister from me, but his deception for years is what makes me hesitant to trust again." She yanked her hair back into a severe twist. "How can I trust anyone after seeing that? Eleven years of marriage where she was happy. Had what looked like an ideal life, and all that time he was like a snake in the grass slithering through their life, living his lies." She let go and shook her hair out.

Alex gazed at her with his piercing eyes. "Again, you can't judge others by his actions. I would never do something like that and neither would the men I know."

"I want to believe you." She met his gaze and clung to it, hoping to find reassurance there, but even if she found it, how could she trust it? She clenched her hands together. "But I just can't."

He watched her with those deep, contemplative eyes, and her desire to believe in him was stronger than ever. But the fear of betrayal was already buried deep in her psyche, and she couldn't eliminate it with a simple look.

"Since you prayed at dinner the other night, I assume you're a woman of faith?"

She nodded.

"Could you turn to God with this?"

"I have, but I'm not making any headway. In fact, my faith is suffering because this sits there like a huge wall in the way of everything else."

"A roadblock," he muttered.

"Yes. Exactly."

"It's like an avalanche closed things off."

"Right. The avalanche. It's a perfect analogy." She nodded hard. "I mean…I haven't completely lost faith in people. If I had, I wouldn't have hired your team, but still, I keep worrying that…that it means I didn't learn anything from Percy. That I trusted you all too easily. Sure, I checked your team out online, but anyone can put up a website filled with lies. And I trusted Yuki and Tomio, too. Why? A need arises, and I give in. What's not to say a need will arise in the future to have a man in my life, and I give into that need, even if the guy's not ethical or is hiding something? I just can't risk it. Easier not to get involved in the first place."

He nodded sadly.

She hated seeing how she was hurting him. "It's nothing personal, Alex."

"No, I know. I got it." He shook his head. "How did we get off on this tangent anyway?"

"McCray being attracted to me."

"Maybe it's best to go back to that."

"Agreed," she said firmly, though she didn't want to do that. Their discussion had been good. Helped her see some things. Maybe see more about him. Not such a good thing, because, of course, he passed the test with flying colors.

The investigation. Stick with that. "So if Percy didn't shoot at me, but John Doe was the target, do you think he was working with McCray?"

"Again, I'm not confirming—"

"That McCray is the gun runner." She laughed.

A reluctant smile crept across his mouth but disappeared when the door lock clicked like a keycard had been slid through it. In one smooth move, his hand went to his gun, and he reached the door with lightning speed.

Sam stepped into the room carrying her coat and wearing a huge smile.

Both Alex and Whitney exhaled at the same time.

"What?" Sam looked around.

"You scared us," Alex said, dropping his hand. Keeping his focus on Sam he said, "I think the murder could very well be related to the gun running."

Sam joined them. "And I just might have the lead that could answer that question."

"How's that?" Alex asked.

She held up an evidence bag and jiggled it. "John Doe's cell phone."

15

Excitement burned in Alex over Sam's discovery, but he quickly tamped it down. The phone had been buried in the snow for days, getting wet, and they might not be able to even turn it on.

On the other hand, it could be the break they'd been needing. "Where did you find it?"

Sam's excited smile evaporated. "On the porch in the area I tarped. I figure John Doe was holding it and it flew out of his hand when he fell."

"Are you positive it's his?" Whitney asked, her expectant gaze one that tightened Alex's gut, as he didn't want her to be disappointed.

Sam frowned. "Not yet, but by now we've interviewed nearly everyone here, and no one mentioned losing their phone. I would think that would've come up. And I asked Tomio about it. No one reported a missing phone."

"Then it's likely his, so what are you waiting for?" Alex asked. "Let's look at it."

Sam shook her head and took the phone from the bag. "It's been in snow for days and is powered down. I don't know if that's due to phone failure or the battery being drained. But before I can assess it, I need to dry it out."

Whitney narrowed her eyes. "How wet could it get when the snow is frozen?"

Sam took it out of the bag. "It doesn't take much moisture to fry electronics. I took precautions and dried it with a towel before bringing it inside and the snow melted on it. But I guarantee I didn't get all the moisture. Powering it up can cause any water inside the device to activate a shortage and render it useless. Even warming it could cause a condensation issue."

Whitney frowned. "Then what do you do?"

"I have no option but to let it gradually dry out. The heat in the room should do the trick. I can also open it to speed things up, but I need to talk to Nate about that before I do."

"Why's that?" Alex asked, as he couldn't think of a single reason the sheriff needed to be involved in this.

"It's evidence in a murder investigation. I'd be altering the state I found the device in, and it will affect the evidentiary value of the information it contains."

"I'm going to pretend I understood that." Whitney smiled.

"Think of it this way." Sam said. "After we turn this phone on, the moment it starts running, it modifies files that might need to be changed to boot up. These changes are timestamped. So just by turning it on, it's no longer in the same state as when I found it. If a jury is going to believe the information we might gather from it, they have to know that we didn't change anything, or the data can't be used as evidence."

"That makes sense," Whitney said. "But how do you do it because you have to turn it on, right?"

"Right. We make a copy of the drive, which I can still do once it's dry without opening it. Someone could call into question that once I opened it, breaking the factory seal, that I altered the hardware, too. Does that make it clearer?"

Whiney nodded. "I'm impressed. You have to know so much to do your job. Blood, fingerprints, electronics, and much more, I'm sure."

"I've already figured out she's one of the best, and she keeps proving it," Alex said, as he was proud of his new teammate. All of his teammates actually.

"That's enough of the gushing." Sam swatted a hand at Alex. "There's one other thing you need to know about this phone model. It has a feature that if John Doe has the fingerprint reader active and the phone isn't opened using a print within forty-eight hours, it will require his numeric passcode to gain access. There's no way we can figure that passcode out here. So the clock is ticking while we can still use his finger to open the phone."

"His finger?" Whitney cringed. "That means you have to use his...you'll need to..."

"Press his finger on the device, yes," Sam said. "And time's of the essence. So let me get this nearer to an air vent to start the drying process, and then I'll call Nate."

She dragged an end table close to a heat vent to set the phone down, then dug out her phone and dialed.

Alex sat down next to Whitney and offered a quick prayer that they were not only able to turn on this phone, but that it would contain information that would allow them to find the killer.

Whitney swiveled to face him. "You all really are something else. I'm so thankful you came to my rescue with McCray, or I wouldn't have thought to ask for your help."

"You weren't happy with me at the time." Alex grinned and got the responding blush he hoped to elicit.

"I was most ungracious." She grimaced. "I apologize."

"Hey." He waved it off. "I blew it, too. I was...um...kind of captivated by you and let it get to me. I should've been more professional. I really botched things."

He couldn't believe he'd admitted that to her, and if he thought she blushed before, she was downright crimson now.

"Perfect," he heard Sam say. "Yeah. I'll let you know what I find."

Alex gladly changed his focus to Sam as he and Whitney were approaching that personal territory that they'd just gotten away from. "He approve opening the case?"

Sam nodded. "Said do whatever I need to do to get this guy's ID."

She grabbed a nearby tool kit from her stack of equipment and knelt at the table. She bent over the phone, her concentration fixed, a half smile on her lips.

"She loves her job," Alex said.

"It's obvious that you all do."

"Yeah, I mean it's unfortunate that our services are needed, but they are. So someone has to do it, and I'm honored that God chose me to be one of the team."

"Me, too," Sam said.

Whitney nodded, but Alex didn't think she really understood how much this job meant to each of them... the impact and difference they knew they were making in helping people in need. For some reason, it was really important to him that she did.

"It's a calling for us. We take the responsibility of people in need as seriously as a pastor takes the spiritual welfare of his congregation."

She tilted her head. "I had no idea it was that personal for you all, but thank you for clarifying."

Good. She got it now. But he was uncomfortable about putting it all out there so he got up to watch over Sam.

Sam glanced up from removing tiny screws on the end

of the iPhone, a miniature-sized driver in her hand. "I'm hoping I won't find a lot of moisture and it will dry quickly."

She grabbed what looked like a cloth log that was an inch thick and a foot long from her bag and heated it in the microwave then laid it on the end of the phone. "Melts the glue that holds the screen in place."

Alex grinned. "I probably should've asked if you've done this before I agreed with opening it, but it looks like you know what you're doing."

She looked up at him, a hint of unease in her expression. "Actually, I've never done it on the job. We sent phones to the regional computer lab for things like this."

Alex didn't like the sound of that at all. "Then how do you know how to do it?"

"I replaced my phone's battery a few months back. I'm too cheap to pay the crazy price service techs charge. I figured someday the special tools could come in handy on the job, so I added them to my work stuff. And voilà. They have." She chuckled and grabbed a tool with a flat edge and slid it along the edge of the phone until she had the case open. She then shone a small flashlight on it. "Crud. Like I figured. It's wet. We'll just have to wait it out."

She looked over her shoulder at Whitney. "I'd like to leave this close to the vent. Or should I put it up out of the reach of little fingers?"

"It'll be fine overnight, but we definitely should move it before Zoey gets up in the morning."

Sam stood. "Actually, I'm hoping it will be dry by then, but you never know."

"You really think so?" Whitney got up, enthusiasm burning in her eyes. "I mean we might know who John Doe is by the morning?"

Sam held up a hand. "Don't get too excited. He's likely put a passcode on the device, and we don't know if he used the fingerprint reader or if the reader will even work with his finger."

Whitney's smile fell. "Why not?"

"Many of today's fingerprint identification sensors on smartphones work through electrical conductance."

"Is that what is sounds like?" Alex asked. "Electrical flow?"

"Basically, yes. Every person has a bit of electricity running through their body. The scanner senses our prints using light and these capacitors use electrical current. But when someone dies, the flow of electricity in the body ceases, and interacting with the scanner can be problematic. This is a newer model phone, and we may have a problem. Or it may work. I've seen anecdotal reports of it both working *and* failing to work."

"Maybe it's all in the way you tilt your head and if you say some incantation before you do it." Alex laughed.

"How can you laugh?" Whitney shuddered. "I find this all so gross. I don't know why I'm so squeamish about you using John's finger, but I am. I see death all the time at the hospital, but something about him being murdered right next to me changes the dynamics I guess."

Alex turned to her, serious now. "A violent death is like no other, and it's extremely unsettling." He wished for about the hundredth time that Whitney hadn't had to see this man murdered.

The memories of it would ease over time. He knew that from his days as a marine, but he also knew it was going to stay with her for the rest of her life and pop up to bother her when she least expected it. He didn't wish that on anyone at all, especially this sensitive woman who captivated him.

∼

Smoke pulled Alex from his sleep, and his chest convulsed as a coughing jag shook him violently. He shot up. Looked around. Swirling gray smoke filled the space. Not the pleasant fireplace aroma carrying pine. No. Acrid smoke slithered around the room like a living breathing thing, and his lungs burned.

The resort was on fire. The suite maybe.

Whitney and the kids. He had to get them to safety. And Sam.

"Sam—fire!" He yelled in the direction of her room. "Wake up, there's a fire."

He had to breathe deeply to be able to yell, his lungs feeling like the fire had already invaded them, burning with each breath. He must've already inhaled a lot of smoke in his sleep. What about the kids? Zoey was so small. She couldn't handle as much as he could.

Fear gripped his body.

He started to run, then remembered his fire training. *Get low.* He dropped to the floor. His hand latched onto a small blanket that Zoey was using with her doll. Placing it over his mouth, he crawled to the bedroom door. He reached up to touch the knob.

Not hot. No fire in their room.

Thank you.

He turned the knob.

"Alex," Sam screamed from across the room.

"At the bedroom getting the kids and Whitney. Go. Get out of here."

"No. I'm coming to help."

Of course she was. She was one hundred percent a team player.

He opened the door. Found it less smoky. *Good.*

"Wake up," he shouted and headed straight for the bed where he'd tucked Zoey in just a few hours ago.

"Whitney! Isaiah! Wake up!" He heard Whitney stir.

Yes!

"Fire," he shouted to break through her lethargy. "I've got Zoey and Isaiah. Drop to the floor and make your way to the exit."

"No alarm," Whitney mumbled as she stirred. "The kids."

He hadn't even thought of the smoke detectors not working. How had that happened? The renovation likely.

Never mind. Not important now.

"I've got Zoey." He scooped her up, placed her blanket over her mouth, and nudged Isaiah awake. "Hey, bud. There's a fire. Grab on to my belt loop, and we're going to crawl out of here, okay?"

The boy lay there unmoving. In shock, his eyes wide.

"I got him." Sam crawled up to the bed and grabbed his hand, pulling him swiftly down to the floor. "C'mon, buddy."

Alex hit the floor again, careful to cradle Zoey in his arm.

"Move. Move. Mo—" His last word was stolen by a coughing fit.

"Whitney, stay close to me," he got out and started forward.

He looked around as he crawled. There was no heat. No flames. Where was all of this smoke coming from? He touched the main doorknob. Cold.

"We're good to go." He frantically recalled the layout ahead of them. "Head for the fire exit to the left of the room."

He opened the door. Burning, watery tears poured from his eyes, but he could see the exit light glowing in high velocity through very thin black smoke. Flame-pushed smoke. The fire was nearby.

He had no time to worry if it was set to smoke Whitney out into the open. The smoke was too thick for anyone to make her out and target her right now, and he had to move.

Quick. Hurry. Hurry. Get this family to safety.

His lungs bursting with the raw rasping air, he made his way down the hall teeming with the same smoke but tried not to cough and scare the others more. Zoey's chest rose and fell with her face protected by the blanket. Whitney, Sam, and Isaiah all struggled for breath behind him, Isaiah struggling more than the others.

Alex wanted to grab the kid. Pull him into his arms and run. But Alex couldn't help them if he didn't make sure he stayed safe, too. He kept going, powered by a pure rush of adrenaline.

He was moving quickly now in a one arm crawl, his precious package in his other arm. One knee in front of the other through the dense brown cloud so thick it obliterated everything in front of him.

He hit another door. The stairwell. Felt for the knob. Still cool.

He pushed it open. Found better air. Whiter smoke.

Yes. Yes! A good sign they were moving away from the fire.

He reached the stairs. Cradled Zoey tight against his body and drew his gun. The others crawled up close. Isaiah was coughing harder now, his little body convulsing with it. Whitney held him close, her spasms shorter and more controlled. Sam was toughing it out like Alex and not making a sound. Alex's instinct was to send everyone down the stairs ahead of him so he could see them reach safety and pick up anyone who might fall behind, but he had to assess the danger first.

He turned around. "It's better out here. Going down now. Stay here until I say it's okay."

"Be careful," Whitney cried. "I don't...I...just be careful."

Her anguish broke his heart. He gritted his teeth and started down with Zoey. He *would* save them all.

He scooted down the steps, more like slid down on his hip. One flight. Another. The air was clearing with each step. Blessedly clearing enough to see a few feet ahead. He hit the exit door. Shoved it open and burst outside.

The whirly snow and bone-chilling wind bit into his face, but he could breathe. He gulped in deep breaths and searched the swirling snow for any foe. Found nothing save the howling wind. No lights on within view. Not a single one. He turned back to the landing, looking for the flames in the building. Clear.

He hovered in the doorway, keeping the door cracked and lifting the blanket to get fresh air for Zoey.

"It's safe to come down," he yelled.

"Roger that," Sam responded.

Zoey startled.

"Shh, baby, it's okay. Everything's okay." He kissed her forehead and stroked her hair.

She blinked a few times, snuggled into his chest, and went back to sleep.

He stayed in the doorway, waiting for them to emerge from the smoke. Whitney came down with Isaiah first, and his heart sang. Then Sam, her expression tight and pinched.

He hustled them to the door and opened it more so they could step out. They gulped in snow-laden air, hands on their knees as they gasped for more.

Sam stood tall and strong, her weapon in her hand, breathing deeply but on high alert. They shared a look understood only by those who felt the heavy responsibility of protecting innocent life and nearly failing.

Alex took several long breaths, his chest a mass of pain as he tried to form a game plan.

Why had he moved them to this building? This situation could turn out to be deadlier than a direct attack on his original suite would have been.

"Now what?" Sam asked, a fit of coughing catching her for a moment, and she doubled over. "We can't survive this cold for long, but we need the fresh air."

Yeah, what? Think, man. Think. "The tent, maybe? It has a heater in it, and it's not far."

"You can't take the kids in there," Whitney said as she cradled Isaiah's head protectively against her body.

"We might not have a choice." Alex took a look around to evaluate and decide.

A gunshot split the quiet. Pain razored into his upper arm, stunning him. A second shot rang out. Went wide.

"No!" He whirled. Grabbed Whitney's arm. "Back inside. Hurry!"

16

Fear nearly smothered the little breath Whitney could gain and gripped her heart like a vise as she grasped Isaiah's shaking shoulders. The poor boy. She had to keep it together for him. She clutched him close as Alex forced them swiftly to the floor. He joined them, selecting a spot where they were protected but he could look out the door that he propped open with his shoe. She scooted Isaiah closer to the air, but safe from any direct bullets.

Alex swiveled and held Zoey out to Whitney. The girl slept so deeply that nothing much could wake her. Apparently not even a fire or gunshot.

"We'll keep the door propped open just enough for air flow," Alex said. "Stay nearby but low. Sam, I need you to stay with them while I find a way out of this."

"No!" The word shot so powerfully out of Whitney's mouth it scared even her, and Isaiah jolted. She took a calming breath. "No. We need you here. You can't go outside or you'll be a sitting duck and the fire's in the other direction."

"I can't just stay here and wait to…" His words fell off but she knew he meant to finish with *die*.

She reached out to touch his shoulder and found moisture. Sticky liquid. Blood, she knew from her days as a nurse. "The bullet. Did it—"

He shook his head and directed a pointed look at the wide-eyed Isaiah. "Flesh wound. Nothing more."

His usual confidence was missing in his tone, and her fingers were covered in blood, but he was right. Isaiah was terrified already, and no point in scaring him more. But she did need to assess and treat the injury as soon as possible.

He looked around the area. "Something's odd about the fire."

"You mean no flames," Sam said. "Just smoke."

"Maybe that's all it is. They just wanted to smoke us out. And if that's the case, smoke rises so the first floor might be fine."

"Good, yes," Sam encouraged.

"I'll check it out and clear the route to the main building, then come back for you."

"No, please. No," Whitney begged, as she couldn't imagine seeing him disappear into that smoke again.

"I'll go," Sam offered.

Whitney should be as distraught thinking about Sam heading into danger, but the thought didn't sting quite as much.

"I'm lead on the protection detail, and it's my responsibility," Alex said firmly.

"Sorry," Whitney whispered when she wanted to say more, but her years in the ED taught her to follow a qualified leader in an emergency.

He eyed Sam. "I'm counting on you to protect them."

"With my life," was her measured response.

As Alex started to rise, Whitney grabbed his hand and squeezed. "Be careful. Please."

"Yeah, please," Isaiah said through shaking teeth.

Alex squeezed her hand and released it, then touched Isaiah's shoulder. "I'll do my very best for all of you, bud. Now don't worry. I've been in far tougher situations than this one, and I'll be back for you. You have my promise."

∼

Alex was such a fool. Promising the kid that he'd be back. He could no more promise that than he could tell the boy that getting over the loss of his mother was going to be easy.

Shaking his head, Alex inched toward the interior door leading to the first-floor hallway. With the outside door open, the stairwell had cleared significantly of smoke, and he could breathe without coughing. The knob was cool. He jerked it open and shot a look into the hallway, searching for danger before jerking back.

A slight haze of smoke filled the short hallway with six rooms but nothing like the second floor. Okay, so fine, the fire must've started up there. He raised his gun and entered the space. He didn't think their shooter could've made it from his stand outside to one of the rooms, but he quickly made his way down the hall, checking each door to be sure it was locked. He reached the exit to the lobby that was chained from the other side to keep guests out. He tugged on it and confirmed it was still securely locked.

He turned to the stairwell and climbed to the second floor. Smoke grew in intensity with each step. He jerked open the fire door, covered his mouth with the back of his arm and plunged into the smoke that was even thicker on this end of the hall. Only a few steps in, he found the source of the fire. Smoldering flames and smoke curled from a large metal trash can. The lid to the can lay on the floor, and he clapped it on top, ending the billowing cloud.

So the fire was deliberately set. Not to burn down the

place or the arsonist wouldn't have contained it in the can. Just to smoke up the hall and rooms and force Whitney out into the open while not killing anyone else. At least that was the only reason Alex could think of.

She was in serious danger, and he'd left her behind.

He turned and charged down the stairs. Bolted down the hallway, but when he reached the end he slowed. Calmed his nerves. Calmed his racing heart. Isaiah and Whitney were already terrified. He wouldn't add to that.

He turned the corner. Saw the little group huddled by the door.

"You're back. Thank goodness." Whitney came to her feet and directed a radiant smile his way.

Joy in seeing her safe rocked his world. He almost gasped but managed to keep his focus on the danger. "Fire was set in a metal trash can upstairs. No real fire danger, just smoke. The air in the hallway is much better so let's secure this door and move in there."

He signaled for Sam to go first, and then pulled the door closed, trying it several times to make sure it latched.

Isaiah got up, his gaze so wary, Alex rested a hand on his shoulder. "You're handling this really well. I'm proud of you."

A tight smile quirked up the boy's thin lips, and he started off behind Sam. Whitney and Zoey next. Alex thought to take Zoey, but he had to keep his hands free. He got out his cell and was thankful to see two bars. He dialed Tomio and prayed the man answered, because the only way out of that hallway was if Tomio unlocked the other exit door. Until that happened, as Whitney said a few minutes ago, they would all be sitting ducks.

Whitney's hands were shaking as she tipped the overhead lamp and studied Alex's gunshot wound. Tomio had come to their rescue, and Alex lay on the sofa in yet another suite, his arm draped over an end table that she'd cleaned with disinfectant wipes. She probed the three-inch-long wound, and he didn't even flinch. Just looked up at her as if bored. He'd been grazed, as he said, but also as she suspected, he'd downplayed an injury that went deeper than he let on.

"How bad is it, Doc?" he joked.

Ah, the joker he'd told her about was here, not the Alex she'd come to know. Meant he was stressed, but not letting on. Or maybe that was his way to let off the residual adrenaline from their near-death experience.

They hadn't talked about the fire, but she was smart enough to know that it was started to get her out of the room so someone could fire a shot at her. She had to believe Percy was here. But she was still so shaken that she wasn't up to having a rational discussion about him. Better to treat Alex and then take time to think about her—their—next move.

She separated the damaged flesh and knew this could only be sutured if the wound was excised, and even then, she shouldn't do it. "I'll clean it thoroughly with the iodine and then rinse with saline."

"So it's going to hurt."

"Yeah. I'm not going to lie to you. Thankfully you have lidocaine in the first aid kit, but it's still going to hurt." She watched his face for a reaction and had the urge to swipe away smudges of sooty ash but resisted.

She forced her attention to the job at hand. "Speaking of the lidocaine, it's prescription-only to be administered by a doctor. I could lose my license if anyone found out I injected you."

"Then you shouldn't use it."

"I'm not going to let you suffer if I can prevent it."

"And I'm not going to let you lose your license."

"No one will find out if you don't say anything."

"I won't, but I don't want to ask you to compromise your code of conduct. So please, just skip it."

"Have you ever been injected with lidocaine before?"

"Yes."

"Any adverse side effects?"

"No."

"Good. Good. I mean, you could still have a reaction, but the odds are low, and I'm comfortable with using it." She frowned. "With it being prescription-only, how on earth did you get it for a first aid kit?"

"You'd have to ask Gage that," he said, but his tone told her that he'd rather she didn't. "Will you stitch me up, or is that something nurses don't do?"

"As a rule we don't do sutures, but nurse practitioners and clinical nurse specialists do. I don't have that advanced training so I haven't done them." She eyed the wound. "But it may not matter because unless I can ensure there are no foreign materials in the wound, I wouldn't close it anyway. The risk of infection is too high."

"You mean like fragments of cloth from my shirt or gunpowder from the slug?"

"And dirt, too, because it's been exposed now for a few hours."

"Sorry, Mom, if I got my boo-boo dirty." He grinned. "I was kinda busy."

She did sound like a scolding mother, and she couldn't help but respond to the adorable smile that displayed a dimple in his cheek. Their gazes locked, and right there over his bloody arm, recognition of their attraction flowed between them, and she was suddenly aware of touching him even through the gloves.

She reached for the lidocaine. "I'll go ahead and get started."

"Are you sure you want to do that? Your ethics and all." His face blanched.

She uncapped the syringe. He took one look, gritted his teeth, and looked away.

"You don't like needles."

"Hate them."

Interesting. This guy had been shot without a single complaint, and he couldn't handle looking at the tiny little lidocaine syringe. This chink in what she'd seen as an impenetrable armor of solidness left her even more interested in him. It made him more human. More real. More interesting.

"Don't worry," she said. "I'll be gentle."

"Just do it. Fast. Get it over with." He glanced up at her, the smile and dimple long gone.

His hair was in disarray from the fire, his face smudged, and she wanted to lay down the syringe and brush away a lock of hair on his forehead like she might a distressed child in the ED. Instead, she smiled at him. "I'm sure we can find a lollipop for you if you lay extra still."

He gaped at her for a moment then laid his head back and laughed hard. While he was distracted she made several injections around the wound and then got his attention. "I'm done."

He blinked a few times. Looked like he wanted to let out a sigh but gave a clipped nod instead.

"Now comes the hard part." As she thought of hurting him, she frowned. "Sorry, but it has to be done."

"Not the first time this has happened to me. So I know what to expect."

"Then let's get to it." She worked hard to put on her professional nurse persona—caring, yet emotionally detached—and poured the cleaning solution into the wound.

A quick rise of Alex's chest was his only response. More of a reaction than she'd thought, so she knew it was still very painful. She worked quickly and turned back to the first aid kit that was professional enough in its supplies to be carried on an ambulance.

"Gage must really care about you all to provide such a kit."

"Sure. Yeah, he does. We all carry one when we're in the field, but it's not just for us. We're all first aid trained so we can use it in the event one of our protectees gets injured."

"Oh, right. Yeah, that could happen." A protectee like her or the kids.

She looked at the kit, and her gaze landed on a hemostatic device called an XSTAT. A large plunger-type syringe, it was filled with pill-sized medical-grade sponges that were coated with a hemostatic agent that stopped bleeding. This would be reserved for a large wound and the plunger placed into the wound to release the sponges deep inside. They expanded and stemmed bleeding. No need for direct pressure.

So yeah, they were prepared alright with the latest technology. Prepared for life-threatening injuries. She closed her eyes for just a moment and prayed that none of them would ever, ever have to use the XSTAT.

Alex was embarrassed. What kind of a guy was afraid of a stinkin' needle? He was a marine, for Pete's sake. He'd faced bombs. Bullets. Grenades. RPG's. But a tiny needle. Just the sight of one left him woozy.

Worse, he had to go all girly-boy in front of Whitney. He

shouldn't care about that, but man, he did. Way too much. He opened his eyes and looked at her as she packed and dressed his wound. She would leave it open to drain and prevent infection from setting in.

She clinically appraised his arm, her eyes narrowed in concentration. The tip of her tongue poked out the corner of her mouth, and she looked so adorable. He started to lift his hand to touch her face and caught himself before doing so.

She met his gaze, that concerned nursing expression back on her face, and he had to admit he found it very enticing.

"There," she said, her brow furrowing. "All finished. On a scale of one to ten, how's your pain level?"

She had a heart of pure gold. That was obvious, and he knew she was one of those extraordinary nurses who made their patients feel like they were the only person she cared for. And that she cared. Deeply. It wasn't an act. She was the real deal, and he liked everything he'd seen in the last thirty minutes. Liked it too much. Well, not the needle.

"Pain level," she asked again.

"Not even worth mentioning." He struggled to get up, and the not-worth-mentioning pain radiated through the wound in all directions sending out pain signals like a sonar ping. He tried not to respond but had to take a quick breath.

"Ah, so 'not worth mentioning' is what? A five or more."

He didn't answer.

"I'll grab you a couple of Tylenols." She turned back to the first aid kit.

He let out a long silent breath. He wasn't a martyr by any means, but she already felt bad about him getting shot while protecting her, and he didn't want to add to that guilt because none of this was her fault. She was the victim as much as he was.

She handed him two tablets. "I'll grab some water."

"No. Please. I got it." He swung his feet to the floor, and his head swam for a moment. He paused to let it pass and thought to take a deep breath, but his lungs were still tight. He suspected he would cough, and it would raise Whitney's alarm, so he took a shallower breath. It still made him hack once.

"I heard that," she said.

"Nothing gets by Nurse Whitney does it?"

"Nope. Nothing, and you might as well accept that and stop trying to hide your symptoms." She eyed him. "How's your breathing?"

"Lungs are still a bit tight, but I honestly think it will be fine."

"Promise me you'll let me know if you feel anything odd. You could still have a reaction to the lidocaine."

"The phone—evidence," Sam cried out and jumped up from the table across the room. "It's in the room. We left it. I have to go get it."

She charged for the door.

"Sam!" Alex yelled to stop her, causing that coughing fit he'd tried to avoid and making his arm scream in pain.

She paused, turned, and stared at him.

"We need the evidence, sure," he said. "But take a beat and be careful."

A sheepish expression crossed her face. "Right. Thanks."

"Any hint of danger—leave it. And make sure you don't lead anyone back here." He kept his warning gaze on her.

She gave a quick nod and exited the room.

Whitney closed the first aid kit, which was more like a large tackle box than a small kit. He knew Gage procured items that he shouldn't have, but in more than one instance they'd come in handy. Alex could've handled the cleaning of his wound without the lidocaine, but he was sure glad she had it available, and he was also glad Whitney knew how to use it.

Shaking her head, she came to sit next to him. "You know, I realized from the beginning that you all were in an elite class, but with every minute I spend with you and Sam, I discover skills that I couldn't even imagine were necessary to know."

"Yeah. I wish what we did wasn't necessary, but if it needs doing, I'm your guy." He tried to smile, but she was sitting so close, her soft gaze open and inviting, that he only wanted to kiss her.

"Seriously. I have nothing but respect for you." She sighed.

"And that's a bad thing?"

"Yes...no." Another long sigh. "I don't want to like you, all right?"

He hated hearing that, but he got it. They weren't in a place where liking was the right thing for either of them. He gently touched the side of her face, her skin creamy and soft. "I don't want to like you either."

Those full lips dipped in frown.

"But I do," he said, hoping to erase it.

She flashed him a surprised look, and when he thought she might pull away, she leaned into his fingers for just a moment. Time stopped. No sound. No motion.

Just the two of them locked in each other's hold.

The wind slammed something against the window, breaking the spell. They both looked over, alert. When there was no sign of danger, she got up to clean up the packaging.

He struggled to his feet, and on his way to the kitchen he looked around their new digs. The two-bedroom suite was the mirror opposite of their last room, and he felt as if he knew the space but it was backward. They'd chosen the location because it was at the end of a hallway where they could have one of the police officers stand guard twenty-four seven and the only way to the access the room was to get through him and his weapon. Alex didn't like that there wasn't a more secure location, but they only had so many options. He'd almost thought about moving back to Whitney's apartment, as the killer might not think to look there again, but Alex didn't want to take them outside and expose them to additional gunfire.

He swallowed the pills and took a second to compose himself before turning back to Whitney. "I don't want to say this, but you realize this was a blatant attempt on your life, don't you?"

She looked up, her eyes clouded with unease. "I get it."

"Which means Percy is likely here, and he's the shooter, not our gun runner."

"Yeah, I get that, too." She wadded up a gauze bandage package and fired it into the trash can with enough force that it bounced back out.

"Unless." He crossed the room toward her, trying to come up with a way to ask this question.

"Unless what?" She sounded so tired, and there was a raspy tone to her voice from the smoke. It was lower. Husky. Sexy. But thinking about what made it so deep—the smoke that could have taken any one of their lives—and he was chilled to the core.

"Unless there's someone else in your life who might want to kill you."

She snorted. Loud and very unladylike. She clamped a hand over her mouth and looked mortified. "Sorry, but come on. Until Percy killed Vanessa, I lived *the* most boring life on this planet. I worked long shifts, often pulling in overtime on a weekly basis. Going home and crashing to get up and go back to work. Family dinner once a week at my parents' house was my only social outing. Who in that world would want to kill me?"

"Maybe you were at odds with a doctor at the hospital."

"I'm pretty easygoing when there isn't a killer after me." A wry smile tugged on her lips. "I got along with everyone. Even the biggest egocentric ones of them all. No point in making a hard job even harder."

He was coming to believe that very thing about her. "How about a romantic relationship gone bad?"

"You have to date for that to happen, and I haven't been on a date in too long to remember."

Odd. He was sad for her, but more than that, it made him unreasonably happy that there wasn't a man in her life. Something he wasn't going to devote more thought to because what was the point with their current views on relationships?

He got back on track. "Give it some thought, okay? Just in case you can come up with someone."

The door lock snicked, and his hand went to his weapon. Whitney's eyes flew open, and she dropped the package.

Sam stepped into the room, her gaze jubilant.

"Got it." She held up an evidence bag holding the phone. She'd tucked several of her equipment cases under the other arm. She set everything on the table and sat. "I'm going to check it out. Hopefully it's dry."

She reopened the case and ran her phone's light over the device. She grabbed a magnifying glass from her kit and studied it. "It's looking drier, but I would feel better about waiting until the morning at a minimum to fire it up. What do you think? Can we afford to wait, or do you want me to risk frying it?"

"We should wait," Alex said. "We're all exhausted after

the scare. We need to sleep, and we can't really do anything tonight anyway. Let's get up early and check it out then."

"Agreed," Whitney said. "I want to know who John Doe is, but if we don't manage our health," she paused and eyed Alex, "especially you since you're injured, we won't be able to keep up the investigation."

"That's our plan. We all get some sleep, then check it again in the morning." He heard the words coming from his mouth, but could they sleep?

Not him. He wouldn't be asleep on the job when danger came knocking at Whitney's door again.

17

The morning broke with one piece of good news, and Alex would take it even if it didn't provide significant help. The wind speeds had died down. Just a notch. Sure, they were still blizzard force, whipping the sides of their tarp enclosure that was attached to the building as he heaped miniature shovelfuls of snow into a makeshift sifter. But maybe it was a sign that the storm was abating, and the team would be able to chopper Nate to the resort. Then Alex could get Whitney and the kids to the Blackwell compound for safety. Not happening today, though, so they had to focus on and develop the few viable leads that they'd uncovered.

Like the phone. He thought they would've turned it on already. Sam thought differently after she slipped thin paper into a questionable spot, and when it came away damp, she pronounced starting it up was too risky. Give it a few hours while they looked for the bullet, she'd said. So here they sat instead. On small plastic stools in the freezing temps.

He lifted his shoulders and stretched his back out from bending in the cold. His thoughts went to Whitney. Man, he'd hated to leave her in their new suite. His every instinct said to stand guard and watch over her and the kids, but Sam impressed upon him the importance of helping her locate the slug. Finding it could lead to the murder weapon, hopefully identifying the shooter. Alex was seriously leaning toward Percy now, but where was he?

Alex sighed and instantly regretted it when Sam looked up at him from where she sat cross-legged on her stool. "You're worried about them."

"Yeah," he admitted.

She stopped sifting. "You have all three PPB officers standing watch in your stead. They'll be fine."

He scrubbed his chin. "I know that, but still..."

Her eyes speared him. "You can't let it go. Maybe praying will help."

"Yeah, maybe." He scooped up another shovel of snow and dumped it onto the screen. He watched the powdery white flakes sift through, leaving nothing behind.

He needed some sifting in his own life, too. Wouldn't it be great if he could take the mountains blocking his way and sift them out like this? Sure, his issues were monstrously sized and no screen could hold them, but could God? He moved mountains, Alex knew. In other people's lives. He'd seen it. Believed it possible. God had just never moved any major ones in Alex's life.

Maybe because you're in the way.

Wait, what? How was he in the way? The first thing that came to mind was his past. He *was* holding onto it. That was now clear. What if he forgot about it? Let go of the hurt and pain he still felt from the way he lost his mother? But he had so much anger, too. At her and God. So was his anger blocking God, preventing Him from working in Alex's life?

Sam shifted, her gaze concerned now. "Let's give this another fifteen minutes and then take a break to warm up. You can check on them, and I can check on the phone."

"Sounds good," he said, still trying to figure out his issues.

He returned to shoveling and sifting, and an image of Whiney caring for his wound popped into his mind. Sweet, compassionate, funny, beautiful Whitney. What would it be like to be in a relationship with her?

He let himself imagine her and the kids in his life on a permanent basis. Living at the compound. A regular family. Him helping Isaiah. The boy learning to move beyond his pain and embrace life again. Alex liked every bit of what he was picturing, and he wanted it. Wanted it more than he thought possible.

"Look!" Sam shot forward, kneeling on the porch and gently swiping snow from the wall.

He peered over her shoulder and spotted the telltale bullet hole in the siding.

She flipped her evidence kit open, grabbed a plastic marker along with her camera, and started snapping pictures. "I need you to step outside so I have more room to take pictures."

"And then can you remove the slug to determine the caliber?"

"Depends," she said, shooting photos. "If removing the slug might damage it, I'll have to leave it. I have what I need to move forward. Knowing the bullet location, I can do my trajectory calculation."

He got up. "How long will that take?'

"Fifteen minutes. Maybe less." She shooed him toward the entrance flap buffeted by wind. "Now get out of here so I can get it done."

"I'll wait in the lobby for you so we can head out to the shooter's stand." He slipped into the blustery wind, and for once didn't feel the cold. But he wasn't foolish enough to stand outside when the lobby would be nice and warm.

He hurried inside and brushed off his jacket and cap then took them off. He thought to check on Whitney, but it would be so much better if he could arrive and tell her that they'd found the shooter hunkered down in his stand and apprehended him.

Percy? Maybe. Likely. If it was, then she could go back to her normal life.

Alex frowned. He didn't much like that thought. When this all ended, he wouldn't see her again. Ever. Even *if* he changed his mind about dating her—she lived and worked in Portland. Besides, she'd have to say yes to a date, and she had her own issues. He doubted going out with him was on her horizon at all.

"Can I get you something warm to drink?" Yuki called out as she came from behind the desk.

He shook his head. "That's kind of you, but no. Sam will be here in a minute, and we're going back out."

"Are you making progress?"

He nodded but didn't elaborate.

She tilted her head and studied him in the intense way she had of making him feel like he was transparent, and she could see clean through him. "You're not going to tell me what you've found, are you?"

"No. Sorry."

She planted her hands on her waist. "I don't like that violence has found its way to our little resort."

"I don't like it, either."

McCray, in his perfect timing, stepped into the lobby and leisurely strolled toward the dining room. Alex didn't want the jerk anywhere near Yuki or Tomio or the guests. "When this is all over, we'll have to have a talk about how you can better secure the resort for your guest's safety."

Her eyes narrowed. "Do you think we need to do that?"

"In today's world it's a good idea to be as prepared as

possible without going overboard and ruining the experience your guests expect. I mean, metal detectors at the front door might turn them off a bit." He chuckled to lighten the mood.

"It's safe to say that will never happen." She swatted a hand at his arm before a deep frown found its way to her face, and she stepped closer. "How are Whitney and the kids doing after the…well…the incident last night?"

"She's a strong and brave woman. She's holding up."

"I am glad you are seeing this in her." Yuki smiled mischievously. "She is single you know. Very single."

Alex rolled his eyes. "Subtlety isn't your strong suit, Yuki."

She mocked affront. "Life is too short to be subtle. Just keep noticing our girl. She's a special one."

Alex had to agree, but the noticing wasn't the problem. He'd noticed her. Plenty.

The front door flew open, and Sam stomped in, bringing with her a tornado of snow. Her cheeks were red and her eyes alive. "Let's go."

"You have the location?"

She glanced at Yuki, then nodded.

"Don't worry, I know better than to waste my time asking for details from the pair of you." Yuki shifted her gaze to Alex. "Tell Whitney and the kids that I miss and love them."

"Will do." Alex wondered what it would be like to be this free with emotions. Not needing to hold them in so tightly that it physically hurt. He knew his mother's death impacted him, but until he'd found a woman who triggered the long-buried emotions, he'd had no idea just how much.

"C'mon, hotshot," Sam said. "Stop staring and get that jacket on."

Alex slipped into his jacket and cap, but Sam was out the door before he could pull up the zipper. She was already stepping off the porch into waist-high drifts, and he hurried to catch her before she disappeared into the storm.

"We need to stay together!" he yelled against the wind and reached for her arm.

She slowed her pace. "Sorry. Got carried away."

He dug a small rope from his pocket that he'd brought for just this reason, knotted both ends, and held out one end. "Don't let go of this if you're on the move."

She took the far end, and he clutched the other. He patted his pocket to make sure his gun was ready to draw in an instant then nodded for her to set off. She led him along the front of the building toward the ski slopes. They passed a small ski and gift shop, and the long wooden rack out front that would normally be overloaded with skis.

They continued on, slogging through snow, the battle hard, his thigh muscles straining. He had to lean into the wind. Head down. Pick his feet up high. He was thankful for sections blown clear where he could almost step normally.

Sam paused outside a small outbuilding designed to look like a Swiss chalet. From their search the other day, he knew it housed maintenance equipment. After searching it, he'd locked it up tight with Tomio's keys.

She released the rope and gave him a pointed look. This building was a perfect place for their shooter to hunker down. Alex quickly shoved the rope into his pocket and drew his gun. Sam pulled her gun, too. Alex tried the knob —it was unlocked. At his signal, they burst into the small space. He scanned the room. No one was there, but food wrappers and water bottles littered the floor. Those items weren't there when they'd first searched.

He shot back outside. Keeping his head on a swivel, he dropped to his knees to make a visual search of the snow.

He'd long ago learned to track animals on the wooded property where he'd grown up, but tracking people was a different story. Easier actually, as people left many more signs than animals, like trampled leaves. If he turned one over, he could usually find a signature print on the other side. It could show the type of shoe and the direction the person headed.

All of it took patience and time, something he had in spades when he was tracking. One step. One minuscule lead. Then another. He was all over that challenge.

The snow was even easier. Virtually anyone with little training could track someone in the snow. He located a set of prints. The firm snow compression, large boot size, and length of stride indicated these prints were made by a man.

"What do we have?" Sam asked from above.

"Large boot prints leading away and up the hill toward the ungroomed area. It's a man by the large tread size. Heavy or muscular—from the snow compression. Tall—from the stride length. This could fit Percy." Alex stood. "I can still see most of the treads. Means they're fresh, but they're filling in fast."

"Then we need to hurry. Go after him."

Alex shook his head. "Too dangerous to follow him without supplies and proper gear. The snow isn't stable and one of us could get hurt and be caught unprepared. I won't risk that."

She frowned. "I know you're right, but I don't much like your answer."

"Safety comes first." He couldn't believe he was being the cautious one here, but with his wilderness training, he knew the extreme danger better than Sam.

"Then let's keep searching for the weapon. I placed the shot's origination about fifty feet ahead." She started forward.

Alex followed and kept glancing behind, his gun still in his hand. Despite it being the prudent thing to walk away, his gut urged him to track the suspect. When it came to his own life, he wasn't one for playing things safe, but he wouldn't risk Sam's life or anyone else's.

Whitney came to mind. What if he went out and didn't come back? Would she be upset by that? She was a caring and compassionate woman, so of course it would trouble her, but he was thinking of her as a woman. One who had feelings for him. Did she?

Sam stopped. He was so distracted by his thoughts he almost plowed her down. Instead, he skirted around her and faced the direction their foe had bolted. He alternated his gaze between Sam and trying to make out any danger from their suspect. He could only see a few feet out. If the killer was packing his gun, he could easily shoot them.

He swallowed down his anxiety as Sam took out her phone.

"Odd time to try to make a call isn't it?" He joked.

She laughed. "I have a metal detector app on my phone."

She sank down into the snow that came up to her waist and waved her phone over the fluffy pile. She slowly inched around until an alarm sounded and the screen flashed.

"You found it." He bent down to carefully sweep away the snow.

"Found something," she corrected and also tried to dig it out.

They soon reached the ground, and the object that set off the detector lay in full view.

She looked up at him. "Well, we found something all right."

He nodded. "Just not what we were expecting at all."

18

Whitney watched Alex remove his ski gloves and was shocked to see latex gloves underneath. His short beard was laced with ice crystals and underneath he wore a frown. Sam unwound her scarf, revealing red and frosty cheeks. They both looked deadly serious, raising Whitney's concern. They pulled their heavy jackets off and hung them up by the door.

Their jackets were so pelted with snow it looked as if someone plastered them with white paint. Whitney waited for one of them to explain why when they were in a protected tent. Neither spoke.

Her stomach tightened, but she tried to remain light-hearted. "You must have a serious opening in your tent."

Sam firmly met Whitney's gaze. "We located the slug embedded in the lodge's wall. From that, I figured out the bullet trajectory, allowing us to search for the shooter's location."

"And?" Whitney held her breath.

Alex stepped closer to her and took out a grayish plastic gun from his pocket. "We found where he was hiding when he shot John Doe. Nearby, this is what we found."

Whitney frowned as she examined it, then looked up. "I've seen something like that before. In the news. It's a 3-D printed gun, right?"

Alex gave a solemn nod. "There's a man who released blueprints of how to print them on the Internet."

"What? If he gave out the plans then anyone could print a gun. Even criminals."

"Which is exactly why he's doing it." Sam's tone was laden with disgust. "He believes all people have the right to bear arms no matter what. Even the most depraved of criminals."

Whitney gaped at the gun—just a hunk of plastic that looked like someone pounded a metal nail in it—and tried to wrap her head around the discovery. "And that's what John Doe was shot with?"

"Looks like it," Sam said. "But until a ballistics test is done on the weapon we won't know for sure."

Still trying to process, Whitney shook her head. "Where did you find it, and why would the killer leave it behind?"

"I can't begin to know why he left the gun," Alex said. "But we located it between the maintenance shed and ski lift. The nail set off a metal detector app on Sam's phone. It's chambered for a .38 caliber bullet which is the size of slug Sam removed from the wall. Odds are good that it's our murder weapon."

He set the gun on the table and shifted his attention to Sam. "Doesn't match either of the guns we've taken into evidence."

Thank goodness. "Which means I'm in the clear and can have my gun back."

"It does," Sam said.

Whitney was glad to have the extra protection and glad that the bullet matched a different gun.

"Hey wait," she said suddenly realizing Alex had been

keeping things from her. "You never told me about another gun."

"Sorry. It was on a need-to-know basis," he said.

Seriously? How could he so easily deceive her? Sure, it wasn't like he lied to her, but it was kind of a lie of omission, and she didn't like it one bit. She locked gazes with him. "What else are you keeping from me?"

"What?" His eyes narrowed in confusion.

She put her hands on her hips. "This is just like Percy. One little seemingly innocuous thing comes out, and then it leads down a path to complete deception."

"You're overreacting here, Whitney. It's part of the investigation where Sam and I cannot divulge the details outside of the team." His gaze was dark. "I thought by now you realized the kind of man I am, but I guess I was wrong."

"Um, we should probably move on, and you two can circle back to this later," Sam said. "You should also know there's evidence of a person staying in the shed."

Whitney let go of her upset with Alex to focus. "What kind of evidence?"

"Food wrappers and water bottles. Plus fresh boot prints lead up to the ungroomed area of the nearest slope."

"Did you follow the trail or get a look at who it was?"

"No," Alex said, his tone rigid and unyielding.

It was clear Whitney had hurt him or made him mad, which she didn't know, but he wouldn't be feeling either emotion if he'd been deliberately deceiving her.

"We weren't prepared to be out long in this weather, and it would've been dangerous to follow," he continued. "Plus, I didn't see a person. Visibility was limited. I don't know how he could possibly have seen us coming."

"Maybe he didn't," Sam said. "Maybe he was planning to move anyway."

"I'd like to think we didn't tip him off, but we can't be

sure." Alex firmed his shoulders. "I'll grab some supplies and head back out there to do some recon."

"Not alone." Whitney's tone was sharper than she intended. Bossy and demanding and all wrong for the woman who'd all but said he was as deceptive as Percy.

Alex arched a brow like he dared her to stop him, but he didn't speak.

"Don't worry," Sam said. "I won't let him do that."

He swung his gaze to Sam. "Like to see you try to stop me."

"I'm the law, remember?" She grinned. "You have to obey me."

He stared for a long moment then shook his head and chuckled. "Actually, I have to obey the laws, not you specifically. Unless you're planning to detain me."

"I will if I have to." She laughed with him.

Whitney couldn't find a lighthearted mood again. She had to believe Percy was living in the shed, and if he had another gun, he could've hurt Sam and Alex. Maybe shot one or both of them. And if Alex ignored her and Sam's advice and went back out, Percy could take him out. But maybe he didn't have another gun.

"I still don't get why Percy would leave a gun behind like that."

"First, we don't know it's Percy," Alex said. "Second, he likely figured the snow would hide it and it was better than if we found it on his person. And third, it looks like the bullet deformed the barrel and it wouldn't work so he just ditched it."

The implications of everything, especially if she assumed it was Percy out there, was unreal. "Is it just me or is this bizarre?"

"It's bizarre," Sam said.

Whitney's brain was running on high octane now, filling

with questions. "Where would Percy even get something like this made? I mean if he didn't have access to the plans, what are the odds he could develop his own 3-D gun?"

"I didn't read anything to suggest he's knowledgeable about ballistics," Sam said.

"He isn't that I know of, but then it's clear I never really knew him."

"Without that knowledge, he couldn't create a blueprint for an operational gun. He would've needed help," Alex said, his earlier upset with her seeming to be gone. "And we have to also consider this might not be Percy. Could be related to our gun runner. Maybe he's gotten into printing 3-D guns."

"We have no indication of that," Sam said.

"True, but we don't know everything about him, and it would be a natural offshoot for a gun runner to begin selling 3-D guns." Alex dug out his phone. "I think our best bet right now is to find out where this gun came from. I'm going to call Eryn to see if she can help us track the weapon down."

Sam nodded. "And while you do that, I'll grab my camera and get set up to shoot the gun."

Whitney watched Sam dig through equipment bags. "Do you always travel with this much equipment?"

Sam gave a resounding nod. "Plus, in this case, we were hoping to recover evidence of our target's illegal activities so we needed additional equipment."

"And this situation with Percy has derailed you."

"Actually, I think the storm more than anything has hindered us because our target's people can't get through."

"Eryn, good," Alex said, sitting down. "I'm going to put you on speaker with Sam and Whitney." He changed the setting then tweed coatbetween them and explained about the 3-D gun. "Sam will take detailed pictures and email them. Can you use those to identify a potential source from the Internet?"

"I can try uploading the pictures and do an image search. Though I don't think the chances of it returning anything are very good."

Alex furrowed his forehead. "Why not?"

"If the killer printed the gun himself, I supposed he could've shared pictures on the web somewhere, but if he bought it from an illegal gun dealer he isn't likely going to advertise anywhere other than the dark web."

"Dark web?" Whitney asked.

"It's a deep layer of the Internet where criminals buy and sell illegal goods. The average person never goes this deep as it requires a special browser and special hacking skills. But if someone is printing and selling these guns on any scale at all, that's where I'll find them."

"Are you going to search there?" Whitney asked.

"No," Eryn said. "The dark web doesn't work the same way as the Internet you know. I'd be happy to explain it in more detail if—"

Alex groaned. "No please. Not that." He looked at Whitney. "You don't want that, trust me. You'll still be standing right here tomorrow."

Eryn laughed. "Fine. Just know that I will look there, but it's not easy, okay?"

"Okay," Whitney said, liking the way Alex had been able to get to a joking mode so quickly from the earlier tension. It honestly felt good to have a few moments of light banter, especially when talking about dark webs or whatever Eryn called it.

"What do you know about 3-D printers, Eryn?" Sam asked.

"You mean besides that I've been bugging Gage to buy one?" She laughed.

Alex rolled his eyes. "Yeah, besides that."

"Basically, there are many models and prices. Like anything else in life, the lower-cost models don't provide you with a stellar product. To print a gun yourself, you'd have to buy an expensive printer."

"Like how expensive?" Alex asked.

"I'd say eight—maybe ten thousand dollars. And that would likely be buying it used, not new. Though, I do have to admit that I haven't looked at prices lately. Once I mentioned the cost to Gage, he shut me down."

"So if Percy printed this gun, he would probably have to do it at a company with a top-of-the-line 3-D printer?"

"Hold that thought for a second. I need to mention it's looking like Percy isn't at the resort."

"What?" the word shot from Whitney's mouth. "Why do you think that?"

"Piper and I believe we have an actual sighting of him. He was caught on camera at a convenience store yesterday."

"You *believe*?" Alex asked before Whitney could ask the same question.

"The image isn't clear enough for facial recognition."

"Can it be enhanced?" Whitney asked, her heart thumping over the strong possibility that Percy might not be at the resort.

"No. I've given it to my contact at the Marshal Service, and he's talked to the store owner who recognized Percy's picture. But the owner can't be sure that Percy really was the man in the store or if he'd seen Percy's picture on the news so many times that he looks familiar."

"Essentially you don't have definitive proof, then." Sam sounded as disappointed as Whitney felt.

"Exactly. But my guy at the Marshals continues to work the lead, and my gut says it's going to pan out."

"Going to pan out?" Alex stared down on the gun. "For

now we still have to assume Percy could be here, and this could be his gun."

"Really?" Whitney asked, deflating. "Just like that you ignore this possible sighting?"

Alex leaned forward. "I'm not ignoring it, I'm putting your safety first."

She couldn't argue with that.

"So back to the printing, then," Eryn said. "It takes time to do 3-D printing. Especially the many pieces of a gun. Means he would need access to this printer for some time to complete all the pieces."

"Doesn't seem likely for a man on the run," Whitney said.

"Agreed," Alex replied. "Eryn, can you run the gun info by Riley? Maybe he has some insight that we're missing."

"Glad to," Eryn said. "And if he has anything to report, I'll have him call you."

"Thanks, Eryn. Keep me updated, okay?"

"Yeah, I'll get to work on the gun and have Piper get those CCTV files."

Alex disconnected the call and picked up the gun to stare at it.

Something about his look worried Whitney. "What is it? What's wrong?"

He shook his head. "It's just so bizarre, as you said. This isn't simply a case of murder, but using a gun like this means it's likely premeditated. The killer didn't go out and buy a gun, he made it or had it made for him. Percy wouldn't have had time to think about that or prepare in that way."

"Maybe he met someone in jail who gave him a source for this gun so when he escaped he knew where to go," Sam suggested.

"But why go to all this effort?" Alex asked.

Whitney shrugged. "I don't know. What do you think?"

"Perhaps because it's untraceable. Maybe to make a statement of some sort. Or he simply had access to a 3-D printer at his former company, and that was the easiest way for him to get a gun."

"I can ask..." *My sister.* She wanted to ask Vanessa, but she would never be able to do that again. Never be able to reminisce about old memories. Their childhood. Anything at all. Hot tears threatened again and she had to swallow them down before she could speak. "My sister might have known about the printer, but I have no idea. We could call my parents. They might know."

"Not on your phone and not from here. If Percy isn't here, he might be able to use it to track you. I'll have Gage call them." Alex widened his stance as if he thought she might argue.

She got that she'd upset things between them with her overreaction on withholding the gun information, and he likely thought she wouldn't listen to him, but she wouldn't risk the kids' safety like that. "Mom and Dad aren't going to trust him. Not when they don't know him."

"Then we'll have to figure out something we can tell them so that they know we're really working with you." He held out the gun again. "Because we need to do everything we can to figure out where this gun might have been printed."

"I agree."

The bedroom door opened, and Isaiah stepped out. "Aunt Whitney, I..."

Alex shoved the gun in his jacket pocket and smiled at Isaiah. "Hey, bud. Come on out."

Oh, man. What a guy. He was this big, tough guy intensely focused on his job, and yet, he was sensitive enough to think of how Isaiah would react if he saw that gun. She couldn't reconcile Alex's thoughtful side to the way Percy behaved.

In just a few days, she'd witnessed Alex's consideration many times when in all the years she'd known Percy she'd never seen this special kind of caring for his own children. He was of the old-school belief that children were to be seen, not heard. Vanessa didn't like it and had always said his behavior was a result of his upbringing, but in hindsight, Whitney could see he was simply a cold, hard person.

Alex was nothing like that. Not at all. She was just trying to give herself a reason not to fall for a guy who was working his way into her heart faster than she thought humanly possible. And at the moment, with her defenses down, she wasn't opposed to that idea at all.

19

Alex took the evidence bag from his pocket and set it on the dresser in Sam's bedroom.

Carrying her camera equipment, she followed him into the room and closed the door. "Good job out there with not letting Isaiah see the gun. I have to say, I've never had to take a child into account while processing evidence before."

"Makes things a bit trickier, doesn't it?" Alex thought about how upset Isaiah would have been if he'd been exposed to a gun. How life in general would be harder with children who complicated things. But then Isaiah's brief smile when Alex had broken through would be worth a million inconveniences if he could help the boy smile again.

Sam unfolded a small tripod. "I can get these to Eryn if you want to go back to them."

"Actually, I wanted to talk to you about our next step."

She mounted the digital camera on the tripod. "I can tell you have an idea."

He nodded. "I feel certain Whitney was the target of that fire. To smoke her out."

"I agree."

"That says Percy is our shooter, but as we discussed, it

makes no sense that a guy on the run is going to take the time to stop and print a gun."

"Agree with that, too."

"Which means he probably bought it. Logic would say it was a local purchase as he sure doesn't have the time to wait on mail order."

She positioned the camera over a white mat. "Makes sense, I guess, but overnight shipping would take care of that."

"Still, he'd need a shipping address. Would he want to take the time to set it up, and then could he even be sure he'd be at the delivery location?"

"Yeah, both are problematic." She looked up for a moment. "A local buy is more likely."

"I know there are Portland companies that contract to do 3-D printing of various items, but no reputable company will print gun parts."

"Okay, then." She tilted her head and stilled her hands. "We're looking for someone who owns an expensive 3-D printer and has questionable ethics."

"Percy ran in pretty high economic circles. Could simply be a friend of his." Alex was already forming a to-do list in his head. "I'll ask Whitney about that, and we can also look for online contacts in connection to Percy who might have access to a printer."

"We should check out LinkedIn. A lot of professionals network there, and he might have, too. Until his address became a prison cell."

"I'll check it out," he said, adding it to his mental list. "I know I said I believe this is all about Whitney, but I could be wrong about her being the target last night."

Sam looked up and met his gaze. "Then what was the point of the fire and who set it?"

"Not sure, but we have to consider everything, right?"

She nodded as she snapped on gloves and took the gun from the bag.

"We should listen to the interviews and review our notes again to see if any of the people we talked to might have access to a 3-D printer. We could check out their employers. Hobbies. Then anyone who has a hint of a lead, we go back to them for a follow-up."

"Which do you want to start on first? Percy or the others?"

"What if we split this up? I take Percy and you take the interviews?"

"Sounds like a plan once I've gotten these photos taken and off to Eryn." Sam laid the gun on the white mat and set a ruler next to it for scale. "And I have to check on John Doe's phone."

In the excitement of finding the gun, Alex had totally forgotten about the phone. "You sure you don't want to do the phone first? It could've been a while since John Doe looked at it, and we're off on our timing."

She glanced at her watch. "We're good. I figured if the phone was in his hand, then he'd recently unlocked it. Besides, not many people let hours pass without checking their phones these days so I also left a few hours' buffer just in case."

"Good job, Sam." He smiled sincerely. "Like I said, you're the best."

"And don't you forget it. Oh, and maybe tell Gage, too." A mischievous gleam brightened her eyes and she laughed.

He rolled his eyes. "Let me know when you're ready to turn it on. I don't want to miss it."

"What about McCray?" she asked. "Any way you see him fitting in with this?"

"Not with the attack last night," Alex quickly answered but then gave it some thought. "I suppose I could be wrong about Whitney being the target. After our contentious interview with him, he could've started it just to mess with us."

"Oh, yeah. I could totally see him doing that, but shooting you? That's a little extreme, don't you think?"

"Maybe." Alex ran a hand over his hair and wanted to pull it out in frustration. "I guess what it all boils down to is I don't want Whitney to be the target."

Sam watched him. "You really do have a thing for her."

Alex thought to deny it, but why? "It's not going anywhere. So if you're worried it'll be a problem, you don't need to."

"Here's the thing, Alex." She set down a marker next to the gun and put her hands flat on the dresser. "I have to count on you to have my back here. I can't afford for you to be distracted. Not even the least bit. Are you sure you're up for this? Because if you aren't, tell me now so I know to be prepared."

He hated to be questioned about his ability to do his job almost as badly as he hated Whitney drawing a comparison between him and Percy when no similarity existed. Maybe Sam had a right to voice her concern because her life could depend on him having her back, but Whitney had been way off base. Either way, he had to take a step back from Whitney and think like a Blackwell operator on a serious mission.

He clenched his jaw, stepped forward, and held Sam's gaze. "You can count on me."

She gave a firm nod. "Your word is good enough for me. I'll finish up here and get to the phone."

"I'll be out in the living area." He found the room empty and heard Whitney talking to the kids in the bedroom, the TV playing in the background.

He took a seat at the small dining table to begin his research. He knew a lot about weapons from his military days, but he knew little to nothing about 3-D guns. Eryn and Riley were charged with officially gathering information, but he needed to do his own research, too. It would help him figure out where Percy might have gotten his hands on this style of weapon.

Alex used his phone to access the Internet and started reading about 3-D printers first. He wanted to confirm Eryn's comment about the quality of machine that might be needed to create a gun. As she'd said, it required a pricey printer or the weapon became deformed in firing. But so what? If the barrel got deformed, the gun had removable barrels that could be swapped out in seconds. He found the gun blueprint and the gun consisted of fifteen printed parts, most of which were small and would print fairly rapidly. But four main body parts would take hours as Eryn mentioned. The barrel alone took four hours to crank out.

Sam came into the room and dropped into a chair across from him and took out her phone. "Photos done. Gonna email Eryn now."

He shook his head. "This is crazy. The guy who developed the blueprints now plans to adapt his method to work on cheaper printers."

She tapped her thumbs on the screen. "So more people will have access to DYI guns."

"Exactly. And forget about metal detectors to find them at airports or like you did. The only non-printed piece in this plan is a common hardware store nail. It's non-functional steel inserted into the body to comply with the Undetectable Firearms Act."

"Like our gun has." She stopped texting and looked up. "If it's non-functional, they could just leave the nail out then."

"Exactly. The gun designer said that he didn't have to

add the pin, and that others who printed their own weren't required by law to do so. He hoped they would."

Sam snorted. "Right, like the kind of person who needs to print their own gun will even consider it."

"My thoughts, too."

"But our gun has one, so that's a bit odd, right?"

"Maybe the person who made it is more legit than we thought. He wants to comply with laws, but he still can't legally sell firearms."

"Or it's a legit dealer."

"That would be an interesting dynamic." Alex didn't even want to open that can of worms as it could take them down rabbit trails and waste their time. "Just thinking about this gives me the creeps. Imagine a world with an unlimited supply of non-detectable guns. The black-market value of such an endeavor would be through the roof. The printer cost puts it out of reach now, but if the blueprint guy updates the plans for cheaper printers or even an open source printer where someone can design and build their own, then the floodgates really are open for creating an undetectable gun."

"I can't even wrap my head around it." Sam shoved her phone into her pocket and got up. "I'm glad to have the phone to work on to keep my mind busy."

"And I have to search for Percy's contacts." Alex turned back to his computer and opened LinkedIn.

Sam crossed over to the TV cabinet where the phone had been placed in a drawer for safekeeping and got to work.

"Let me go ask," he heard Whitney say before she entered the room, and her gaze went from him to Sam and back again.

After her reaction to McCray's gun, he didn't know what to say to her.

She approached Alex. "The kids were wondering if you wanted to have lunch with them."

Okay, not the question he expected. "I really should keep working."

She came to sit next to him. "Is this about my overreaction earlier?"

Another slap in the face. "You think I'd be childish enough not to have lunch with them because of that?"

Her eyes widened. "No, wait. I'm making things worse, aren't I?"

"You're sure not making it better."

"It just sounded like you might still be mad." She placed her hand over his.

He couldn't believe he didn't jerk it away. He should. He wanted to. But even worse—he wanted her touch. What a fool he was.

"I'm sorry for what I said and how I handled things. I have no right to expect you or Sam to tell me things you can't share. It just hit a nerve."

He lowered his voice so Sam couldn't hear. "And maybe you're looking for a reason to dislike me."

She lowered her voice as well. "Probably. Am I forgiven?"

"Yes," he said. If he ever did get into a relationship with her, it would be hard to stay mad at her.

"Thank you for being the true gentleman that you are." She squeezed his hand and took hers away.

He instantly missed her touch. "I'd like to eat with the kids, but I think we're onto something here, and I should keep working."

"I get it."

"Phone's charged enough to boot up." Sam sat, finger hovering near the power button, the phone plugged into an outlet.

Alex forgot all about lunch as a feeling of great

expectancy hung in the air. He got up and joined Sam, his heart beating a little harder over the very important lead that could go sideways with one push of her finger. Whitney was right behind him.

"Ready?" Sam asked.

"Go for it," Alex said.

Whitney took a deep breath and nodded.

Sam pressed the button.

The start-up screen displayed, and Whitney leaned forward. Her anticipation was infectious, and Alex caught himself mimicking her eager watch.

"It's turning on!" She grabbed his arm and held tight, her focus glued to the phone.

"Don't get too excited yet," he warned, trying to ignore the jolt of emotions her contact released.

"This is when it will fail if it's going to," Sam added.

But the phone continued through the start-up screens, and Whitney's fingers tightened. He glanced at her. She didn't seem to have any idea that she was holding onto him, but man, he was all too aware of the warmth of her hand on his arm.

"Okay. Looking good," Sam said as the welcome screen with clock boasting the correct time came up. "Let's see if he's protected his phone with the touch ID."

She pressed her thumb on the button and the message *try again* displayed on the screen.

"That means he did, right?" Whitney asked.

Sam nodded. "And I need to use his finger to keep from getting locked out of the phone for tying too many times."

Whitney shuddered.

"I know this bothers you," Alex said. "But if you remember we're doing it to find his killer and justice is served, it might be easier for you."

"Yeah. That helps." She let go of his arm and ran her

hand through her wavy hair. "I've honestly been thinking only of myself and the kids when this poor man lost his life and deserves to have his killer found... even if it isn't Percy."

Alex shook his head. "Don't beat yourself up about that. It's natural to think about your safety. God gave you that instinct. Don't discount it."

Sam got to her feet, unplugged the phone, and pocketed it. "Okay, this has enough of a charge now, and I'm out of here. I have only so many tries for this to work. Pray that I succeed."

"You got it." Whitney excitedly threw her arms around Sam and hugged her. "Thank you, Sam. You're amazing, and I owe you so much. After this is all over I hope I can somehow repay you."

Sam eased free, her face red. "Nothing to owe. Just doing my job."

"Oh, I'll find a way to repay you." Whitney smiled.

Sam gave Alex a sober look as she slipped into her jacket and exited the room. All the excitement drained from the space, leaving behind cloaking tension, and the space seemed to close in on Alex. He searched for something to say and could only think to revert to his usual humor.

"Hey, I'm amazing, too. Where's my hug?" He forced a grin to his mouth, though he didn't really feel it. He didn't like being the joking guy with Whitney.

"You're right. I owe you even more." She locked gazes with him and started to close the distance between them.

"Wait." He held up a hand. "I was joking."

"Well, I'm not. You deserve my thanks, and I'm going to give you a hug whether you want it or not." She kept her focus on him and gently pressed his hand out of the way.

Her arms went up. Her eyes darkened.

He knew how this was going to go and shouldn't let this happen, but he couldn't step back. The temperature in the room soared, and he felt flushed. He inhaled a steadying breath while planting his feet in expectation of having his world rocked.

She slid her hands up his chest. Circled them around his neck. Her touch should have been filled with gratefulness, but it was loaded with the unspoken emotions that had been zinging between them for days.

She raised up on her tiptoes, and he leaned down. Her hair caressed his face like a soft kiss, and he almost gasped. She tightened her hold, and he slid his arms around her slender body and drew tight. Then he held on. For dear life.

Emotions from the last hug he'd had where he'd felt such deep emotion flashed back. His mother. The day before she took her life. She'd already decided by then. She had it planned. Arranged things for after her death. Had seemed peaceful when she was planning such a horrendous act. She'd said her goodbyes. He didn't know it at the time, but in hindsight he could see it.

One final encompassing hug. One final kiss on his forehead. Eliciting a promise to always look out for Faith. He should have seen it.

Why didn't I, God? Why?

He shook his head as he had for what felt like an endless lifetime. He'd asked this question a million times with no answer. What was the point?

Whitney leaned back. "What's wrong? Do you really not want a hug?"

"No, it's...I..." He stepped back and shoved a hand in hair. "It reminded me of my mother."

Her eyes flashed wide. "Your mother. *Man*. That's not the kind of feeling I got from you."

"I know. It just morphed into that."

She took his hand and led him to the couch. "It's time

for you to tell me about your mother. Not just the overview but details."

"I don't—"

"It will help." She nudged him to sit, and sat next to him, still holding his hand and gazing intently at him.

He fidgeted, then pulled his hand away to rake it through his hair. "I don't know what you're expecting me to say."

"Tell me how she died."

He took a long breath in and let it out slowly, sounding like a leaky tire. Once she heard the specifics of his mom's death, things could change between them. They always did when someone found out the details of what happened, like he had a plague or something. But he wouldn't look away or feel less than because of her actions. At least he'd mastered that skill over the years.

"She took a bottle of pills while my sister and I were at school," he said flatly and waited for her response.

She blinked, then sorrow filled her eyes. Finally she whispered, "I can't imagine how hard that must have been for you."

She didn't say anything else. Didn't look disgusted. Just supportive. Could she be the first person to simply accept that his mother's actions had nothing to do with him?

He hoped so and for some reason he wanted to tell her the whole story. "I got home from school before Faith's nanny brought her home from preschool. I called 911 so by the time Faith got there, I could shield her from seeing them take Mom out in a body bag." A vision of the bag laid out on the gurney, the shape of his mother's body molded through the plastic when it rolled past was almost too much. A long shudder wanted to work its way through him but he held it at a bay.

"No wonder you can relate to Isaiah. Your loss was sudden and shocking, too."

He nodded. "In hindsight, I can see she was preparing for a few days. Saying goodbye. She was suddenly so peaceful after such a long bout of depression. I've since learned that just making the decision helps some people relax...but I...I didn't get it." He stopped. Swallowed hard.

She rested her hand on his. "I know this seems clichéd, but I am so sorry for your loss. For you having to go through that. Especially as a child…"

He nodded and ignored the moisture forming in his eyes.

"You're still troubled by what happened." Her voice was low and gentle.

He shifted uncomfortably, then exhaled a long breath. "I didn't think it was still an issue, but yeah, seems that it is." He looked at her. "Meeting you. Isaiah. It's all become obvious to me."

She nodded. "I've seen families in the ED after a loved one has taken their life. They were confused and hurt and desperate to know what they did wrong. Why they couldn't have stopped it. Do you feel that way?"

He couldn't sit under her close scrutiny any longer. He got up to pace. "I thought I'd given up on the what ifs. What if I'd seen her mood change and realized it was a bad thing? That she was saying goodbye. Thought about her pills. I didn't, and I can't change that. I know in my brain that it was the depression and it had nothing to do with me, but still, I feel a need to make up for it."

"How?"

He'd never told anyone this, and his heart was already ripped open, but more than anything he wanted her to know the real Alex Hamilton. Not the joker everyone else knew. That meant putting it all out there. "By making sure people around me are happy. Not letting anyone get too discouraged. Joking around to make that happen. It's ingrained in me now, and I have a hard time turning it off."

"That surprises me." She got up and joined him by the fire. "I know you've mentioned that, and I've seen it some, but I wouldn't say you were a particularly joking kind of guy. I've found you more serious and contemplative."

He met her gaze. "That's because of you. When I'm with you I'm different. I want to see you smile, because, well, it's amazing, but I don't feel a need to crack a joke to make it happen. I think I'm the Alex I'm supposed to be when I'm around you."

"Interesting."

He had no idea what *that* meant. "Interesting good or interesting bad?"

"Good." She bit her lip for a moment. "Because I feel comfortable around you, too. Like we fit together."

Yeah. He felt that way, too. But could he trust those feelings? Trust that she wasn't going to rip his heart out as his mother had done? Could he have a relationship where he could relax and trust the other person completely? He didn't know, and until he did, he wouldn't do anything to lead her on. Nothing. Not even kissing her—when that was all he wanted to do.

20

The door burst open, and Whitney spun, but not before Alex drew his gun and jumped in front of her.

"Damien Vose," Sam said, holding up the cell phone.

Whitney's knees wobbled and wouldn't hold her. She sank down onto the sofa and blinked a few times to get her focus back.

"Seriously, Sam." Alex seated his gun back in his holster and let out a breath. "You can't come busting in here like that. I might've taken you out."

"Sorry," Sam crossed the room. "I was just excited at succeeding. I thought you might be, too."

"Yeah, sure, I am," Alex said. "Just let my heart rate slow down."

Sam approached Whitney at the sofa. "Does that name mean anything to you?"

"Damien Vose," Whitney said, trying the sound of it. "No. I don't think so."

Sam shifted her focus to Alex. "What about you?"

"No."

Sam held up the phone again. "Hopefully once I get into

the phone it will give us more to go on. I need to copy the files, but first I need your help. Both of you."

"You know how to image the phone?" Alex asked.

Sam grinned. "Sure do. I took a continuing ed class in it, but the Northwest Regional Forensics Computer Lab did all the imaging for PPB. So I've never done it on the job, but I've practiced plenty of times, and I'm confident in doing it."

Alex gave a single nod. "What do you need from us then?"

"Protocol says I image before I do anything, but I'm worried with the water issue that the phone could still fail before we get anything from it. So I want to write down all the calls and text numbers in case it does fry."

"Won't that change things in the memory?" Alex asked.

She nodded. "But I talked to Nate, and we agreed it's better to do this than risk losing it all. I'll call the numbers out to you, and I'd like you each to jot them down as a fail-safe check. You know, in case digits get transposed."

"Then let's do it." Alex went to the desk in the corner and grabbed a yellow legal pad and two pens.

Sam headed for the dining table and plugged the phone in again. Whitney got up and joined her. Alex ripped some paper free and set the pad and pen in front of Whitney. She picked up the pen as Alex sat next to her.

Sam looked up from the phone. "Okay, let's start with calls. I'll give the time and date of the call along with the number. Oh, and the name, if one shows up in the log. Ready?"

"Ready," Whitney said.

Alex nodded.

Sam started down the log, enunciating the information clearly, and Whitney did her job until they'd reached the end of the calls.

Sam tapped the screen. "Let me scan the most recent

texts to see the gist of the conversations so I can prioritize them."

Whitney set down her pen and watched as Sam scrolled through them. Her facial expressions changed as she read until she snapped her head up. "Bingo. I think he was meeting our gun runner."

Alex leaned forward. "Why?"

"This thread starts with him saying he's arrived at the resort. The response from our target says, 'Did you bring two boxes or thirty-two of the widgets?'"

Alex stared blankly at Sam.

"The numbers two and thirty-two," she said.

Alex drummed his fingers for a moment then his expression cleared. "Oh, right, clever. Yeah. Right. Vose was here to meet our guy."

Confused, Whitney shot a look between the pair. "I don't get it."

Alex gave Sam a questioning look, and she nodded.

Alex looked at Whitney. "Our guy's room is 232. And you're right. It's McCray. I can't have you sharing that with anyone else."

"Thank you for trusting me with it. I won't let you down." Whitney leaned in. "What else do his texts say?"

"Basically, that it's all clear and to bring the product with him. McCray was waiting. So here's the phone number for the text." Sam rattled it off.

Whitney concentrated on writing it down right. "Here's your link, then. Between them. And with the likely sighting of Percy, it could mean McCray killed Vose."

Alex shook his head. "We have no proof of that and the sighting still hasn't been confirmed. We can't assume anything."

Sam looked up from the phone. "I'd like to think we can

track this phone number Vose called back to McCray, but odds are good he was using an untraceable phone."

"And if I know McCray, he got rid of that cell the minute Vose was killed," Alex added. "We can still ask Nate for a warrant to search him and his room. That will put him on alert, but it can't be helped at this point."

"If he threw the phone in the trash in any of the common areas," Whitney said. "It would still be sitting out back. Room trash is bagged and in the same place, too."

"He'd be more careful than that. Maybe take it outside and bury it. Or hide it in the building." Alex's fingers started up again. "Still, I'll have the PPB officers search the trash cans."

"There're gonna love you for that," Sam said.

"At least I'm not tossing them in a dumpster of rotting garbage." Alex grinned.

"Ew, gross." Whitney shuddered.

"Tell me about it," Sam said. "As a criminalist I've been in my share of them on sweltering summer days. But now..." She sighed contentedly. "At the balmy coast, I've got it made."

"Um, I hate to burst your bubble, but think ahead to summer and seafood season." A boyish smile crossed Alex's face.

She held up a hand. "Enough said. Okay, let's finish up these texts."

"And then?" Whitney asked.

"We'll have Eryn run a phone lookup on this number and we'll do a background check on Vose," Alex said a gleam in his eye. "And then...then it's time we paid McCray another visit."

∽

Alex scanned the Internet search results for Damien Vose on his computer screen and clicked on the next one. He'd wanted to rush out to confront McCray, but his interrogation would go better if they had additional information on Vose. So Alex was searching the Internet while Sam and Whitney sat at the small dining table with him listening to the guest and staff interviews to find someone who might have access to or knowledge of a 3-D printer. So far both efforts had been a bust.

He quickly scanned the new article for content, zoning in on the important details. "Here's something. Vose was convicted for possessing and selling an illegal weapon that resulted in a death during a gang drive-by shooting. He was charged as an accessory to murder."

Whitney's eyes narrowed. "I don't get it. You said that the fingerprint database contained convicted criminals' prints. So why didn't his prints show up?"

"Says here he was only seventeen," Alex said. "Maybe as a minor the records were sealed."

"I'm surprised the reporter used his name then."

"Me, too, but he did." Alex squinted at the screen. "Don't know if this website is reputable or not, but if they used the name, maybe they're not."

"Regardless, we now know he's been convicted of a crime," Sam said. "And Alex is right. If the record was sealed, he wouldn't show up in a regular search. As far as the records go, it's as close to having never committed the crime as possible."

"So how does this help us?" Whitney asked.

Sam frowned. "Maybe just that he sounds like someone who might do business with McCray. He didn't deserve to die, and I'm sorry he did, but any guy who sells illegal weapons is a real lowlife in my book."

"Mine, too. Especially in the military," Alex said, and

didn't care if he ever offended anyone with his position. "I never understood how there could be a black market for weapons that wind up in the hands of the very people who are trying to end someone's life."

Whitney shook her head. "I've led such a sheltered life compared to you two."

Alex wanted to say she'd lost her innocence in the worst possible way with Percy, but he didn't want to bring up her sister's death. So he went back to his research and kept digging. He finally pulled up a picture of a major weapons bust.

He enlarged it and squinted to make out the background.

"Yes!" He pumped his hand up and swiveled his computer. "Look at who we have here."

Whitney bent close to the computer. "That's Vose being hauled off in cuffs."

Sam leaned over Whitney's shoulder. "And McCray in the background."

"This is the proof of a connection I need to confront McCray." Alex turned the computer back and sent the picture to his phone.

He stood and looked at Sam. "I'm assuming you want in on this conversation."

"Absolutely."

"I'll keep listening to interviews." Whitney looked up at him, and he didn't like the worry he saw in her expression. Worry put there by Percy. Worry that might always be triggered when a loved one was in a dangerous situation.

Not that he was a loved one, but with each minute that passed, he could easily imagine it more and more.

She grabbed his hand. "Please be careful. Even if he's not the killer, he's still a dangerous man."

Alex waited for her to let go of his hand and swing her concerned gaze to Sam, but she kept her focus on him.

He switched his thoughts to the meeting with McCray but decided to try for a lighter tone. "Hey, I've got Deputy Sam with me. She's got my back."

"Maybe you should bring Officer Everett with you, too," Whitney suggested and let go of his hand.

Sam shook her head. "That would be overkill and would put McCray even more on the defensive."

A hint of a plan niggled Alex's brain and he let it blossom. "That gives me an idea. Maybe we can use Everett to trap McCray."

Sam cocked her head. "I'm listening."

"We think he ditched the burner phone, right? But what if he wasn't as careful as he should have been and tossed it into one of the public trash cans like Whitney suggested? Or hid it to be able to retrieve later?"

Sam gave a clipped nod. "I think that's possible."

"So say we interview him, and when we leave, we make sure the door stays open a crack. We have a conversation in the hallway about Everett searching the trash. McCray thinks we're stupid for not closing the door and he eavesdrops on us."

"Oh, I get it," Whitney said, a smile forming. "You think he'll go get the phone before Everett can find it."

"Exactly. And we can have Officer Umbel or Yablonsky tail him because McCray will be looking for us or Everett, but not the other two."

"And then if he does grab it," Sam jumped in. "We'll have the proof that Vose had called McCray."

Alex nodded.

"I say we go for it." Sam pointed at the door. "Everett's still in the hall waiting for us to leave. I'll arrange things with him."

She hurried across the room, and once again Alex was struck by her capabilities and willingness to adapt at a moment's notice. She'd proved to be a valuable asset to the team, and Alex fully planned to give Gage a glowing report on her.

While waiting for Sam to return, Alex sat back down and returned his attention to his computer to keep busy and not stare at Whitney like some love-struck fool.

Man, how did he let himself fall for a woman after all these years of avoiding it?

Everything just seemed so natural with Whitney. Yeah, well so did loving his mother. Natural until it wasn't, and he was looking at her laying in a coffin, his heart ripped open. He shook his head to knock the thoughts away.

"Everything okay?" Whitney asked.

"Fine."

She tapped his laptop. "You didn't find something there that you're not sharing, did you?"

"No. I've told you everything I know about this." *Not about you. And me. Me and you.*

He read the next story, keeping an ear out for Sam to swipe her key in the door lock. When he heard the click, he stood.

Sam poked her head in. "We're a go. Umbel is already on his way to stake out the hallway so he's ready for us, and Yablonsky will take the lobby."

Alex took one last look at McCray's growling picture on his laptop and closed it. "We'll be back in a flash."

"Right. Okay." Whitney's head bobbed, and it kept bobbing as if she didn't realize it. "Be careful, then. And yeah, come right back so I know you're fine."

At her worried frown, Alex patted her shoulder, earning a raised eyebrow from Sam, but he didn't care. He squeezed and smiled at Whitney. She beamed up at him.

His heart stuttered at the power a simple smile had over him.

"Be back soon," he managed to get out and spun to leave.

He kept up a quick pace, moving ahead of Sam so she couldn't ask about his obvious display of affection for Whitney. At McCray's door, he relegated thoughts of Whitney to the back of his brain and pounded hard.

A few minutes passed before McCray answered, a frown drawing down his long face. He scratched the whiskers on his chin and eyed Alex. "What do you want?"

"To ask a few questions," Alex said, ignoring the attitude. "Can we come in?"

McCray widened his stance and straightened his shirt. "No."

"You want to air your dirty laundry in the hallway then?" Alex challenged, as it would be easier to ask the questions inside and quickly move into serving the warrant afterwards.

McCray smirked. "Don't have any dirty laundry."

"Okay, suit yourself. Give me just a sec." Alex got out his phone and dialed the number from the texts Vose had received in the off chance that McCray had kept the phone and it was somewhere nearby. It rang in Alex's ear, but not in the room or on McCray.

So fine. He got rid of it.

Alex eyed him again. "I wanted to talk to you about a buddy of yours who came to visit you here."

"I told you. I'm alone." He relaxed back against the wall crossing his feet at the ankle as if this visit was of no consequence to him.

"Yeah, see, I get that, but what would you say if I have a phone with texts saying this person had arrived at the resort and you asked him to bring the widgets to your room."

A muscle jumped in the man's jaw, but his face remained

unchanged. He was good at this cat-and-mouse game, Alex had to give him that.

"I didn't have any text communications like that. I can show you my phone if you like."

"First," Sam said. "You could have deleted the text. Second, you didn't use your phone. You used a burner, and you know it."

"Burner?" he asked a slight smirk on his lips. "I'm not sure what that is."

"Right," Sam nearly growled at him. "It's a prepaid untraceable phone."

"Why would I need that when I have my own phone? I have nothing to hide." The smirk blossomed into a full-blown sneer.

"How about the widgets?" Alex asked. "I'm sure you don't want us finding those."

"I'm not really sure what you're referring to."

"Then how about the name Damien Vose. That ring a bell for you?" He watched McCray, that muscle twinging again, but no other response.

"We have pictures of the two of you taken in an undercover sting that you wiggled out of." Alex tried hard to keep the frustration from his tone so McCray didn't know he was getting upset, but he failed.

The creep just stood there.

Alex changed his focus to Sam and gave her a pointed look.

"In that case," she said and pulled the warrant from a cargo pocket in her pants. "We have a warrant to search you and your room."

"Now come on." He pushed off the wall. "You have no probable cause for that."

"Look at the man who suddenly understands the law." Alex jeered. "Hands against the wall for that search."

He glared at Alex and turned, his eyes never leaving him until he faced the wall. It was then that Alex saw the depth of evil in this man's eyes. Alex could almost see the thoughts of revenge and payback trailing across McCray's mind like an old-fashioned ticker tape. Alex didn't doubt for one second that the man would be capable of killing Vose—killing him and taking great pleasure in doing so if Vose crossed him.

Alex put on a pair of booties over his shoes and snapped on latex gloves then patted McCray down. He was aware of Sam putting on her protective clothing and gloves but kept his attention on McCray. Alex was looking solely for a weapon and phone at this stage, but he never knew what he might find.

His hand passed over what felt like a Leatherman in McCray's front pocket. "I'll take the Leatherman nice and slow."

McCray removed the multi-purpose tool and slapped it into Alex's open palm. Carrying a knife like this wasn't odd for some people, but not a lot of businessmen—like McCray claimed to be—would carry one. A skier and outdoor enthusiast might, however.

Alex finished his search. "Step inside and empty your pockets on the dresser."

He strolled into the room so slowly a slug would have won a race with him, and Alex was tempted to give him a shove, but no point in poking the bear.

Sam bent down to grab her equipment bag and followed Alex into the room. The judge signed off on getting a DNA sample from McCray to compare to any touch DNA Sam could lift from Vose's hand in the event that the pair shook hands. And she was authorized to look for other forensic samples that might link them, such as dirt matching small clods tightly embedded in Vose's shoe treads.

McCray complied without further prodding, dumping out his pockets on the long dresser. Out came a key ring filled with keys, a room keycard, loose change, a money clip thick with bills, and breath mints. So the guy was conscious about his breath. Odd for a criminal if you asked Alex. Maybe it was to hide his alcohol habit.

"Where do you want him?" Alex asked Sam.

"At the table."

Alex pointed at the small table sitting between two chairs by the window. "You heard her."

McCray did the slimy slug crawl to the table while Sam dug out the DNA swab.

McCray watched her every move. "What's that?"

"We have authorization to take a DNA sample."

"What?" He shot to his feet. "Why?"

"In case you shook hands with Vose."

Some of the color drained from his face, giving Alex a strong feeling that they were on the right track.

McCray glared up at Sam, but finally opened his mouth, and Sam swabbed the inside. He made a production of swallowing and gagging, but she ignored him to store the swab in its tube.

"Tell me when you're done with forensics so I can start searching," Alex said to Sam and rested against the dresser.

She nodded and went back to her equipment bag to remove special lights. Alex glanced around the room as he waited, and now wished he hadn't removed the gun from the drawer so they could've taken it into evidence. Not that the caliber matched the murder weapon, but it might become significant as the investigation advanced.

On the flip side, if McCray was the killer, he might have used the gun in the meantime to kill someone else and that trumped taking it into evidence.

Sam moved around the floor, setting down evidence

markers then snapping pictures before picking up minuscule things with tweezers, bagging, and labeling it. She continued for about an hour then stood. "Okay. You can search."

Alex started with the same dresser that he'd looked through before. McCray relaxed back in his chair, his arms clasped behind his head. His sudden relaxed posture said they weren't going to find anything beyond what Sam had lifted. Still, Alex did a thorough search, then he and Sam headed out the door.

"Hey, thanks for the laugh," McCray called after them. "It was like watching Inspector Clouseau bumble his way through an investigation."

Alex stifled the growl of frustration and anger that wanted to escape and exited the room. He used his foot to stop the door from closing and faced Sam.

"What time did you say the PPB officers were going to search public trash cans for that burner phone?" he asked loud enough for McCray to hear.

"As soon as we get back to the room."

"Then let's go. I really want to find McCray's burner." He slowly released the door and glanced down the hallway to where Umbel remained in position.

Alex nodded at him. Umbel eased back into the shadows where he would wait for McCray to take the bait and go retrieve the burner phone.

21

Alex stormed into the suite, irritated and exasperated. McCray didn't fall for their plan. Alex wasn't surprised. Not really. The guy didn't become a successful gun runner because he was sloppy and impetuous. But Alex had to try it.

Now they were left with *what* as a lead? Nothing. Not really.

He dropped on the couch, feeling like having a big pity party. That was so not him. He didn't give into his emotions. Ever. Correction—hadn't given into them until a certain someone named Whitney showed up in his life. Now it was all he could do to keep them in check.

Why? Why her? Why now and here?

The bedroom door opened and sweet little Zoey came running out. Whitney was directly behind her, and Isaiah in the rear. Whitney cast Alex a questioning look, and he had to assume she was asking if McCray went for the phone or otherwise told them anything. He gave a quick shake of his head.

She frowned, and he wanted to do anything he could to

erase that frown and put a smile on her face. She deserved happiness. Not all this sadness and negativity.

What about that, too, God? I understand having mountains in my life. I deserve them. But not Whitney. She's a caregiver. A nurturer. She deserves all the best.

Including the best guy, which was so not him.

Zoey rushed up to him and climbed up on his lap with her rosy face, curls wet from a bath, and soft fuzzy pajamas. She cupped her blanket against her cheek and plugged her thumb into her mouth. Her eyes sleepy, her long lashes blinking hard to stay awake, she sighed and rested her face against his chest as if this was the most natural thing for her to do.

It felt natural. Trusting. Caring. Loving. It was all natural. Every bit of it. What God created man for. Alex knew that love once. His mother. His father to some extent, but totally his mother. Until she taught him the most difficult lesson he'd ever faced in life. The things with the most power to impact you also held the most power to hurt you. And were the most challenging to get over.

People could never understand or explain suicide. Never. Not on their own anyway. But you could learn to live with the loss. He just hadn't really examined his feelings. Dealt with them. It had been far easier to avoid.

But now? Now, he wanted to circle his arms around the warm little body trusting him with her affections. Around the woman who captivated his heart. Around the boy who was hurting with such powerful emotions. Protect them from everything bad in this fallen world. And to do that, to be the kind of man who could put others before his needs in the most profound way, he had to show up emotionally and be present. Not be the shell of the person he'd been since his mother died, but the man who could love with abandon. The man God wanted him to be.

The question was, did he want this badly enough to do the work to make it a reality?

~

The storm would break tomorrow. That was the broadcast on their weather radio, meaning it would be Whitney's last night with Alex because she was going to ask Gage to assign someone else to her protection until Percy could be caught. The thought took a bite from her heart, leaving an ache behind, precisely the reason she needed to get away from Alex.

She picked up her brush and tugged it through her hair. She stared at her reflection in the bathroom mirror.

She was about to step out into the other room, and she didn't know what to expect other than heartbreak. She'd brought it on herself. Despite her warnings, despite Percy's betrayal setting a fresh and still-raw example of why not to fall in love, she'd fallen for a guy who she didn't know enough about to really trust with her heart.

Sure, Alex had proved his tenacity. His compassion. His goodness. His kindness. But he also proved he was skittish when it came to a relationship. His mother's death still affected him.

What if they got involved? Got married? Parented Zoey and Isaiah together? She could totally imagine it—imagine the joy of sharing that responsibility and of being together. But he wasn't over losing his mother and could one day freak out over the commitment of love and bail on them. He wouldn't want to do it. He was honorable, but he could do it.

But even understanding the risk, just like that, she gave her heart away to him.

She eyed herself with disdain. "So what are you going to do, girl? You might as well admit falling for him. Not that you'll follow through on it. Thankfully, you still have the common sense not to do that."

She tossed the brush on the counter and marched into the adjoining space, ready to thank Alex for his help and tell him that she was going to talk to Gage about a change.

"You're sure." His excited voice met her at the door as he talked on his phone. "One hundred percent sure."

He listened, his expression astonished.

"I need proof, Eryn," he said, sounding demanding, and yet, thrilled at the same time. "Then get me a picture of him sitting in his cell."

Sitting in a cell? Did they arrest Percy?

She hurried into the room. "Did they...is he?"

He held up a finger, his attention remaining on the call. "Figure out a way and then call me back so we can talk about it when you all will arrive tomorrow." He shoved his phone into his pocket and met Whitney's gaze. "Yes. The Marshals have Percy in custody."

She gaped at him. "In jail? He's in jail? Percy. For real? He's in jail?"

He nodded. "I asked Eryn for a picture as proof, but honestly, we don't need it. He's been arrested."

Joy bubbled up inside. Incredible, delightful, breath-stealing joy, and she didn't think but hurled herself at Alex and threw her arms around his neck.

He stood stock-still for a long moment then circled his arms around her back and drew her close to him. His skin was warm, and he smelled of a musky aftershave. She eased even closer, and an emotion she'd never felt came rushing in.

Pure, unfettered love for a man. She'd never really loved anyone like this. She'd had crushes, relationships, but if this untainted rush of joy told her anything, it told her that she'd never before truly been in love.

He eased back. Peered into her eyes. Emotions raced across his face so fast she couldn't pin them down. He tenderly caressed the side of her face. Slid a lock of hair behind her ear.

"Whitney, I..." he said, then shook his head and lowered it.

He was going to kiss her and seemed to be asking permission.

She didn't think twice but slid her hand into his hair and drew his head down. His lips touched hers. Warm. Soft. Full. Heat rushed through her limbs, and she felt his touch clear to her toes.

Incredible. Oh, how incredible. She'd waited her whole adult life to feel genuine love and now she had. He deepened the kiss. She matched him. Wanted it go on and on. To start a relationship with him.

Shocked at her thoughts, she stiffened in his embrace and tried to push free, but he held fast for a moment longer.

His head came up. His honey-brown eyes darkened with reluctance. Confusion. Frustration.

"I shouldn't have done that," he said, his voice hoarse and throaty but he didn't completely release her, and she didn't try to escape.

Hopeless. She was hopelessly in love and wanted this moment to last. Because the second she broke contact she was on her own again, and her heart would be shredded. Twisted like a roller coaster. She was a mass of confusion and longing.

"But I..." He shrugged, lifting her arms with the rise of his shoulders.

"I know."

"Do you?"

It had felt so right for him to hold her. To kiss her. To love her, and she had to acknowledge that to herself. Maybe to him. She touched his cheek—she just had to do it. One time. The last time.

He sucked in a quick breath.

"I don't want to feel anything," she admitted. "But I do. Deeply. Still, I can't pursue it."

If possible, he looked mad and thankful at the same time as he took a step back, breaking their hold. "Yeah. Me too. I can't. I know that now. Wish I could, but…"

"Hey, I get it. I'm there, too." She looked around the room for something to say. Saw her tote bag. "Since Percy's been arrested, it's safe for me to move back to my apartment, right?"

"Um…yeah…well, sure."

"You have reservations?"

He seemed to ponder that. "The fire still troubles me, but honestly, that seems like a McCray thing directed at me and Sam. So yeah, it should be fine to resume your normal life."

"Normal. Weird to think about. I don't even know what that might look like now." She let her mind wander. "Guess I'll give Tomio time to find a replacement and then move back to Portland. Maybe start fresh in a new job. New hospital. Or even a doctor's office where I'd have more regular hours for the kids. And I have to call my parents to tell them we're all safe now."

Alex's phone chimed, and he dug it out to display a picture of an angry Percy sitting in a small jail cell.

Whitney stared at, and even in seeing him sitting in the tiny boxy room, she could hardly believe he was back behind bars. "Wow, Eryn works fast."

"She said her Marshal buddy was still at the jail, and she'd have him snap a picture." Alex's phone rang in his hand. "It's Gage. I need to take the call and arrange for the team to bring Nate and the medical examiner in when the storm clears."

She nodded. "And I need to pack."

They shared one final look that acknowledged everything they were giving up by going their separate ways, and in a flash their moment ended. Her heart clenched. She'd never, ever forget their time together or him.

22

A helicopter whirred overhead, and Whitney grabbed her jacket to step outside of the restaurant for her lunch break. The morning broke sunny and calm—blindingly sunny with heavenly warm rays sparkling off white undulating snow, and she had to squint to take in the scenery and bustling activity around her.

Tree branches encrusted with the white powder bent toward the ground looking like abstract sculptures in white. Beauty beyond imagination unfolded everywhere around her. Beauty only God could create.

It all remained undisturbed except for where Tomio's crew had been working all morning clearing the area around the lodge and grooming the slope, allowing the lift to open in an hour. But now, snow whipped into a frenzy at the base of the run while a large helicopter settled down to the ground. Sam stood waiting for their team to land, but not Alex. He'd gone out early to try to track the killer, and she hadn't seen him all morning. Maybe he was avoiding her.

The helicopter touched down, bringing Blackwell's team along with the sheriff and medical examiner so they could take over the investigation into Vose's murder. She'd hoped that Alex would have located the killer this morning. It could still be McCray, but they had no proof that he'd fired the deadly shot. Couldn't prove he didn't, either. There just wasn't any evidence. Maybe the sheriff would do a better job, but then she didn't think so. Not with as thorough as Alex and Sam had been.

Whitney shielded her eyes against the sun, wishing Alex stood by her side. She missed him all morning, and her heart was cold and dark and filled with a flurry of emotions so powerful she could hardly think. Emotions piling up against the wall of her heart. Swirling wildly. Wanting to blow open at the least little problem. Just like the blizzard.

Oh, Father, why can't I be happy that no one else got hurt and Percy is once again behind bars? Why this gloom?

Sam turned to look her way and curled her finger, summoning Whitney over to the team. She eagerly stepped across the cleared area, skirting several clumps of snow left behind by the plow. She dodged skiers dressed in vivid colors excitedly headed toward the ski lift. Guests were so tired of being inside, they were rushing out to wait in line for the lift to open.

The rotors thumped an even rhythm as they slowed, and Alex's teammates poured out of the helicopter like ants from a mound.

She ran her gaze over them and recalled names from the video call. Of course, Eryn was the easiest to remember as she was the only woman in the group. She was two inches or so shorter than Whitney, but physically fit. She probably worked out a lot like Sam.

The final guy off the helicopter was in his sixties and carried a medical-type bag so she assumed he was the medical examiner. He stopped to talk to a man dressed in a khaki uniform—Sheriff Nate Ryder, she assumed. He was over six feet tall, had broad shoulders, and was powerfully built. His expression was confident, and she felt comfortable just seeing that.

All over six feet tall, Alex's other teammates wore intensity like a coat of armor as they scanned the area. She hadn't noticed that intensity in the video call, and she was taken aback by the strength of it. Though Alex was intense and driven, he seemed more laid-back than these guys. Or maybe he tempered his intensity for her as he knew she was still reeling from Percy's aggressiveness.

She didn't recognize one of the guys, and Trey, who she'd met the other night, was missing. She reached the group, and they all turned to look at her.

Gage stood directly in front of her. He was as fierce-looking in person as on the screen. But as he shot out a hand and a smile spread across his face, replacing intensity with sincerity. "Gage Blackwell. Glad to meet you in person, Whitney."

"I'm the one who is so glad." She shook vigorously and ran her gaze over the others. "To meet and thank all of you in person for locating Percy and working so hard to protect us."

"We're glad we were able to help." He stepped back and nodded at a guy she hadn't met. "You've met the team except Coop. He's one of our helo pilots."

He nodded, a serious expression on his face. He had dark brown hair, laser-eyed focus, and a steady hand as she shook it. "Glad to see Alex and Sam were able to keep you and the kids safe."

That she could smile sincerely about, and she did. "They did an amazing job. You all should be very proud of them. And I am forever in your debt. If you ever need anything, please ask." She thought about what she'd said. "Of course, as a nurse, you probably don't ever want to need my help there, but..." She chuckled.

"I really need to get moving before the sun thaws our victim," the medical examiner said.

The thought sent acid curling through Whitney's stomach.

"Right," Gage replied and quickly introduced him and the sheriff.

"I'll show you where he is," Sam said, her focus going to Gage. "I'll come back to update you."

"Any idea when Alex will be back?" Gage asked.

She shook her head. "He said when he hears the helo if he's in a position to return he will. Otherwise he'll call you."

"Ma'am, we need to get moving," the ME said pointedly to Sam.

"Right this way." She spun and marched across the courtyard toward the tent, the ME struggling to keep up.

"I need to go, too," Whitney said. "My niece and nephew are waiting to have lunch with me." She smiled. "Thank you again, and I mean it. If I can ever repay you, please ask."

Gage offered his hand again, and then she took off. Feeling their piercing gazes on her back as she walked unnerved her, but she resisted the urge to turn and try to read their expressions.

She forgot about them and wound through the snow piles to head down the side path to her apartment. Tomio had done a quick pass-through with the snow blower there and cleared a strip just wide enough to walk. Didn't matter as the staff were all working, too busy to be out back here and the area was deserted.

She reached the stairs and took the first step.

"Aunt Whitney, help," Isaiah's terrified voice came from behind the breezeway.

"Isaiah?" She turned to look. Saw nothing.

She knew he planned to play outside this morning. Had he gotten stuck in a snowdrift? She could just imagine his thin little body wedged in a pile of snow but unhurt, and it brought a smile to her face.

"Help!" His tone was high and frantic now, and her smiled evaporated.

This was more than a stuck-in-a-snowbank cry. He was in serious distress.

She bolted toward the area where she heard his voice. She raced through the second breezeway, and her footsteps faltered.

A tall, angry-looking man held Isaiah against his broad chest, a 3-D printed gun in his hand.

The killer. He was the killer. And he had Isaiah!

No! Not Isaiah! God, no, please. Don't let him be hurt. Help me!

"Isaiah." She rushed toward him.

Her nephew's eyes glistened with tears but he was fighting them and his chin was up. She'd never been so proud of him. But he needed her, and she needed to be calm.

The man raised the gun and planted his feet wide in the snow. "Slow your roll, Whitney, or the kid gets hurt."

Whitney stopped in her tracks, her heart pounding in her ears. She searched the man's face to place him—to figure out why he was threatening her nephew and how he knew her name.

She'd seen him before, but where?

He was unique-looking and should be easy to place. He wore a heavy parka with the hood up, shadowing his face, but she could still make out his features. A square jaw. Small, thin lips. Large nose resembling a ski slope. Several moles on his cheek. Big and muscled, he looked like a hardened criminal.

Know him or not, she had to get Isaiah away from him. But how? He had a gun.

Panic crawled up her back and weighed her down. "Did Percy put you up to this?"

"Percy?" Confusion flashed across his expression.

"Do I know you?" she asked searching for anything to help.

"By name, no. We met for just the briefest moment at the hospital. You can call me Ibson."

"What do you want, Ibson?"

He stabbed a finger at snowmobile behind him. "For us to take a little trip."

"But why? What do you have to do with me?" she asked, actually sounding calm when her insides were quivering like a bowl of gelatin.

"Think back to your last day at the hospital. You came to check on the guy who was admitted from the ED. You poked your head into the room. Said you were off for the day and wished me well."

"A patient?"

"No."

"Staff."

"Ding, ding, ding."

"MD or nurse."

"Neither."

"Please. I'm confused. Just tell me."

"Posed as a nurse to visit Mr. Bingham."

"Oh right. You were giving him pain meds in his IV. I remember now." She remembered seeing him standing over the very wealthy investment banker who was sound asleep. "Wait. It wasn't pain meds. He wasn't in pain. He was sleeping."

"Bingo. You caught me giving him a dirt nap."

Her eyes widened. "You killed him. And I saw you.

Could have stopped you, but I was too preoccupied." Guilt flooded through her. "Did you? Did he?"

"Yeah, he's in never-never land for good."

No. "But why?"

"It's what I do."

Do? "You're a hit man?"

"I prefer being called a cleaner, but yeah." A sick smile crossed his mouth. "And I don't like leaving loose ends. I've even taken to printing my own guns so they're not traceable. But you seeing me and then disappearing? Not something I could let go. Took me weeks to catch your trail."

She stood in shock. She had no idea. None. "How *did* you find me?"

"I have my ways." He said, shifting Isaiah and aimed the gun at her. "Now let's take that ride so I can tie up those infuriating loose ends."

"You and me only, right? And you'll leave Isaiah here?"

"Sorry. Can't leave a witness behind."

"You shot at me in the courtyard and started the fire, too."

He grinned but didn't speak.

"Aunt Whitney?" Isaiah cried out. "I'm scared."

"Hey. Hey, buddy. It'll be okay. I'll be with you," she tried to comfort him. "Let's go for that ride together. It's so sunny and pretty after the storm. And it'll be fun."

Ibson jabbed his chin at a black-and-silver touring snowmobile that Tomio used to drive around the resort. "You drive. Kid on my lap."

He strode to the machine, carrying Isaiah like he was a ragdoll. He threw a leg over the raised padded seat in the back and settled Isaiah on his lap.

"Please," she said. "Isaiah won't tell anyone he saw you. He knows how to keep a secret. Please just leave him behind. You can't manage me and a kid at the same time."

"Get on," he snarled and lifted the gun. "Before you make me use this."

A tear slipped from Isaiah's eye, and Whitney couldn't take it anymore. She bent down and kissed his cheek. "We'll be fine. God has us, and Alex will help. I know he will."

"A-a-are you sure?"

She squeezed his hand. "I am."

"Shut up," Ibson said. "And get on. Now!"

She climbed onto the driver's portion of the bulky machine. Thankfully she'd grown up around snowmobiles and knew how to handle one. She'd never driven this particular model, but she could operate it safely.

She pulled her hat down hard and swiveled to look at Ibson. "What about a helmet for Isaiah?"

He glared at her and shoved a pair of goggles into her hands.

Right. No reason for a helmet from his point of view if he was going to kill Isaiah anyway.

"Get us moving. Climb the rough on the right and just keep going."

"But where?"

"I'll be taking the pass at the top. You..." He shrugged.

"Us what?" Isaiah asked.

"Enjoy the ride." She patted his knee as fury made her feel like a fierce mother lion with a cub to protect. One more try before turning the key. "You know there's room for him to ride in front of me. The seat lets me scoot back. That will give you more control."

He seemed to think about it for a moment then shook his head. "No more stalling. Go now."

She gladly put on the goggles. With the deep snow, she knew she was going to get a face full of powder and reluctantly reached for the key to get the engine running. She pulled the throttle and off they went. It took her a few minutes to get the hang of running it, but soon had them climbing through the deep snow.

Powder peppered her face, and she had to keep swiping the goggles to keep them clean. Her chest was soon caked with snow. Her neck and face were freezing. She hoped her body was protecting Isaiah.

She kept them moving at a steady clip, sinking into the fluff and accelerating to come out, the engine cutting the quiet.

She had to concentrate on driving, but she also had to figure out how to free Isaiah, because free him she would. She might lose her life to this man, but there was no way her nephew was dying today. No possible way.

Alex heard a snowmobile powering up the hill in the scrub just east of him. The fool was likely going to destroy any hope he had of continuing to track the killer. He stepped out from behind the tree to wave the guy down, but he kept coming. In fact, he accelerated.

Not just one person. A trio on a big touring machine. No helmets. Not even for the kid. Irresponsible. The driver kept the throttle pressed as if fleeing a foe. *Fools*. This place was meant to be enjoyed, not raced through. And the snow was too deep for this speed.

The driver barreled straight at him. They got closer. *What in the world?*

It was Whitney driving. Isaiah in back.

A strange man.

"Alex!" Isaiah screamed. "Help us."

The man clamped his hand over Isaiah's mouth and poked a gun to Whitney's head. A 3-D printed gun.

The killer.

No. No. No. The killer had her. Had Isaiah. Alex had failed them.

He reached for his gun in his jacket pocket, but knew if he drew it, the guy would kill her. He held up his hands and backed off. Stood helplessly by as they pulled even with him, flinging up snow.

Whitney met his gaze for a moment. Looking helpless. Terrified. Isaiah crying. The man glaring.

Alex wanted to hurl himself at the sled, but he'd taken off his snowshoes, and the snow was up to his thighs. He couldn't move fast enough.

He couldn't let them disappear though.

Think. Think.

He had to track them somehow. He had to get back to the lodge and hope Gage and Riley were on their way back. Then hope they could spot the snowmobile in the heavy woods.

He needed something else. He frantically searched around him. Saw his bag. GPS dart.

He dove for the bag. Ripped off his gloves and tore it open to find the portable GPS dart system. Police used a similar system mounted in the front of their cars to fire a GPS dart that stuck to a vehicle so they could track it and not have to engage in high-speed chases.

Eryn had modified one for their use, and he'd brought it along mostly because he thought it was cool and had been hoping for a chance to use it. But not like this. Not because Whitney and Isaiah were being whisked away by a killer.

He armed the device. Held it out. Fired. The projectile launched. Attached to the back of the snowmobile seat.

He watched to see if the man felt the impact, but he showed no indication that he was going to rip it free.

Alex could hardly fathom turning away and heading down the hill when Whitney was being hurled in the opposite direction, but her life depended on him making record time down that hill. He would cross over to the nearest ski run and hopefully find someone whose skis he could commandeer. If not, it would still be faster heading down that trail than in the navigating the rough. Time was of the essence—not a moment to waste.

23

Whitney wished she'd been able to stop by Alex. But all she could do was toss him a panicked look and make sure she didn't hit him. Since then, they'd climbed higher and higher, and now her thumb cramped. She couldn't hold the throttle any longer.

She released it and the machine slowed and sank into the deep powder. She shifted to look back at Ibson and patted Isaiah's hand.

"Love you, bud," she said.

"What are you doing?" Ibson roared.

"My hand's cramping, and I can't hold the lever." She hoped he would take over driving, giving her the chance to escape with Isaiah.

"Switch the lever to a finger throttle." He reached around her and twisted the lever, bringing it up and allowing her to control it with her fingers not her thumb.

"I don't know," she said trying to buy time. "I'm still not sure my hand will cooperate. Can I rest it for just a minute?"

"Sure, you can rest. For more than a minute if you want." He lifted the gun and aimed at her head.

She cringed.

"Drive, Aunt Whitney!" Isaiah screamed.

"Okay, buddy." She gripped the throttle. The snowmobile jolted forward, whisking them through the snow, climbing higher and higher. Away from Alex. From help.

Alex noted the location of the GPS dart on his phone then shoved it into his pocket. Whitney and Isaiah were nearing the pass that would take them out of the area, potentially making it harder to free them. He scanned the sky for the helo and found only fluffy white clouds on a vibrant blue backdrop. He wished the helo was sitting in front of him, but at least the team was only a few minutes out on their return trip.

The minute Alex had reached the resort, he'd made a frantic phone call to Gage, who grabbed Nate. The three of them made a plan. Now they needed to execute it. But first their ride had to arrive.

"C'mon, c'mon. Get here already." He paced over the packed snow near the landing zone, his gut twisted in a ball of agony.

"We'll get to them." Nate stood alert and ready by the supplies he'd helped Alex collect.

"But we have no idea if we'll be on time. We don't know who has them or why. They might not even be on the snowmobile anymore. What if he..." No, he couldn't say it. Shouldn't even be thinking it. But a killer had them and hadn't hidden his face. He surely planned to finish what he'd started.

"They're here." Nate pointed at the sky.

Alex cocked his head. Listened for the *whomp, whomp, whomp* of the rotors.

Yes! He heard it, and the helo swooped over the mountain in the distance. He would soon be airborne with Nate and the team—Gage, Coop, Eryn, Sam, and Riley. They would all go after Whitney and Isaiah. Free them. They'd take the killer down, whoever he was. At this moment, Alex didn't even care. Sure, he was curious, but his burning need to save the woman he loved trumped that.

Loved. Yeah, he'd fallen in love with Whitney. How could he not? She was sweet. Kind. Compassionate. Beautiful. Everything he'd longed for in a woman in the moments he'd let himself dream that he could have someone in his life. And now she was in danger.

The helo's rotors rumbled louder as it appeared over the ridge. Alex picked up his equipment tote bag and made ready to hand it to whoever opened the door. Nate grabbed skis and poles, his stance solid and ready.

The helo hovered overhead and swirling snow-filled wind from the rotors buffeted them. Alex planted his feet and lowered his head, keeping his eyes fixed on the spot where Coop would touch down.

One bounce and they were down. Alex was at the door before Gage had it open.

He pounded on it. "C'mon, c'mon, c'mon. We need to move."

"Cool it," Nate said from behind. "Or you're no good to them."

Alex knew that in his head, but he couldn't lose Whitney or Isaiah. He couldn't survive that.

The door slid open. He handed off the bag and bolted for the other supplies. He heard Nate talking to Gage about their plan, about his role as a law enforcement officer, and how they had to handle things by the book.

Forget the book. Alex would do whatever was needed to save Whitney.

Sam jogged across the lot and helped finished loading

supplies. They all boarded, and Coop soon had them whirling up into the sky.

Alex quickly put his headset on and ran his gaze over the team. "Let's review the plan."

Eryn frowned. "Are you sure Whitney's abductor is heading for the nearest pass?"

"Sure? No," Alex replied, as he wasn't sure of anything right now except for his feelings for Whitney and the fear that was churning in his gut. He got out his phone and tapped the screen until he had the GPS tracking program up. "They're still heading due north. At their current speed they'll reach the pass in thirty minutes, but we're good on time."

"And you're positive you didn't recognize him?" Gage asked.

Alex rested his phone on his knee, keeping his eye on Whitney and Isaiah's symbol, and thought back to the brief moments he'd seen the guy. "Positive."

"Then his motive is unclear," Eryn said.

"Exactly," Alex replied. "I don't know if he just happened upon them and grabbed them for leverage in case he needed them to escape, or if he targeted her and the bullet that took out Vose was meant for her."

"Could be an important distinction," Coop said over the headset from the pilot seat. "The first says he may let them go. The second says, no way."

"He didn't hide his face. Says he's not letting them go either way." Nate's tone was grim.

Alex suspected this was the tone he used when notifying next of kin that they'd lost a loved one. Acid roiled in Alex's gut, swirling and rising up his throat. He swallowed hard.

Details. Stick to details. "Okay, so Coop's taking a circuitous route to keep from alerting the abductor. He'll put us down well north of pass. We'll ski downhill. Set up an ambush."

Alex made eye contact with Riley. "You'll take a stand with a clear shot at the pass. When I signal, you'll take out the snowmobile engine, leaving them as sitting ducks. You have the correct ammo, right?"

"The .50 BMG." He lifted his rifle laying across his lap and patted his Kevlar vest pocket where Alex had to assume extra armor-piercing bullets were stored for his rifle. Though he wouldn't need them. Alex was sure of that. Riley aimed with deadly accuracy, and he would nail the engine with his first shot.

"So, he takes out the machine," Nate said. "Then we have an unpredictable hostage taker in panic mode. That's the time I'm concerned about. We have to play it by the book. If this guy is our killer—and it's looking like he is—we don't want him to walk over some technicality."

Sam sat forward. "I think we all agree with that, but saving Whitney's and Isaiah's lives are priority."

"True. But we can't get caught up in the moment and not think." Nate locked gazes with Alex, singling him out.

And well he should. Alex was the loose cannon here. The one with the most to lose.

Nate swung his gaze to Riley. "We've already agreed that a sniper shot isn't our best option, but I want to confirm that you're on board with that and will take direction from me."

"Affirmative," Riley said. "Not only is taking a life a last resort in all cases, but we want to spare Whitney and Isaiah from such trauma."

"So we set up for an ambush," Alex took over again. "Take a moment. Assess the landscape and then I call an audible. Either we'll swarm them as a group or I'll take a more subtle approach. Negotiate if we have to, but for me, that's our last resort. In my military career, I've never seen a negotiation end well."

"Not my experience at all." Gage firmed his shoulders. "If it comes to that, I'll take lead. I've handled plenty of standoffs for Blackwell and come out on top."

Alex knew he spoke the truth, but then, Gage wasn't in love with the hostage in those situations.

"Forget your past. Think about my successful negotiation instead. I mean, I'm freaking awesome at it." Gage grinned.

Alex thought smiling was beyond him, but Gage never bragged and rarely joked, so Alex chuckled.

"Better take it down a notch," Eryn said, her voice deadpan and her gaze locked on Gage. "Or that head's not going to fit through the door."

Laughter broke out, removing some of the tension. That was Gage's intent, Alex knew, but he didn't want them to lose their intensity.

"Nate has lead on calling a sniper shot, but I'll be handling other assignments. Is everyone clear on the plan?" Alex ran his gaze over the group, pausing for a nod of acknowledgement from each person.

"Then we're a go." Satisfied that they were ready, Alex nodded and sat back to pray. Because no matter Gage's confidence level, hostage rescues could go sideways in a flash and people died. Alex always took the time to pray before an op to settle his nerves, but he needed God's comfort even more today.

He looked over the rugged terrain below, far away from the groomed slopes. He was scheduled to ski this area because McCray had a heli-ski tour scheduled. Sam would have sat that out as she wasn't the hard-core thrill seeker. Alex had loads of back-country experience and knew how dangerous heli-skiing could be. That's what he liked about it. Man versus the wild.

Helo pilots flew skiers and guides up to extreme skiing areas, dropped them off, and then picked them up lower on the slope. Because the terrain was rough and challenging, it was generally reserved for experienced, super-fit athletes. The others on the team were fit and could ski but weren't as proficient as Alex. Today would be a challenge for them, but they would rise to it.

They always did. Always.

Remember that.

He closed his eyes. Visualized the op. Prayed about everything that could go wrong, and then left it in God's hands. At least he hoped he'd left it there. He knew from the past that he could pray all he wanted and make a decision about how he would act. Trust God or not trust Him. But it was in the doing that his decision and faith were tested. Not in the planning. Not in the prepping. But in the living of life.

For the most part he'd done well with it in the day-to-day struggles. The doing of his job. The keeping of his personal life on an even keel.

But in the bigger things. Nah, there he'd failed big time.

Case in point—the huge mountain God dropped in his path, blocking Alex's future with a wife and family. No pass in sight as a way out. Okay, maybe God didn't make the mountain. Alex did by the way he reacted to his losing his mother. Once an eleven-year-old lost and stuck behind a mountain of pain and hurt. Now a thirty-four-year-old still stuck there. He loved Whitney, but could he finally man up in his life so he could do something about it?

He glanced at the GPS. She was now twenty or so minutes out. Once they got to the pass, her abductor could ditch her. Kill her. Leaving Alex alone. And he could do nothing except pray.

He could lose her. He really could. He knew what that was like. The pain. The lifelong questioning. An intense ache spread through his body, weakening his limbs.

"Swinging into the landing zone," Coop announced.

Alex cleared his mind and came alert. Adrenaline pumping. All senses firing. He felt like he could see clearly for the first time in a long time.

Here he was thinking the blizzard had been an obstacle from God to disrupt his life and get his attention. It was, but it also was a blessing in keeping him with Whitney, and he now knew what he had to do.

He looked at his team gearing up, game faces on. Ready to rock and roll. To do what they did best—save lives.

24

Whitney didn't know how far it was to the pass, but they were summiting the mountain and it had to be coming up. Soon they would stop. Then what? What did Ibson plan to do with them? How did he plan to kill them?

The finality of their situation settled into her heart.

Father. Please. There's still time. Please intervene. Not for me, but for Isaiah. He's just a child. A boy. Save him. No matter what happens to me, save him.

She relaxed the throttle a notch, hoping to delay their approach, and hoping Ibson wouldn't notice the slight decrease in speed.

She held her breath. Waited for him to jab her in the back.

Nothing. No recognition at all. A small victory, but she'd take it and hope it gave Alex more time to come for them.

Was he coming? Surely he would, but how? He couldn't catch up to the snowmobile. The helicopter might be an option if it had been on site, but they'd taken Vose and the ME away, and Whitney hadn't heard them return. So that seemed out of the question, too.

She could easily visualize Alex pacing at the resort.

Feeling as helpless as she was. She suspected he would call the helicopter back, if he could even communicate with Gage, but if so, how long would that take? Would it be in time to save them from Ibson?

Please. I can't do anything for Isaiah. We're at your mercy. Please let them help us. Please.

∼

Alex swooshed down the slope, laying down the first tracks on pristine snow, an adrenaline rush like no other. His rifle and pack were on his back as he glided over downy-soft pillows and moguls to lead the others to the pass. The powder was perfect. Untouched. His heart pumped hard just as he liked it. The brisk temperature was modified by the radiating sun.

His ski suddenly caught an edge, and he fought to keep himself upright. He needed focus. To concentrate. If he was alone, he would schuss down the hill. No turns. Just maximum speed to reach their location faster, but he had to think of everyone's skiing abilities and bring them all safely to their target.

Alex glanced ahead, searching for the snowmobile so they could take cover if it approached. If he'd mistimed things and the snowmobile was closer than he thought, he hoped they were at least blending into the terrain. He usually wore bright-colored ski clothing for recreational skiing, but he and Sam were undercover and didn't want to stand out for McCray, so they'd worn white suits Gage had recently purchased.

Alex didn't know how Gage managed it, but he'd bought the new gear recently adopted by the US Army. The clothing was all white and the skis were shorter and wider, built more like cross-country skis rather than downhill skis.

They could be used for both types of skiing and easily strapped onto their cold weather boots making them able to quickly maneuver. Nate was the only one who wore any color.

At the location he thought best for Riley to take a stand, Alex turned up slope and used a swift hockey stop. He lifted his goggles to assess the area. Now that he could see the pass and topography, he could finalize their plan.

Riley swung into place next to him, pulling out his scope and surveying the area. "This will work just fine."

"Thought so," Alex said. "I'll give you the authorization to take out the snowmobile, but wait for Nate's go-ahead for any other shot."

He nodded, but he really didn't need to. It was typical protocol for him to wait for permission for his shot. He'd stay here, uphill about a half mile. Not only was it the right spot to take out the snowmobile, but because he would be on overwatch for the team as well, this stand gave him a full overview without putting him too far away. Distance wasn't an issue though. Not really. Riley could make this shot and longer ones with no problem or loss of accuracy.

He bumped fists with Alex and did a kick turn to glide into the scrub for cover.

Alex signaled for the others to move out, and he dug in his poles to get moving. It took little effort as the slope was steep and gravity took him downhill at a quick clip. Just north of the pass he stopped and turned.

"Take cover," he said into their communications device, and his voice came over the earbuds. "Gage go north. Coop and Sam east. Eryn west. I'm south with you, Nate."

They all moved into strong positions that would allow them to step out and surround the abductor once the snowmobile was stopped. A force six-strong plus a man on the scope should be able to stop this foe without any injuries, but they didn't know who they were dealing with and had no intel on him—they hadn't been able to perform a threat assessment and were going in blind.

Alex didn't like that at all. He simply had to trust God. To trust the team. The strong men and women of Blackwell. Nate, too.

Alex waited for Nate to settle into position, and then Alex took a prime viewing spot where he would be able to see the snowmobile as it approached. He unloaded his pack and got out binoculars to aim them downhill. The snow-encrusted windshield of the snowmobile came into view. He shifted and caught the green of Whitney's scarf fluttering in the breeze. She still drove, and Isaiah was in the hands of the abductor.

"Snowmobile is about a klick away," he said into the mic and offered a silent prayer of thanks that they'd arrived on time. "You in position, Riley?"

"Affirmative. I'll let you know the minute I have the sled in my scope."

"Roger that," Alex said. "Others report."

"In position," Eryn said.

"Ditto," Gage replied.

"Same here," Coop said.

"I'm in place," Sam said.

"Yes," Nate said.

"We'll go in as a group and swarm the machine—on my signal. Stand by." Alex zoomed in the binoculars to get a look at Whitney's face. How he loved that face and didn't want anything to happen to her. He switched to Isaiah who he could only see when he poked his head out around Whitney. Poor kid. He had to be terrified. He'd been through so much, and Alex simply wanted to help him. And love him. Let him heal. Maybe finish healing himself at the same time.

"Target locked in the scope," Riley said. "Waiting orders."

Alex shifted the binocs up. Caught the abductor's face. Hoodie tied tight around a wide face. Goggles on. Nothing much to see except a sneer. Maybe a permanent one, warning Alex to take care. Alex wished they would be taking that kill shot, the only sure way to save Whitney and Isaiah. But the trauma would just be too great for the boy. Whitney, too. Alex hoped they didn't have do that to either of them.

The sled drew closer, the sound of the engine getting louder. The machine wasn't running full-out like before. Thankfully, or the team wouldn't have arrived in time. It was time to disable the motor, but it had to be done at precisely the right moment.

Alex counted down in his mind. Evaluated the speed. Evaluated the distance to come alongside them.

"In ten," Alex said and began the countdown in his head, his hands sweating in his gloves as he shifted his rifle over his shoulder with his free hand. "Five. Four. Three. Two. One. *Engage*."

Riley's rifle cracked a loud boom into the air. The snowmobile engine died and the machine came to a halting stop.

"Move. Move. Move," Alex ordered and they poured out of their hiding spots.

The abductor's head snapped up. He looked around. Sat stunned. For only a second. Still holding Isaiah, he hurled his body off the far side of the machine, tumbling into the snow.

A gun discharged. The abductor's gun. Not a team weapon. Alex was sure of that.

"Isaiah," Whitney screamed, and plunged off the side near the boy.

"Cover me," Alex told Nate and let his rifle hang to pole his way to the snowmobile. He quickly assessed the situation and released his skis to launch himself into the air, clearing the snowmobile seat and landing on the abductor's back.

The man reached up and grabbed Alex by the throat. His hands clamped on tight, his thumbs pressing into the middle and squeezing. Alex couldn't breathe. He struggled. Fought back but couldn't budge the vise-like hands. He couldn't let the guy get the better of him. He reached into his jacket pocket for his Taser. Pressed it into the guy's neck and deployed it.

The man's hands fell away, and his body went rigid. He gritted his teeth and moaned.

"I've got him," Nate said from above where he stood with his rifle pointed down.

Alex gulped air, scooted free, and released the Taser. He dug out his zip ties and cuffed the jerk when he really wanted to check on Whitney and Isaiah, but he couldn't turn his back on a potential killer.

The moment he was secured, Alex spun, flailing in the deep snow.

Whitney was sitting up and brushing snow from Isaiah's face. The boy was crying, but alive. An injury or just afraid?

Alex frantically clawed through the thick powder. "Isaiah. Is he okay?"

She nodded. "The bullet didn't hit him."

She jerked Isaiah into her arms and held fast, looking at Alex over the top of the boy's head. "Thank you, Alex. I knew you would come. I knew it. I just didn't know if it would be in time."

Tears started pouring from her eyes, and her chest rose in sobs.

"Shh, honey, it's okay." He scooted closer to them and gently circled his arms around the pair. He held them there.

This little family. The family he wanted. Could have. If he would let himself. If she would let him.

∽

Debrief. That's what the team called this meeting where they'd been hashing out every movement in their rescue efforts. Whitney had never attended such a meeting. Alex said they held debriefs following every op as it helped them figure out what went wrong so they never made the same mistake twice. From her point of view, there had been no mistakes, and she and Isaiah were alive thanks to them.

All she could do was sit back in the resort conference room and answer the few questions they directed her way. Oh, and try to quit shaking, but adrenaline was still lingering in her body even though she'd been back at the resort safe and sound for an hour. She kept thinking about the dangerous positions these brave men and women put themselves in for her—and others—all because they felt called to do the job. She wished there was a special way she could thank them. To let them know how very much she appreciated them. She was determined to find a way.

"That'll do it." Alex looked at his watch and stood. "Thanks, everyone, for the fine job. I owe you all, and I know you'll collect. Just go easy on me."

"Easy?" Coop snorted. "No way that's happening."

"I didn't figure there was, but I had to try." Alex grimaced, but it was all in good humor.

"Okay, people." Gage got up. "We'll be continuing to ferry in needed supplies and carry out people who have to leave the resort today. If we run long, we'll be spending the night. The manager has arranged rooms and meals for us just in case."

The others started to get up.

"Can I say something before you all go?" Whitney asked.

"Go ahead," Gage said, but she could tell he was in a hurry. She'd make this quick.

She stood. "I wanted to say thank you, which seems so very inadequate for what I'm feeling. I mean, how can words express my thanks for saving my life, and more importantly, Isaiah's life? But thank you."

There were mumbles of *you're welcome* and smiles directed her way.

"We're always glad to help." Gage clapped his hands, dismissing his team who scuttled out of the room minus Alex.

He faced Gage. "I'm going to see Whitney back to her apartment, and then I'll come find you."

Gage nodded and followed his team out the door.

"You don't have to do that," Whitney said feeling bad about taking him away from valuable work.

"I know, but I thought we should talk before I leave."

"Oh, right. Yes, you'll be leaving, too," she said, the realization that he was about to walk out of her life a heavy blow.

He gave a solemn nod and gestured at the door.

She headed out, slipping into her jacket as she walked. It felt so weird to see the lobby bustling with people again after the eerie emptiness from the blizzard, but skiers in bright-colored clothes, their faces rosy red from the cold, rushed in to warm up at the roaring fireplace.

Gage stood near the door. McCray, hands fisted, glared at him. "But I need to leave today. You're taking others out who have to go. I demand a spot on your chopper, too."

"Sorry," Gage said, an edge of warning in his tone. "We had to prioritize the list and you didn't make the cut. Maybe tomorrow. Or the next day."

"They'll have the pass cleared by then."

"Exactly." A snide smile crossed Gage's mouth as he started to leave.

McCray grabbed Gage's arm to stop him. He spun at a rate Whitney didn't think humanly possible and had McCray's arm behind his back so fast it was a blur. He issued some sort of a warning Whitney couldn't make out from this distance, but the anger in his eyes made it clear. *Back off now.*

He shoved the man away and marched out the door.

"I have to say since we couldn't get the jerk on gun running that felt good to witness," Alex said.

"But he was hassling Gage."

"I guarantee Gage enjoyed the encounter."

She cast him a questioning look.

"Putting McCray in his place had to feel good."

"Oh. I thought you meant the physical part."

Alex grinned. "He probably didn't hate that either."

She shook her head. "I am—on the one hand—in awe of you all, and—on the other hand—wondering how you enjoy what you do."

"I feel the same way about your chosen profession. Needles." He mocked an exaggerated shudder.

She laughed, and it felt wonderful. They started walking again, and she reveled in feeling safe and having the worry of Percy gone. But she still had two precious kids who needed her help to heal, and she had to take that responsibility very seriously. Especially now that Isaiah had gone through another traumatic experience that would leave emotional scars. Even if he was already trying to pretend it didn't bother him, and he was acting tough like the guys on the team, he wasn't hiding it very well.

They reached the door. McCray stepped in front of Alex.

"Don't even think about it." Alex brushed past him,

clearing the way for Whitney to head out into the refreshing sunshine.

Whitney started down the sidewalk. "When your mom died, did you go to counseling?"

"No. No one offered, and I was too young to realize I needed it."

"Would it have helped, do you think?"

"Yeah. I do."

Exactly what she needed to hear to finalize her plans. "At first, I thought I would work here until Tomio could find a replacement, but now I think I should get back to my real life as soon as possible and find a counselor for Isaiah. Then get him back in his regular school. I know Tomio will understand."

"So you'll be going back to Portland?"

She nodded.

His steps slowed, and she looked up at him to find a frown on his face. "I was kinda thinking that maybe we should try to figure out this thing that's going on between us."

Interesting.

"Yeah?" she asked as she climbed the stairs to her apartment where Yuki was watching the kids.

"Yeah." He joined her on the stairs. "I mean, I think it's more than just physical attraction, don't you?"

Oh yeah. "Way more. Which is odd, right? We've known each other only a little while, but it feels right."

"I think so, too. That doesn't happen very often so we'd be foolish to let it go and not give it a try."

"I suppose."

"You don't sound convinced."

She stopped outside her apartment door. "I'm convinced that I'm attracted to you. That I think you're an amazing, special man. That any woman would be a fool not to jump into a relationship with you."

"But..."

She couldn't believe she was going to say this when all she wanted to do was let this man hold her and kiss her again. "But, after the trauma Isaiah just suffered, I want to focus on him right now and not divide my attention."

Alex's mouth flattened into a grim line, and she almost blurted out that she wanted to change her mind, but Isaiah had to come first.

"So it's a *no* then," he mumbled.

"No. Not no. It's a *later*. Can we give it a few weeks? Let me get settled back in my life. Find that counselor for Isaiah. Make sure that he's headed in the right direction. And use that time to think about what I want. What the kids need." She raised a hand to touch his cheek that was frosty cold. "To think about you. About us."

"You think there will be an *us* when you get done with this thinking?"

"I sure hope so."

His frown deepened.

"Hey, hey," she said. "I don't want you to leave upset."

"See," he said, cupping the side of her face with the gentlest of touches. "You don't want me to leave upset, but I don't want to leave you at all. And that's such a huge difference that I don't know if we'll be able to overcome it."

EPILOGUE

Christmas Eve Day broke with drizzle, and Alex paced the length of his small cabin. Back and forth. He'd lost count of his steps an hour ago. He stopped to straighten the bowl of fruit Hannah insisted he fill for Isaiah and Zoey while they stayed the night with him.

A banana fell out, and he settled it back on top. Then picked it up. Set it down. Turned it. Right, then left. Grabbed an apple and put the banana there instead. Perched the apple on top.

"What're you doing, man?" He groaned.

He didn't do fruit arranging, nothing that even resembled fruit arranging, but he worked hard to make it look good. It all had to look presentable if he was going to convince Whitney to marry him. To live here in the boonies. In his tiny, boring little cabin at first, but then they could get a house.

He'd already talked to Gage, and he was fine with Alex moving out of the compound. Alex didn't want to. He'd be the first one to go. The others would eventually leave, too, he suspected, and it was the end of something they'd built together. Not the end of the team. That would never happen.

Everyone had reinforced that at their big Thanksgiving dinner at Gage's house. Alex felt uncomfortable sitting next to Sam with all the couples surrounding them, and he missed Whitney and the kids something fierce. Man, he wished they would have agreed to attend, but she'd said Isaiah wasn't ready to embrace thanks right now, and it was going be a painful day for him.

Alex couldn't argue with that, and he was overjoyed when she agreed to come to the Christmas party.

A knock sounded on the door. He shot a look at the clock. No. It was too early for Whitney. Besides he had to let her in the gate, so she couldn't be knocking on his door.

He answered the door and found Sam standing there. She'd abandoned her usual work attire for a simple black dress and heels. Her hair was up in a messy bun thing. She was holding a stack of files.

"Wow. Who are you, and what have you done with Sam?" He laughed. "You must be Samantha."

She rolled her eyes and pushed past him. "I have a few files to close out on Ibson and wanted to review them with you."

"Sure." He pointed at his dining table that he'd polished until it gleamed. He'd polished the whole place. And himself. Sure, he took care of his appearance all the time. His mom had a thing about grooming, and he'd always continued it to honor her, but today every whisker was precision length. His clothes pressed to Marine standards.

She set down the files. "I could say the same thing about you, you know?"

"What? That I'm Samantha?" He grinned at her.

"Nah. You clean up nice." She smiled back at him and dropped into a chair. "For your information, I do like wearing dresses for special occasions. Hannah and Gage's party is going to be so fun. We'll get to see everyone's families. Brothers and sisters. Yours is coming, right?"

"Yep. She'll be late, but that's Faith." He shook his head. "Sometimes I think she lives everything by her name including having faith that she'll be on time."

"Oh, I get that. My middle sister never arrives anywhere on time. She was born three weeks late, and my mom says she's been late ever since." She laughed. "I think today will be a lot like Christmas at my big crazy family's place in California."

"Except for the weather." He grinned.

She smiled, then sighed. "I miss them."

"Why aren't you going home then?"

She shrugged, but her smile vanished.

"You can tell me. I don't gossip."

"Not much anyway." She wrinkled her nose. "Seriously, let's stick to the files, okay?"

"Okay," he said, but wanted to dig and find out what she was avoiding back at home.

Now that he'd decided to work on his issues with losing his mother, he wanted to help others do the same thing. But seriously, he couldn't. There was a right time for each person. God's time. Only He knew when they were ready. That's something Alex was now certain of. No question in his mind that God had placed him smack-dab in the middle of a blizzard to slow him down. To take away his high-octane thrills that he now knew he used to avoid facing his past.

He'd thought for years he had to be on the go. To keep moving. His brain worked overtime when he wasn't busy doing something... and those thoughts turned to unhappiness, so why not avoid them?

But, in fact, he was a very patient man. He couldn't have

been a top-notch Recon Marine if he didn't possess extreme patience. And if Whitney turned him down today, he would use that patience and keep going back until he won her heart.

Whitney rang the buzzer on what looked like the strongest, most impenetrable gate she'd ever seen. Alex hadn't been kidding when he said the Blackwell compound was fortified. It left her a bit intimidated and raised her anxieties about a social event with all of Alex's friends. She wasn't the *need a gate to keep people out* kind of person. She was an *open her arms let me help you heal* kind of person. Maybe she and Alex really weren't a good match.

"This place is so cool," Isaiah said from the back seat.

She looked up in the mirror and found his eyes wide open as he gaped out the window trying to get a look ahead.

"I'll release the gate," Alex's voice came over the squawk box startling her and thrilling her at the same time. "Just pull straight ahead, and I'll be waiting for you."

"Okay," she said, sounding breathless.

Three weeks had passed, and she was going to see the man she loved again after no communication except for the Thanksgiving invite and the invitation to this party, which technically came from Gage and his wife, Hannah.

She drove through the opening and down a winding road until she spotted a ranch house with multicolored lights strung along the eves and a giant blow-up snowman in the front yard.

Alex stood at the end of a sidewalk. He wore a royal blue dress shirt, black slacks, and a for her to go first. He had the collar up against the brisk ocean wind, but at least it wasn't spitting drizzle as it had been for the entire drive from Portland.

She stopped the SUV, and he jogged around to the passenger side. She unlocked the doors, and he climbed in.

"Hi." He took her hand, and his smile spread across those full lips that she'd been thinking of kissing from the moment she'd left him.

"Hi," she said back, feeling suddenly very shy.

He shifted his attention to the back seat. "Hey, bud. How you doing?"

Isaiah gave a tight little smile that he'd started using this week. "Okay."

Alex shifted again. "I see your sister is taking her usual car nap."

"Always." Isaiah rolled his eyes but smiled.

Whitney was thrilled with the progress he made. She couldn't wait to hear him laugh. He wasn't ready quite yet. But he'd been in therapy, and his psychologist said he was strong and resilient, and he would laugh again. Once he got over feeling guilty about having joy in his life.

Alex heard a whimpering from the back of the SUV. "What's that I hear?"

"Um," she said. "It's possible I decided we needed a puppy for Christmas."

"Interesting."

"You don't like dogs, do you? I should have waited... asked you...oh no," she rushed on, the words just tumbling out. "...I just...well... I thought it would be good."

"Take a breath." He took an exaggerated intake of air, and she followed suit. "I love dogs. I haven't had one since I was a kid because of my military service, but I was thinking it would be a nice way to round out a family."

"You were?" She sighed. "You're not just saying that to make me feel better?"

"I'm not, but then I guess I should ask if you got one of those little yippie dogs or a *man's* kind of dog. A big strapping one." He laughed.

She mocked outrage at his comment. "Just for that, you're going to have to wait to see."

"It's a—"

"Shh," she gently chastised Isaiah. "Make him wait."

Isaiah shared a conspiratorial look with Alex and spread his hands out to indicate the dog's size.

"Is this what I have to look forward to with the two of you today?" Whitney laughed. "Ganging up on me."

"Quite possibly." He winked at Isaiah who cracked a tiny smile.

Alex pointed to the right. "If you follow the road that way, we can unload your things and the puppy, then you can freshen up before the party if you want to."

She got the SUV going and butterflies fluttered around her stomach. She was going to see his home. The place he'd built himself, as he'd told her that each team member designed and built their own cabins. It had to be a reflection of the man, and she could hardly wait. She soon saw six cabins all designed in a different style.

"Cool," Isaiah said, his eyes going wide again.

"Mine's the first one. The A-frame."

She wouldn't say anything, but she was disappointed in the outside. The others had such character and charm, and his was plain and utilitarian. So opposite of the way he presented himself. Where was the disconnect?

She parked, and they got out to go to the back for the puppy.

"A chocolate lab," he exclaimed in delight. "Perfect."

"She's only two months old, and she sometimes pees on the floor," Isaiah offered. "Aunt Whitney doesn't like that, but she says she's learning and needs us to be patient."

Whitney nodded. "She should have a potty break before we go in, as she gets all excited."

Alex opened the kennel to get her out. "What's her name?"

"Cocoa," Isaiah announced proudly.

"Perfect name for her coloring. Rich dark cocoa."

Whitney nodded. "That was one of the reasons we chose her name, but Isaiah had a great idea. Vanessa loved hot chocolate. She was always drinking it. Even in the summer. Cocoa is a way for us to remember her every day."

"That's a very nice way to do it." He lifted the puppy in his arms, and she lapped his face. "Well, hello to you, too, Cocoa."

Whitney was jealous. Not of the licking, but of the puppy being so close to Alex and held in his arms.

He turned to Whitney. "Would you like me to get Zoey?"

"That would be nice."

As Whitney clipped the leash on Cocoa, Alex opened the door and started unbuckling Zoey's straps. He spoke softly to her to wake her, and Whitney's heart melted over his gentleness.

Zoey's eyes fluttered open, and she squealed for joy. "Awex!"

She always woke up ready to go. No need to take a few minutes to gain her bearings. She went down as quickly, often crashing in whatever location she happened to be in. Whitney had found her sound asleep on her bedroom floor, toys scattered around her more times than not.

"Are we here?" Her eyes were wide with wonder.

"That you are, princess." He smiled down on her, his fond expression warming Whitney's heart. He was so good with the kids. Likely due to helping raise his younger sister.

He lifted her out of the seat and went to put her down,

but she circled her arms around his neck and held on. "I wuv you, Awex."

His mouth fell open, and he glanced at Whitney.

Whitney smiled. "She knows a good man when she sees one."

Alex's face colored, and he sputtered, trying to come up with something to say as he stepped back and closed the car door.

Something about seeing the strong, confident man who'd rescued her from a killer, blushing due to a sweet comment from a three-year-old was really attractive, and Whitney wished they were alone.

She took a deep breath of the salty ocean air as Cocoa sniffed around the yard. She felt at peace in the lovely setting, a feeling that had been missing since Vanessa's death and even before that. She'd thought long and hard about her future with Alex, and if they got married, she could easily live here. *Listen to her*. First, he hadn't proposed. Second, he hadn't even hinted of marriage. And third, she hadn't seen the inside of the small cabin. She didn't care about décor, but with Isaiah and Zoey, Whitney needed two bathrooms. On this, she couldn't compromise.

Alex called to her and before long they were all inside and he was showing them to their rooms. The place was spotlessly clean and the word "utilitarian" described it for her. Nothing personal displayed. No pictures. No sign that he'd actually lived here for four years. And no second bathroom.

Deal breaker? She'd thought so, but when she looked up into his eyes, she knew she would settle for only having an outhouse to be with him.

The kids lost interest in the tour and started chasing Cocoa around the main room. At least there weren't any pricey or precious décor pieces to break. She caught sight of the clock on the wall, and a moment of panic settled in.

"We only have thirty minutes to get ready," she said. "We need to get hopping."

"We can be late," Alex said. "It's not a formal event."

"Still, I don't want to make a bad impression."

"So what can I do to help?"

"Get Isaiah into his outfit, and I'll get Zoey dressed. And if it's not too much, keep an eye on Zoey while I get changed."

"You got it." He turned to Isaiah. "Hey, bud, grab your bag, and let's go to your room to change."

Isaiah frowned and looked like he might protest, but that compliant spirit was still with him, and he picked up his bag.

She corralled Cocoa and put her in her crate, then scooped Zoey up and snuggled her neck. "Time for your pretty dress, princess."

Zoey clapped her chubby hands. She loved dressing up in frilly-skirted dresses and wearing her little white ballet-style shoes. And Whitney loved buying them. Always had.

The memory of picking out and giving the first baby dress to Vanessa as a present slammed into her from out of nowhere and stole her breath. Tears immediately wet her eyes and quickly rolled down her cheeks.

Oh, Vanessa. Sweetie. I miss you so much. I want you here. To see your precious babies growing up. To see who they'll become. I'll do my best for them. I promise. Always. Always. And I think Alex would be a wonderful father for them. I know you would like him.

She concentrated on the joy Zoey would feel in her dress and swiped away the tears. She refused to go to the party looking upset. She would have her cry over this later. When she went to bed and was alone.

In the bedroom, she wrestled three-year-old wiggly legs into a pair of white tights then slipped the dress's white-sequined bodice and pink tulle skirt over the little blond head and got it settled and zipped. Next, she combed Zoey's unruly curls and added a sparkly headband.

"Want to see in mirror."

Whitney accompanied her to the bathroom and held her up to see.

"I'm pretty. Like Mommy."

"Yes, princess. You are pretty and look just like your mommy." Tears started again.

"I want to go see Mommy."

"I know you do. But remember she's in heaven with God, and we can't visit her there."

She turned to look at Whitney. "Need to go potty."

"Right." Whitney nearly laughed as she'd expected to have to handle the child's sadness over losing her mother. "I should have thought of that before getting you all ready."

She started dancing. "Now. Go now."

Whitney whisked her down to the bathroom, and she just made it in time. As Whitney waited, she caught sight of her frazzled hair in the mirror. The ocean humidity was bringing out her frizz, and she looked a mess when she wanted to look so nice for Alex. Tears threatened again.

Seriously. When did she get this weepy?

"Done," Zoey announced.

Whitney put her tights back into place, pulled the dress down, got her hands washed, and gladly opened the bathroom door to send her out to Alex.

"I thought I was going to watch Zoey, but I get a princess instead." He smiled so sweetly at her that Whitney didn't think her heart could be any fuller. "Isaiah helped me find some books. Do you want me to read until it's time to go?"

She nodded solemnly. "But you can't mess up my dress."

"I'll be very careful. I promise."

"You too, Isaiah."

"I got it." He tugged on the collar of his shirt. He didn't like getting dressed up nearly half as much as Zoey did.

Whitney looked at the clock. "Ten minutes. Yikes."

She bolted for the bedroom and closed the door. She went straight to the bathroom and refreshed her makeup, brushed her teeth, and ironed her frizzy hair into soft curls. Then grabbed her dress from the garment bag and had to smile.

She'd splurged on a backless golden embroidery halter bodice dress with a flared skirt in a shimmery blue-black color and paired it with strappy black sandals. She'd never spent so much money on a cocktail dress before, and she likely never would again. But tonight was special. Alex was special and worth every dollar she paid to look nice for him.

She stood before the mirror and slipped diamond studs into her ears, a gift from her parents at high school graduation, added coral lipstick, and decided she looked ravishing. But it didn't matter how *she* thought she looked. There was a certain someone in the other room whose opinion she cared about more.

She turned off the lights and entered the room. She forgot all about her dress, which was foolishness anyway. The important things were right in front of her. Sitting on the couch in front of fireplace, the gas logs burning.

A man and two children. Her future. One she couldn't have imagined just a month ago, but one that she hoped would be a promise before the night was out.

Alex looked over his shoulder. Then back at the book, but suddenly did a double take, and his mouth fell open. "You…wow. I mean…wow."

He put Zoey down. Got up. Locked eyes with her.

Crossed the room. Took her hand and twirled her, her skirt flaring out.

"You look amazing." He smiled and took her other hand. "Maybe we could just send the kids to the party and stay here."

She laughed. "I'll have you know my dress cost way too much not to be seen by at least a dozen other people."

"Then your chariot awaits, my princess."

"But *I'm* your princess." Zoey pouted.

"Can't I have two princesses?"

"As long as you like me best."

Alex threw back his head and laughed, warming Whitney's heart. She couldn't hold back and had to laugh, too.

"Spoken like a true princess." Isaiah said and shook his head. "C'mon, Zo-Zo. I'll put you in your car seat. I'm hungry."

He got her into her jacket and shooed her out the door.

Alex grabbed Whitney's coat and held it out for her. When she slipped into it, he planted a kiss at the base of her neck before sliding her coat the rest of the way on.

She turned to look at him, his eyes sparkling with happiness.

"Does that have you wishing you agreed to stay home with me?" he whispered.

"Maybe," she replied, flirting outrageously and loving every second of it.

He circled his arm around her waist and pulled her close. "I have so much to talk to you about. To tell you. To ask you. Promise you'll save some time tonight at the party for just me."

Her skin tingled from the kiss, and her mind tingled from thoughts of their future. "Of course."

"And now, I apologize in advance, but you're going to have to redo your lipstick." His mouth crashed down on hers, and he kissed her with abandon. Her heart soared and beat hard. Either he wanted to move forward in their relationship or this was the most amazing goodbye kiss ever.

She had to believe the first. Wanted to believe it so badly. And would.

He suddenly lifted his head. Breathing hard, he looked at her.

The kiss had been everything she knew it would be, and she stared openmouthed at him.

He tipped her chin up with his index finger. "You have precisely three minutes to recover from that kiss. I know I won't be able to do it, but maybe you can."

Grinning, he opened the door.

She grabbed her tote bag she'd left by the front door.

Alex peeked inside it. "Gifts?"

"For your team. I wanted to thank all of you with a little something."

His expression was soft, and he touched her cheek. "You really are an incredible person, Whitney. I'm honored to know you."

Embarrassed, she waved away his compliment and dug out the small box she'd wrapped in shiny red foil, the lid separate, so he could open the box with ease. "I have so many more thank yous for you, but I wanted you to have one of these, too."

He took the box and lifted the top. She'd commissioned a bronze coin that had their team logo and name on one side and a Bible verse from Ephesians on the back. He stared silently at the coin as if she'd given him something priceless.

"There's more on the back," she said.

He turned it over and read the verse out loud. "Be strong in the Lord and in his mighty power. Put on the full armor of God, so that you can take your stand against evil. Ephesians

6: 10-11." He ran his finger over the coin then looked up, love burning in his eyes.

"I've never received any gift that means more to me. You captured the spirit of our team and our work, and I'll carry it with me. I know the others will, too." He took it from the box and pocketed it.

"Are you guys coming?" Isaiah whined from the doorway.

Whitney didn't appreciate the interruption, but she did appreciate hearing Isaiah whine like a normal nine-year-old—if there was such a thing. "You got it, bud."

Alex escorted her to the car. His hand on the small of her back left her emotions rocking, and when they pulled up to the house she was still savoring the kiss and thinking about how soon they could be alone together for another one.

She took a long cleansing breath and got out. Lights burned from inside Gage's house and the Christmas lights on the eves were twinkling. As were the stars above in the cold clear night. A magical night all around.

Alex swung Zoey up in his arms, and Whitney walked with Isaiah up the walk to ring the doorbell. She had to look at Alex to see if she could catch even a glimpse of what he was thinking. She met his gaze and held it. The burning in her stomach that only he could fire off started, and she couldn't stand it. She raised up on tiptoes and gave him a soft kiss on the cheek.

He groaned. "Unfair."

"Turnabout and all that." She laughed.

The door opened and a petite woman with shiny red curls smiled at them. Her expression was so welcoming, any nerves Whitney might have at meeting the rest of Alex's friends evaporated.

"Whitney. Good, you're here. I'm Hannah." She stepped

back. "Come in out of the cold and introduce me to these precious children."

They entered the great room that held a large dining table and family room with fireplace blazing. Laughter and conversation flowed around the space filled with team members Whitney recognized. Nate was there, too, but wearing casual clothing, and he looked less intimidating. As did all the others. They were relaxed. Smiling.

"You must be Isaiah," Hannah said as she looked at him. "Gage and I have a son, David, and daughter, Mia. David's six and Mia's seven so not too much younger than you."

Isaiah didn't respond. Just stood chewing on his lower lip.

"I'm Princess Zoey," she introduced herself and yanked on her coat. "Off."

"Yes, you *are* a little princess. Jackets," Hannah said. "Let me take them." She started with Zoey, who immediately wanted to be put down and twirl around in her dress.

Whitney set down her tote, and Alex helped her out of her jacket.

"Ooh, I am so jealous of that dress," Hannah said.

"Why? Yours is lovely." Hannah wore a deep green sheath with a lace outer layer that made her gorgeous red hair stand out.

"Thank you, but it's almost as old as David. I so need to splurge on a day of shopping."

"I could help you out with that," Whitney offered.

"Girl, you have a date." She hung their jackets on hooks by the door and then focused on Isaiah. "David and Mia are in the playroom having dinner. Owen and Bekah are there too, so Zoey could play with them when they finish eating. I'll introduce you and you can have some dinner."

"Cool," Isaiah said, but didn't really sound overly impressed.

Whitney watched him carefully. Where was the boy who was starving not more than ten minutes ago?

"And we have a dog, Barkley," Hannah went on. "He's in his crate because he's only six months old, and he can get into a lot of things he shouldn't at a party like this."

Isaiah nodded, and Whitney expected him to offer that they'd adopted Cocoa, but he didn't even mention her.

"Would you like me to come with you to eat with the other kids?" Whitney asked.

He didn't speak for a long moment, and then nodded, the uncertainty that had been present in his life since Vanessa died evident in unfamiliar surroundings. The urge to hug him was so strong, but Whitney didn't want to draw attention to him and took Zoey's hand. "C'mon, Zoey. Let's go meet some new friends."

They found the other kids in a large playroom filled with toys and arts and crafts supplies. Whitney got Zoey settled with her food but Isaiah hung back, taking his time. She wanted to urge him forward and get him talking to the others, but she stepped back to watch what he decided to do.

"He'll learn to deal with it better," Hannah whispered.

"How can you be so sure?"

"David and Mia. David's my biological child. His father died. And Mia is Gage's daughter. She lost her mother, too."

"I'm so sorry for your loss. I had no idea."

"Thank you." Hannah squeezed Whitney's hand. "So you see we've been through it, and any advice or help we can offer is yours."

"I'm glad to take you up on that. I'll have to get your email and phone number."

Hannah's eyebrow rose. "So you're not staying then?"

"Staying here? Tonight, yes, but we're going home in the morning."

"When I saw you looking up at him when I answered the door, I was sure you were in love with him. But you couldn't work things out, I guess?"

"We haven't had a chance to talk yet."

Hannah clamped a hand over her mouth. "Me and my big mouth are going to get me in trouble one of these days."

"One of these days?" Alex piped up from behind them and chuckled. "It's more like when *aren't* you in trouble?"

She swatted a playful hand at him then shooed them down the hall toward the family room. "Go. Mingle. Make nice and introduce this beautiful woman."

Alex looked at Whitney. "If you think she's beautiful on the outside, wait until you get to know her. Now that's real beauty."

Heat rushed up Whitney's neck and flooded her face. The color of her skin must resemble Santa's red suit.

"Aren't you two so cute together?"

"Cute?" Alex mimed choking. "Anything but cute."

"Okay, adorable, then."

He rolled his eyes. "Me and my big mouth."

Hannah hugged his arm and looked at Whitney. "You have no idea what you're getting yourself into with this one, but I promise you, he's a real catch."

"My turn to blush." Alex fanned his face and pretended to be embarrassed.

Whitney had seen him crack some jokes and play around, but never this much in such a short time, and she was baffled by it. Maybe she didn't know him as well as she thought she did.

Shaking her head, Hannah set off and worked her way through the others, heading toward Gage.

Whitney faced Alex. "You're different tonight."

"Different how?"

"Funny. Sarcastic. A real joker."

"Right. Yeah. Like I told you, I'm kind of known as the team joker. I never did much of that around you, did I?"

She shook her head and worry niggled its way into her brain. "Who are you really?"

"That's what I wanted to talk to you about. Should we do it now or go mingle?"

He was worrying her, but she'd come to talk to the team and thank them personally for their support, too, so she would do that first.

Or maybe you're afraid to find out what he has to say.

"Well, we came for dinner... and I'd like to hand out the gifts. Don't want anyone to go home and miss them."

"Dependable, too," he said and motioned for her to go first.

She stopped to grab her tote bag then followed Hannah into the room. Hannah went straight for Gage. He slid his arm around her waist and didn't miss a beat in his conversation with Sam, Eryn, and Trey.

"Would it be possible to get the whole team together so I could say something?" Whitney asked them.

"Sure," Hannah said. "Let me grab the others."

"Look at her," Alex said as Hannah moved through the room. "She's rounding them up and herding them together like cattle."

"Well, a lot of us are bullheaded," Trey joked.

Whitney laughed, though she didn't know them well enough to know if it was true. But they were all very confident and that had to bring its share of bullheaded moments. She hunted through her bag for Gage's box and gave it to him.

"What's this?" he asked, clearly confused.

"Just a small token of my thanks for your work in keeping us safe and apprehending Percy." She gave Sam, Eryn, and Trey their packages, too.

"That wasn't necessary," Gage said. "We were just doing what we're called to do."

"It's necessary to me, so I hope you can accept it."

"Of course. We'll wait for the others to join us before opening them," Gage said, offering a pointed look at his team.

A man she had to assume was Jackson headed their way as he was the only team member she hadn't met. He held hands with a woman—his wife, Maggie, Whitney assumed—who had golden blond hair pulled back into a bun. Taller than Whitney, she was regal looking in a simple black dress as she almost glided across the room.

She held out slender fingers. "Maggie Tur—Lockhart." She glanced at Jackson. "I will get the hang of having a different name. I promise."

"Newlyweds," Gage explained. "What? All of ten, twelve days now."

"Thirteen, but who's counting?" A dreamy smile crossed Jackson's face. This guy was so in love.

Coop arrived, a big smile on his face, and he looked like he had a secret that was about to burst. The woman by his side had russet brown hair to her shoulders in sleek waves and a shy smile.

Alex introduced them and Whitney shook hands.

Last to arrive was Riley and a woman who looked very familiar to Whitney, but she couldn't place her at first. She was movie-star gorgeous with flowing blond hair and a sparkling dress. Her vivid sapphire eyes sparkled as well.

"You've met, Riley," Alex said. "This is his fiancé Leah—"

"*Kent*. You're Leah Kent. Recording artist. Oh, my, it *is* you."

"Nice to meet you, Whitney, but I am retiring from that life to marry this big lug of a guy." She caressed Riley's arm and beamed up at him.

As Hannah joined them again, Whitney handed Riley's and Jackson's boxes to them. She suddenly felt shy. "Just a little something...that I had made for you all—to thank you for your help."

Everyone stared at her.

"Go ahead." She waved her hands. "Open them."

They did and had similar reactions to Alex of silent reverence.

"How lovely," Hannah exclaimed and gave Whitney a quick hug. "That was so thoughtful."

Whitney would have to be blind not to see that Hannah took a strong mothering role in this group.

"There's more on the back," Alex said, pride in his tone, and he drew her to his side, too.

"This is perfect. Just perfect." Eryn hugged Whitney. "Please tell me you're going to marry this guy."

"Um...well."

"I haven't asked...yet."

"Then why are you here with us? Shoo. Shoo." Eryn waved her hands.

Whitney blushed. "I...I wanted to hand out the coins, and I'm so glad you like them. It really sums up what I think of what you all do."

"Trust me, we're grateful for the coin," Eryn said. "I will cherish it always. And for your kindness." Then she winked. "But we'd be even more grateful if you'd marry this guy before he becomes a confirmed bachelor in his old age and is a third wheel all the time."

Alex gaped at her, and she wrinkled her nose.

Whitney laughed. "Guess we should go have that talk."

"Stay here and let me grab our jackets."

Jackets? Why were they going outside?

"Hey, wait a minute, man," Coop called out. "There's

something I've been busting a gut to say all night. Since we're all standing here, it's the perfect time."

Alex growled a frustrated warning low in his throat. "Make it fast."

Coop drew Kiera in front of him and placed his hand on her belly. "Kiera's pregnant. Four months along."

"Oh my stars, that is just the *best* news." Hannah charged across the circle and hugged Kiera. "Do you know if it's a boy or girl?"

She shook her head. "We want to wait or maybe even be surprised. We're just not sure what we want to do yet."

The guys were pumping Coop's hand and slapping him on the back. He beamed like a proud soon-to-be dad, and his gaze landed lovingly on his wife.

Whitney remembered when Vanessa announced her pregnancies. She used cupcake filling to declare the sex of each baby.

Oh, sweetie, I miss you so much.

Tears came and Alex took her hand. "You're thinking of Vanessa."

She nodded.

"Then come on. Let's get our coats and change the subject."

She nodded, and they stopped on the way out to the back patio to tell Isaiah where they were going and to keep an eye on Zoey.

Alex flipped on a switch and a million sparkling white lights lit up the patio. A table was set with fine white dishes, champagne glasses, and sparkling grape juice filled an ice bucket.

She looked up at him. "You did all of this for me?"

He blushed and nodded. She rushed over to him and hugged him hard.

"I'm feeling kind of insecure about this and thought the ambiance might help."

"It's beautiful, and you're so sweet."

Another blush and he toed the ground with his shoe. "You asked me before who the real Alex is."

Her stomach clenched. "Yes."

"Honestly, I'm not sure, and I'm working on figuring that out. I told you how I started joking around and it stuck with me and then at the resort with you, I didn't feel that way. At least not most of the time. I thought I could be real with you, you know?"

She nodded. "The connection was there and made it seem like we knew each other for a long time."

"Yeah…yeah. Like soul mates, if you believe in that kind of thing. But there was more for me, too. I figured out I still had issues with my mom taking her life and leaving me like that. I've never met anyone who motivated me to face that pain and come to terms with it. But I want to be with you, and you deserve for me to get my stuff together. So I promise I will."

He got down on one knee, reached into his coat pocket, and opened a ring box. "I love you, Whitney. So incredibly much. Will you marry me? It doesn't have to be right away. Give us time to figure everything out. Me with my mom. You heal from losing Vanessa. The kids. But I want my ring on your finger so we both know the commitment we're prepared to make."

"Yes," she said, tears flooding her eyes from happiness. "I love you, too, and yes, I'll marry you."

He slid the ring on—a white gold band with a large round diamond in the center, additional diamonds on either side. He got to his feet.

She held out her hand and gawked at her finger. "The ring is breathtaking, Alex. It's so beautiful."

He tenderly took her in his arms and held her like a precious jewel. "I haven't known this kind of peace in my life. Ever. You're the reason, and I never want to let you go."

"You will never have to." She looked up, memorizing everything about the man looking at her with such warmth, she felt it to her toes.

He slid his hand into her hair and lowered his mouth. His lips settled on hers. They were cold, but quickly warmed, and she twined her arms around his neck and got lost in his kiss.

The door burst open, hitting the wall with a bang. Whitney reluctantly drew back to see Zoey charge out after a puppy with giant paws. Isaiah came running after them. Then David and Mia and Bekah. Hannah was hot on their heels. Gage followed.

The kids ran out into the yard.

The adults stopped and stared at Whitney and Alex.

"Well," Hannah said, not at all shy about breaking into their big moment. "Did she say yes?"

Whitney wiggled her ring finger.

Hannah whooped and came running.

"Just so you know," Alex said. "This is what you're in for if you hang around us for long."

Whitney grinned. "Hey, I come with a ready-made family. You might as well, too. But I warn you, when your family of big grown-up men gets unruly, *you're* in charge of disciplining them."

He laughed and hugged her hard before Hannah swept her out of his arms and into a hug of her own.

"Welcome to the family," she said and released Whitney.

"Now come on, honey." Gage took her hand. "We have kids and a dog to round up, and these two obviously want to be alone."

"Right. The kids." Hannah brushed a strand of hair out of her face. "Maybe we need a vacation."

"Or just a good night's sleep."

"Yeah, that, too," she said as they trudged out into the yard.

Alex put his arm around her, and they watched as Isaiah came wandering back from the yard.

He looked up at Whitney. "Are you going to marry him?"

"Would it be okay with you if I did?"

"Yeah. Alex already asked. He's cool like that."

Alex offered an exploding fist bump to Isaiah. "I asked if it was okay if he had to move here, but it was only speculation. I'm willing to live wherever you choose."

"Here," Isaiah said. "I want to see all the cool stuff you have."

"It's not something you'll get to be involved with on a regular basis," Alex warned.

"Yeah, I know, but I bet the kids at school wonder what goes on here. I'll be like a rock star."

Whitney had to smile at his naive take on life, but he could be right. "I can be a nurse anywhere, but your job is pretty specific."

"Yeah, like you can't fly in helicopters and shoot out engines just anywhere," Isaiah said, sounding impressed. "And you'd be nuts to quit that kind of job. Crazy, you know?"

"Then it looks like we might be moving," Whitney said. "We'll all talk about it later and decide."

Alex jumped in. "We don't have to live in my cabin. Gage is cool with us not living on the compound."

"I'm gonna go eat," Isaiah said. "Unless I have to watch Zoey some more. But I don't think it's fair that I have to do that all the time." He stomped a foot on the concrete and looked up with a dare in his eyes.

"You're right," Whitney said with a serious expression when she was rejoicing inside that he was complaining. "I've got it from here tonight. Go have fun."

He looked up at Alex. "We gonna go look at the cool stuff in the morning?"

Alex nodded. "You better believe we are."

A smile crept onto Isaiah's mouth, and he headed back inside.

Whitney moved closer to Alex. "It's looking like everything is going to be just fine with him. I know he has a long way to go, but he's made a bit of progress. That complaint was just awesome."

"I'm going to remind you of that when he's thirteen and sullen. But for now..." He pulled her against his solid body, kissing her forehead and the tip of her nose before settling his mouth to hers, his touch tender and insistent at the same time.

Her emotions exploded. She slid her arms around him and held on for dear life. When the kiss ended, she rested her head against his chest, something she'd been wanting to do since they parted at the resort.

She thought about that day. About how she'd been crazy to let him go without a proper discussion of what had transpired between them. "I've been thinking. Mountains in your life really aren't a bad thing. And I don't mean the physical ones. Not when God puts them in our path to slow us down to see what we need to see."

He pulled back and looked at her. "You're thinking about the blizzard."

"Yeah. I don't pretend to understand His plan, but I do know one thing. He moved mountains in both of our lives for us to be together, and I plan to honor that by making sure we're one of the couples who grow wrinkled and old together."

"I like that thought." He smiled. "But you know there will be more mountains coming."

"I do, but I also know God has a plan and those mountains are moveable. And now..." She smiled back at him. "Now I have help with them. I have you."

∼

Enjoy this book?

Reviews are the most powerful tool to draw attention to my books for new readers. I wish I had the budget of a New York publisher to take out ads and commercials but that's not a reality. I do have something much more powerful and effective than that.

A committed and loyal bunch of readers like you.

If you've enjoyed *Cold Pursuit*, I would be very grateful if you could leave an honest review on the bookseller's site. It can be as short as you like. Just a few words is all it takes. Thank you very much.

Don't miss Samantha and Griff's story in book 7, COLD DAWN!

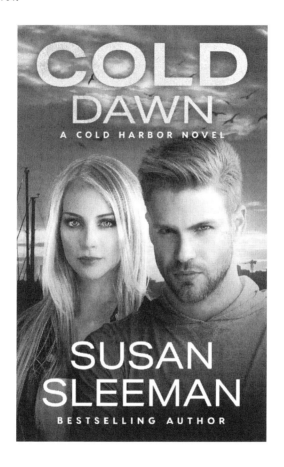

An inferno meant to destroy...

Blackwell Tactical operator and former criminalist Samantha Willis discovers forensic evidence to prove her friend has been murdered. But before she can gather the evidence, an explosion erupts and a fiery inferno traps her in a building. She helplessly watches the evidence go up in flames and prays that she can escape before the encroaching flames take her life.

Or an act of revenge…

Firefighter and former Navy SEAL Matt Griffin knew his friend's death was no accident, and he arrives at the building to gather his own evidence. But he sees the building engulfed in flames and discovers a familiar car parked in the lot. Sam, his former girlfriend, had to be trapped inside. Despite his training, despite his captain's protest, Griff takes off without a threat assessment, risking his life to enter the building and drag Sam to safety. When he does, he can't help but wonder if the fire was set to destroy evidence or if it was set to kill Sam. Either way, if Sam survives, he vows to hunt down the answer.

Chapter One

Andy died here. Yesterday. Alone. In a fiery inferno.
What was he doing in an abandoned crab cannery in the first place? He didn't live in Lost Creek. Wasn't a fisherman.

Forensic expert Samantha Willis' eyes clogged with tears, and she blinked hard to clear them and evaluate the scene. But her heart felt heavy as lead, and the tears kept coming. One after another, rolling down her cheeks and dripping onto the charred floorboards.

Oh, Andy. Why?

He was once her best friend. Then he'd asked her to marry him. She loved him, but only as a friend. She turned him down and things got awkward. Too awkward. So they didn't stay in touch. At least not regularly.

Now he was dead. *Dead.* She couldn't even believe it yet.

Her heart clenched, and she touched a charred wooden

support beam, ashes whispering to the scorched floor. She took a long breath of air laden with the lingering aroma of scorched wood. Not the pleasant smell from a campfire or fireplace. This was bitter and caustic smelling.

She wanted to sit down and have a good cry, but she was there for a reason. She swiped her tears away with her sleeve and snapped on latex gloves to take a look around the room that was—for the most part—still intact. The fire department arrived to extinguish the flames before the shell of the building suffered tremendous damage. But still, Andy didn't make it.

Did someone lure him here to murder him? Sam didn't know. But she would when she was done.

"I promise, Andy," she said to the large empty crab-packing room. "I *will* find out and make them pay. For you, my dear friend. For you."

She set down her forensic kit by the sliding metal door and propped it open with a metal pole. The heavy door to the canning room had closed and locked behind Andy, trapping him in this room. That wasn't going to happen to her.

She pulled her hair up into a ponytail to keep it out of her face as she worked. She grabbed her camera from the bag and lifted her legs carefully over large chunks of wood, scorched like firewood burgeoning to life in a campfire and then doused with a bucket of water. Except no one roasted marshmallows here. Here they killed her friend.

She snapped pictures. Randomly. A shot here. One there. She tried to focus. Tried to set priorities, but her usual professional eye evaded her. As a former criminalist for the Portland Police Bureau and now the forensic specialist for Blackwell Tactical, she had years of experience and had never failed to do her job. But then, she'd never investigated the death of a friend.

The urge to bolt out the door grabbed her by the throat, tears welling in her eyes again and clouding her vision.

Yes, go. Now. She turned. Took a step.

No. Suck it up. Andy needs you to find out what happened here.

Blake Jenkins, the local sheriff, was called in when the firefighters discovered Andy, but the arson investigator hadn't located a source for the fire and couldn't declare it was arson.

She'd counted on Blake's forensic team to gather evidence, but they found nothing to prove arson and let the investigator's report stand. Which meant they hadn't opened a homicide investigation. That could change after the autopsy, but for now, she was the only one looking into Andy's death.

Her phone pealed out the ringtone "Anchors Aweigh," startling her and cutting through the silence. She'd assigned this ringtone to her boss, former Navy SEAL Gage Blackwell. She didn't want to answer. Not now. Not with her heart breaking. But she would.

She owed Gage so much. She would never ignore his call.

Trying not to sound down, she hung her camera around her neck and answered. "What's up, Gage?"

"Sorry to bother you when you're taking some personal time." His sincere, caring tone almost sent her bawling like a baby.

She swallowed hard. "No worries."

"It's about the fire," he said. "The one that your friend died in."

Say what? "Andy? You know something about that?"

"It's looking like you're right. It might not have been an accident."

Her mouth fell open. She believed the fire had to have

been started on purpose, but only because she wanted to blame someone for his death. Wanted a place to direct her anger. But now...

She took another look around the room. "Did they find arson evidence after all?"

"Blake's being closemouthed about his findings as usual, but I talked to the fire marshal. He believes there were two recent fires that were highly suspicious and could be related."

Thoughts pinged in her brain as she tried to make sense of this news. "Were those fires intentionally started?"

"Inconclusive. The fire marshal said the fires burned fast with excessive heat and they all followed a specific path. Plus the utilities were turned off to the buildings, so the source of ignition was either lightning or arson. No lightning in the area any of the nights. Leaves arson. The investigator didn't recover any proof, though. Not in any of the locations."

"Finding arson evidence isn't like a homicide or burglary scene. The evidence often burns up in the fire." She looked around the space. A waterfall of tears started again, and she quickly snapped her gaze to look out the window to gain control and think. "Wait. I'm confused. Why are you involved in this?"

"Blackwell Tactical has been hired to investigate the fires."

Color her surprised. Her team? Hired to find her friend's killer? "But we don't have any experience with arson."

"We *do* know criminal investigations, and we can hire fire experts if we need them."

"True."

"I figured you'd be glad to have a first-rate team looking into Andy's death, so I took the job."

"I'm glad you did," she said with vehemence. "Trust me. I really am."

Silence filled the phone. She hoped she hadn't offended him. Or made him think she didn't want the team's help. She was extremely grateful for their expertise. Plus the friendship and support that came along with working with an incredible group. She'd joined the team less than a year ago, but they were already family.

"You're in mourning, and I hate to ask this," he finally said. "But could you cancel your personal leave to run the investigation? We'll need a forensic expert on this one for sure."

Could I ever!

"I'm in," she said tempering her enthusiasm. She didn't want him to question her ability to keep a level head when investigating a friend's death.

"Good. Good." Relief was nearly palpable in his voice.

She understood his concern. Most of her teammates were former military, not law enforcement. Sure, they taught classes for officers, but the courses were tactical in nature, not investigative. So she, plus Eryn who was a former FBI agent, and Riley who once served as a Portland Police Bureau sniper, were charged with making sure the team followed proper evidentiary protocol.

"I'd like you to get over to the cannery ASAP," Gage continued. "If there's any evidence to be recovered, you'll find it."

"I'm at the scene right now."

"Figured you'd be going there this week, but I should've known you wouldn't wait."

He already knew her so well. He took a personal interest in each of his team members. Maybe too much of an interest at times, but she didn't care. She'd sustained a shoulder injury in her PPB job and faced riding a desk until he'd hired her for the team. In addition to Gage and her, the other six members were also injured while serving their country in the military or in law enforcement.

"Do you need any help or equipment?" he asked.

Now guilt heaped on her head. She'd borrowed team equipment to process the building without asking. She didn't want to do it, but asking for his permission would've started her crying. Crying in front of Gage or the team wasn't optional for her. Ever. At least not if she could help it.

"It's okay," Gage said. "I'll take your silence to mean you've got what you need. That's all that matters."

Of course he figured out that she'd taken the equipment. That was Gage through and through. Nothing got past him. Nothing.

Her phone beeped a low battery warning. *Right.* In her hurry to get here, she'd left her charger in Cold Harbor and needed to buy one soon.

"I gotta go. My phone's dying."

"I'll get the team started on the investigation from our end," Gage said. "You report in the minute you finish the scene."

"Will do." She disconnected and glanced at the battery icon. Five percent charge remaining. Her phone was her lifeline. Like most people these days, she used it for everything. She had to get this place processed and head to the store for that charger.

She lifted her camera again to document the space where tons of crab had been packed over the years. When she'd arrived at the building, she still detected hints of a fishy smell, but nothing seeped through the fire odor in this room. Backing up to the door, she snapped wide shots of the space to capture placement of every table, stool, and the conveyor belts, then moved in to take closer shots of the ruins.

She zoomed in on blackened wood. Ashes. Piles of debris. Charred metal. She followed a grid pattern to get every inch of the room recorded in photos, and then grabbed her kit and went back to the corner where the report stated the fire had started.

She shoved plastic evidence bags in one pocket, tweezers, a tube of swabs in another, and a ruler in her back pocket. In her hands, she carried numbered markers and small empty paint cans. The white-hot burn left little in way of evidence other than ash, and she set markers on the ground where she would select samples. She took even more pictures, and jotted her impressions in a small notebook that would later be transferred to her official report.

Sure, the investigator had taken samples from around the room, but after rush processing, he reported that ignitable liquid residues weren't found in his samples. Either an accelerant wasn't used to start the fire, or he didn't take good samples. She would collect her own to test.

She selected wood pieces boasting liquid stains and placed them in the unused paint cans. She might have something. Might not. The stains could be from accelerants or from years of processing wet crab. She sealed and labeled the paint can, the standard container for storing ILRs, as the cans were impermeable and didn't taint the samples.

She moved on and found glass fragments. Molotov cocktail? Maybe.

Following the same procedure, she placed an evidence marker, snapped a picture, and bagged fragments in a clean can. If the glass came from a bottle or jar holding an ignition source, analysis of the glass could prove it. The investigator surely would've processed glass samples, too, and she didn't expect it to return a positive result for ILRs, but she was always thorough in her work. Forming a hypothesis before collecting all the evidence could taint her mindset and blind her to looking for every piece of possible evidence.

She grabbed her magnifying glass and searched every inch of the room looking for bloodstains, shoe prints—arsonists often stepped in the liquid flammables they used—and anything else she could find.

Coming up with very little, she sat back on her heels to think. She'd been trained in arson evidence collection, but hadn't actually processed a fire scene. But Andy deserved the very best, so she'd done something she vowed never to do again. She called Matt Griffin, the man she once believed she would spend the rest of her life with, and asked him to meet her here.

A retired Navy SEAL, Griff had picked the perfect second career. Firefighting fit his thrill-seeker personality. Battling fires gave him the adrenaline rush he always sought. Mountain climbing. Hang gliding. Skydiving. He did it all. The riskier the better. She didn't like the way he endangered his life, but that was who he was, and to be with him, she'd had to accept that when they were together.

She sighed at the memory. Between his deployments and outdoor adventures, she prayed more during that year than she had in any prior year. And now after seven years, she was about to see him again.

What was that going to be like? She couldn't even imagine, but tingled with the thought. And her hands trembled when she'd called him. Clearly, she still had some feelings for him. Unexpected feelings.

Focus, girl.

She lowered her magnifying glass and spotted hairs or fibers stuck between floorboards. She held the glass closer. Most likely pet hair. Could be from the killer. Or could have been there for years, but she bagged it anyway. Long hairs. Silvery-gray. Coarse like a dog. Andy was allergic to dogs, and they wouldn't have come from him unless he'd picked them up outside his home.

She sat back on her heels to look around and mentally list out the remaining items to follow up on. There was a metal door in the corner with an unusual latch that she needed to check out, and she still needed to go downstairs and look for any accelerant that might have seeped through the floorboards.

She closed the hard-shell case on her camera and stowed it in her tote then knelt to make sure the paint cans were tightly sealed and packed them in her bag.

A loud bang sounded behind her.

She whipped around. The door had closed.

"Scared me to death," she muttered and got up. She must not have wedged the metal bar well enough.

The sound of the wide bar that was used to lock the door scraped into place on the other side. She glanced at the floor. The firm length of steel she'd used to prop the door open was missing.

Why wasn't the steel lying on the floor in this room?

Griff? He liked to play practical jokes.

She crossed the room and tried to push the door open. It wouldn't budge.

She pounded on solid metal. "Griff, if you're playing a joke on me, it's not funny. Open the door."

Silence. Nothing but silence. The caustic odor of gasoline filtered under the door.

Was someone out there? Starting another fire?

Her heart seized up, and she pounded harder. No one answered. Panic sent her pulse racing.

She couldn't unlock the door. Not with the one-inch thick bar on the other side. The very reason Andy got trapped in this room, and why she'd taken precautions to keep the door open.

She dug out her phone and woke it up. The wheel spun and spun, then it shut down. "No. No. No. Not the battery."

She heard movement on the other side of the door. She pounded again and decided to use Griff's real name which he hated. "Matthew Griffin. This isn't funny. Open the door."

No response.

Of course not. Griff would never pull a stunt like this. No way he would make fun of something like fire. Especially when it had killed Andy in this very location.

She rested her head against the cool metal to think and looked down. Smoke slithered under the gap, long fingers creeping into the room and over her feet.

"What? No." She jumped back.

The volume of smoke increased, curling up into her breathing space. She pulled her shirt over her nose and looked around the room. Sought an exit.

"The windows!" She raced across the floor, dodging debris. Climbing on a metal table, she pulled herself up to take a quick look from the second floor. Could she bail out?

She looked down. The building sat on a hill overlooking the river with large boulders directly below. Certain death if she jumped.

She turned back. Dark clouds swirled over the floor and pooled on the ceiling.

Panic raced up her spine—clutched at her throat as smoke burned her eyes.

She ran a frantic gaze over the area again. Searching. Seeking. Any way to stay alive. Found nothing.

No. No. It can't be.

She was trapped, totally trapped. The only way out—another deathtrap.

∼

Griff turned onto Rivercrest Drive and shook his head. How had he driven for an hour and still not come up with what to say to Sam when he saw her again? What could he say?

"Hey, honey. I'm sorry you broke up with me. Sure it's been seven years, but I'm still in love with you, in case you're interested."

Yeah, right. Like he'd ever bare his soul to her again. To any woman. After losing his parents, it took everything he had to open up to her in the first place and risk being hurt again. And now visiting the place where his childhood friend and houseguest Andy died at the same time? The flames taking his life.

Not something Griff would wish on his worst enemies, and he'd seen his share of bad operators in his SEAL days.

He stopped at a red light and glanced down the road to take in the old crab cannery. Smoke billowed up from the building. Thick black clouds of smoke coupled with bright orange flames.

"Say what?"

Someone had set the building on fire again, and the front was fully engulfed.

Sam was there. His heart plummeted.

Did she go inside or wait for him in the lot?

Please let her be waiting.

He floored the gas and shot through the intersection on the deserted road. Punching the emergency button on his dash, he reported the fire to 911. He kept his eyes ahead, trying to see the parking lot. A Jeep was parked there, but no one was inside the vehicle.

"No. Sam. *No*. I told you to wait for me." He swallowed hard to keep his mounting panic at bay. He could handle putting himself in danger, but knowing someone he cared about was in harm's way filled him with terror.

He parked in the lot and jumped from his pickup. The

heat radiated from the building. Glass was breaking. Wood snapping. White smoke curled up and over the black. This side of the building was fully engulfed.

Hurry. Hurry.

He reached into his gear bag stowed in the jump seat to grab a flashlight, bandana, Nomex hood, and fire gloves, then bolted for the other side of the building. Smoke rolled out a window, but so far it was flame free. With the front mostly engulfed, it wouldn't take long for the back to go up, too.

He spotted the exterior stairs and charged up, donning the hood as he moved. It was odd to enter a burning building without full turnout gear or his SCBA and helmet. He'd often considered keeping more of his gear in his truck, but firefighting wasn't an individual activity. It was a team sport, and he wouldn't likely need the gear off duty. The medic in him did keep a large first aid kit in the box of his truck, but he hoped he wouldn't need it today.

He felt the door for heat. Still cool.

Good.

The lock was snapped off.

Did the arsonist know Sam was inside? If so, the person intended to kill her.

His heart lurched, and he doubled his resolve not to let them succeed. He tied the bandana around his mouth and nose, donned his gloves, and jerked the door open.

Smoke flooded out, and the stench of gasoline carried through. Like he suspected. Someone set the fire.

The building plans he'd reviewed earlier told him he had twenty feet to reach the room Andy died in, and he could easily hold his breath that distance. He gulped in air and headed into the smoky haze that darkened the space. Flames dancing along the rear wall illuminated the area.

He placed his hand on the side wall to keep his bearings

and moved deeper into the smoke, counting his steps until the door to the canning room appeared under his hand. What if Sam was trapped inside? He felt the door. It was cool.

He lifted the heavy bar and jerked open the door. Tried to see through the smoke, but it was too thick.

"Sam! Sam!" He listened for a moment.

Heard nothing.

Could she have succumbed to smoke inhalation? Or worse?

Panic edged ever closer.

Stay calm. She needs you.

Wait! Was that a tapping sound coming from the corner? He couldn't see a thing through the concentrated smoke. The urge to rush in hit hard, but he had to find a way to brace the door so he didn't end up trapped, too. He felt around and touched a steel table. He let the door close for a moment and dragged the narrow table to the doorway to wedge it firmly in place.

He got as low as he could and headed straight for the corner where the clanking sound continued. "Sam!"

He reached the back wall. Ran his hands over the area. A metal door. Where it led he didn't know.

God, please. Please let Sam be here and let her still be alive.

Available at most online booksellers now!

For More Details Visit -
www.susansleeman.com/books/cold-dawn/

Dear Reader:

Thank you so much for reading COLD PURSUIT, book six in my Cold Harbor series featuring Blackwell Tactical.

> Book 1 - COLD TERROR
> Book 2 - COLD TRUTH
> Book 3 - COLD FURY
> Book 4 - COLD CASE
> Book 5 - COLD FEAR
> Book 6 - COLD PURSUIT
> Book 7 - COLD DAWN

I'd like to invite you to learn more about the books in the series as they release and about my other books by signing up for my newsletter and connecting with me on social media or even sending me a message. I hold monthly giveaways that I'd like to share with you, and I'd love to hear from you. So stop by this page and join in!

www.susansleeman.com/sign-up/

Susan Sleeman

BOOKS IN THE COLD HARBOR SERIES

Blackwell Tactical – this law enforcement training facility and protection services agency is made up of former military and law enforcement heroes whose injuries keep them from the line of duty. When trouble strikes, there's no better team to have on your side, and they would give everything, even their lives, to protect innocents.

For More Details Visit -
www.susansleeman.com/books/cold-harbor/

THE TRUTH SEEKERS
People are rarely who they seem

A twin who never knew her sister existed, a mother whose child is not her own, a woman whose father is anything but her father. All searching. All seeking. All needing help and hope.

Meet the unsung heroes of the Veritas Center. The Truth Seekers – a team, that includes experts in forensic anthropology, DNA, trace evidence, ballistics, cybercrimes, and toxicology. Committed to restoring hope and families by solving one mystery at a time, none of them are prepared for when the mystery comes calling close to home and threatens to destroy the only life they've known.

For More Details Visit -
www.susansleeman.com/books/truth-seekers/

HOMELAND HEROES SERIES

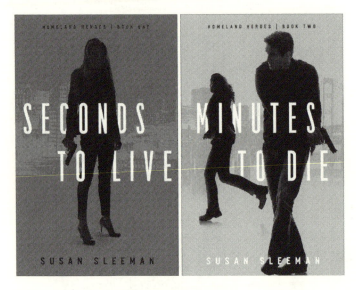

When the clock is ticking on criminal activity conducted on or facilitated by the Internet there is no better team to call other than the RED team, a division of the HSI—Homeland Security's Investigation Unit. RED team includes FBI and DHS Agents, and US Marshal's Service Deputies.

For More Details Visit -

www.susansleeman.com/books/homeland-heroes/

WHITE KNIGHTS SERIES

Join the White Knights as they investigate stories plucked from today's news headlines. The FBI Critical Incident Response Team includes experts in crisis management, explosives, ballistics/weapons, negotiating/criminal profiling, cyber crimes, and forensics. All team members are former military and they stand ready to deploy within four hours, anytime and anywhere to mitigate the highest-priority threats facing our nation.

www.susansleeman.com/books/white-knights/

ABOUT SUSAN

SUSAN SLEEMAN is a bestselling and award-winning author of more than 35 inspirational/Christian and clean read romantic suspense books. In addition to writing, Susan also hosts the website, TheSuspenseZone.com.

Susan currently lives in Oregon, but has had the pleasure of living in nine states. Her husband is a retired church music director and they have two beautiful daughters, a very special son-in-law, and an adorable grandson.

For more information visit:
www.susansleeman.com

Made in the USA
San Bernardino, CA
22 December 2019